Notes from Underground
and
The Grand Inquisitor

Dostoevsky marked the beginning of the [Slavic?] ... ian Lit ~1800s
-belonged to the "intelligentsia" - control of [censorship?] regime ((tsar))
seldom was eliminated at the same time _Notes_ was published
On the more liberal side of critics
Dost. was arrested and imprisoned under one of the harsher Czars

notes published in 2 parts in _Epoch_

Notes from Underground
and
The Grand Inquisitor

BY

FYODOR DOSTOEVSKY

WITH RELEVANT WORKS BY CHERNYSHEVSKY,
SHCHEDRIN AND DOSTOEVSKY

Selection, translation and introduction by
RALPH E. MATLAW

A PLUME BOOK

PLUME
Published by the Penguin Group
Penguin Group (USA) Inc., 375 Hudson Street, New York, New York 10014, U.S.A.
Penguin Group (Canada), 90 Eglinton Avenue East, Suite 700, Toronto,
Ontario, Canada M4P 2Y3 (a division of Pearson Penguin Canada Inc.)
Penguin Books Ltd, 80 Strand, London WC2R 0RL, England
Penguin Ireland, 25 St. Stephen's Green. Dublin 2, Ireland
(a division of Penguin Books Ltd.)
Penguin Group (Australia), 250 Camberwell Road, Camberwell, Victoria 3124,
Australia (a division of Pearson Australia Group Pty. Ltd.)
Penguin Books India Pvt. Ltd., 11 Community Centre,
Panchsheel Park, New Delhi – 110 017, India
Penguin Books (N.Z.) 67 Apollo Drive, Rosedale, North Shore 0632,
New Zealand (a division of Pearson New Zealand Ltd.)
Penguin Books (South Africa) (Pty.) Ltd., 24 Sturdee Avenue,
Rosebank, Johannesburg 2196, South Africa

Penguin Books Ltd, Registered Offices: 80 Strand, London WC2R 0RL, England

Published by Plume, a member of Penguin Group (USA) Inc. Previously published in Dutton and Meridian editions.

First Plume Printing, November 2003
10 9 8

ⓟ REGISTERED TRADEMARK—MARCA REGISTRADA

CIP data is available.
ISBN 978-0-452-28558-3
Library of Congress Catalog Number: 60-9687

Printed in the United States of America

PUBLISHER'S NOTE
This is a work of fiction. Names, characters, places, and incidents either are the
products of the author's imagination or are used fictitiously, and any resemblance
to actual persons, living or dead, business establishments, events, or locales is
entirely coincidental.

for Betty and Karen

CONTENTS

INTRODUCTION

Dostoevsky's impact on the modern literary mind is unrivaled in its scope and vitality. Nowhere does his art appear in so quintessential a form as in *Notes from Underground*; nowhere is his thought presented with such authority as in "The Grand Inquisitor," an episode, in one sense even a digression, in his last and greatest novel, *The Brothers Karamazov*. The connection between them is unmistakable, as is their direct relation to Dostoevsky's own life, a life as sensational, harrowing and frenzied as some of his own fiction.

Dostoevsky was born on October 30, 1821, in a wing of Moscow's Foundling Hospital, where his father was a resident physician. He early showed a marked interest in literature and extensive acquaintance with it and was able to maintain both while studying at the School for Engineers in St. Petersburg. After graduation in 1843 he served in the Engineering Corps for a year, then resigned to devote himself to literary work. He translated French novels—his first published work was a translation of Balzac's *Eugénie Grandet*—and his first original work, *Poor Folk* (1846), was hailed by Russia's leading critic, Belinsky, as an outstanding production. Dostoevsky's subsequent stories met a less favorable reception. His literary fame was ebbing when his career, indeed the whole course of his life, was dramatically altered. In April 1849 he was arrested as a member of a group that met periodically to read and discuss various subjects, including the utopian socialist Fourier. As this was the bleakest period of Nicholas I's autocratic suppression, such apparently innocuous activity was viewed as a dangerous political plot. After eight months' imprisonment, early on the morning of December 22, Dostoevsky and a number of the other "conspirators" were taken to a public square, sentenced to be shot, prepared for death and divided into groups of three to face the firing squad. At the very last moment a courier galloped up with a reprieve from the czar: the whole procedure was a mockery, designed the more effectively to demonstrate his great mercy. One of the men near Dostoevsky went insane. What Dostoevsky himself experienced can only be conjectured, even though he memorably describes the feelings and thoughts of a condemned man in two famous passages in his novels. Yet surely this experience underlies the paradoxical emphasis on the insignificance of life and its infinite value that pervades Dostoevsky's fiction. His sentence was commuted to four years' hard labor in Siberia, in the living hell he describes in *Notes from House of the Dead* (1861–62). For another five years he served in the ranks of a disciplinary regiment in Siberia before he finally obtained permission to return to Petersburg, where he was now completely unknown.

He worked indefatigably to rebuild his literary reputation. With his brother he started and edited the journal *Time,* and in 1862 made his first trip to Europe. There he had his first glimpse of the decay and corruption of Europe, which he proceeded to expound in *Winter Notes on Summer Impressions.* In 1863 he made a second trip, marked by a tempestuous love affair with Apollinaria Suslova, who was to provide him with ample material for certain traits of his more "infernal" heroines, by a mania for gambling that he could not shake for many years, and by recurrent attacks of epilepsy, the disease that had been aggravated by his Siberian experiences.

The year 1864 marks the nadir of Dostoevsky's career. *Time* had been suspended by the government and its successor, *The Epoch,* was a failure almost from the first. For that journal Dostoevsky wrote *Notes from Underground* while his wife lay on her deathbed and he himself was in ill health. Shortly thereafter his brother Michael died, and Dostoevsky assumed all his obligations. Another friend and important contributor to the journal, A. Grigor'ev, also died. To escape creditors, Dostoevsky had to go abroad. He returned to finish *Crime and Punishment,* which, like all his work, was published serially in Russian periodicals. He had also contracted with a shrewd but unscrupulous publisher to provide a new work for a collected edition of his works, and, if it was not ready by a certain date, to forfeit author's rights to those works permanently. To meet his deadline, Dostoevsky started to dictate *The Gambler* (based on the passions of his second trip to Europe) to a young lady who subsequently became his second wife. Again he left Russia, and for the next four years in Germany, Switzerland and Italy underwent great poverty and privation, but also had a period of great productivity, writing *The Idiot* (1867), *The Eternal Husband* (1870) and beginning *The Devils.* He returned to Russia to finish the last.

For years he had mercilessly driven himself, hastily writing an incredible quantity to meet various pressures and obligations, complaining that he was exploited, rushed, that he had no chance to rework and polish his material, to show himself at his best. In the last years of his life, when he was already renowned and sought after, his material lot greatly improved. In 1873 he edited a periodical. In 1875 he published the weakest of his novels, *The Adolescent* (known in English as *A Raw Youth*), at excellent rates. The year following he began to issue serially a public *Writer's Diary,* reminiscences and running commentaries on art, literature, politics, and the Russian scene. The *Diary* had a wide following, and was both an intellectual and financial success. The last three years of his life were spent on the composition of *The Brothers Karamazov.* While this novel is the crowning glory of Dostoevsky's career, he viewed it merely as the first volume of a projected novel of much greater scope. His death in 1881 was almost an occasion for national mourning, a fact given authority by the estimated 40,000 who attended his funeral.

While Dostoevsky's early works have considerable merit, it has become customary to consider the *Notes from Underground* as ushering in his mature production, as a prologue to the tragedy depicted in the five large novels written subsequently. This view no doubt results from very un-Dostoevskian oversimplification; yet the *Notes* do mark a change in ideas and a refinement in techniques.

Dostoevsky had, of course, meditated profoundly on the nature of man and had ably expounded his views in *Notes from House of the Dead.* Now a series of external stimuli helped him to recast his thoughts. He had earlier abandoned the naïve sociological theories that attracted him in his youth, not for the imprisonment and deprivation he had suffered for studying them, but because they no longer corresponded to his deeper insight into the nature of man. His trips abroad disclosed to him the corruption of Western Europe, the inadequacy, the blindness of conceiving man and his destiny in terms of mechanically ameliorating his lot. In *Winter Notes on Summer Impressions* Dostoevsky already adumbrated the beginnings of his own positive views, though he was never to state them effectively except in the highly complex and dramatic world of his novels.

Meanwhile, the Russian so-called liberal and radical camp, basing its arguments on European notions of man's rationality and perfectibility, and making utility the ultimate criterion for man's achievements, expounded its notions and the hope for progress in a series of works that infuriated Dostoevsky. The most important of these was the novel *What Is to Be Done?,* conceived by its author, the critic N. G. Chernyshevsky, as an alternate version of his projected *Encyclopedia of Knowledge and Life* "in the lightest, most popular spirit, almost in the form of a novel, with anecdotes, scenes, pictures, so that it will even be read by people who read practically nothing but novels." There is no other example in world literature of so shoddy a work capturing and maintaining its hold on a large section of a country's "reading" population—both under the czars and in the Soviet Union. Here the ideas of reason, rationalism, man acting for his own advantage, the doctrine of environment, the notion of man's perfectibility and his ceaseless striving toward a perfect, harmonious society are artlessly repeated. In the appendix to this volume the reader will find the excerpts from Chernyshevsky's novel pertinent to the *Notes*. Only the lengthy tale of Kryukova's regeneration and reintegration into society, the immediate predecessor for Dostoevsky's satire in the *Notes* on the theme of the redeemed prostitute, is omitted. Everything about the book sounded false to Dostoevsky. As a journalist and publicist of great abilities he eagerly welcomed the opportunity to criticize the novel in the first issue of his new journal *The Epoch*. The form his criticism finally took was the *Notes from Underground*. Naturally, mutual recriminations between the radical camp and Dostoevsky resumed immediately after the publication of the *Notes*. A slashing satire on Dostoevsky, his journal, and the *Notes,* ostensibly written by Shchedrin, elicited a vigorous rejoinder by Dostoevsky. In the appendix, both are presented in English for the first time.[1] The rivalry between Dostoevsky and the liberals continued for many years, both in periodical literature and through easily identifiable references in Dostoevsky's fiction. For there was more than a temporary rift between the two—there was a fundamental and irreconcilable difference in their views of man.

This need not imply that Dostoevsky's ideas were shaped as a momentary and point-by-point refutation of his antagonists, for many of these ideas had already been formulated elsewhere.

---

[1] In addition to the excerpts from Chernyshevsky's novel, the satire on Dostoevsky by Shchedrin and rebuttal by Dostoevsky, the appendix also contains basic formulations of the problems from Dostoevsky's *Winter Notes on Summer Impressions* and excerpts from his correspondence indicating the germination and progress of the *Notes from Underground*.

But the immediate polemics did determine the direction of the *Notes.* The first section of the *Notes,* the jeering, venomous monologue of the narrator, is directed against the basic materialistic and scientific assumption of civilization in the nineteenth century, and nothing, even the self, is spared from his relentless analysis. That view, propounded in Russia by Chernyshevsky and others, holds that man is good, that he seeks his own advantage, and will seek everyone's communal advantage as he becomes more enlightened, that a new golden age, a new Eden, will dawn as soon as man behaves according to rational, scientific principles. The truths of science are unquestionable and final, and lead inexorably to a recognition of doctrines of determinism and necessity.

For Dostoevsky, the tawdry liberalism that resulted from these ideas led inevitably to the most barren form of Utopian socialism founded on man's reason, on his ostensible goodness and nobility. Through the narrator of the *Notes,* Dostoevsky draws up a powerful indictment of these theories. Man will never desire these things, for he is not so constituted. Man is irrational, capricious; he refuses to be categorized and limited, precisely because he is a man. The narrator scoffs and rails at "two times two makes four," "the wall," "piano key," the recurrent abstractions that stand for rationalism and scientific determinism, as they indicate to him an inhumanity, a reduction of the will, a finality that signifies death. He finds further symbols for man's social organization in three communal organizations: the anthill, the chicken coop, and the crystal palace.

The anthill is a perfect and permanent community where each member's instinctive duties and attendant rewards are clearly defined. The anthill will never change unless nature itself does, for it satisfies the ant's physical needs perfectly. But man has a rational faculty in addition to physical needs: he will not limit himself to his animal nature. Next, through an oblique reference to *Don Quixote,* the narrator proceeds to another possible form of communal life, the chicken coop—an imperfect form of the anthill. It has a deceptive reality and must not be accepted as anything more than a temporary convenience. For chicken coop we can also read apartment blocks, the impersonal and very defective shelter that man has come to create for himself. Finally, there is the crystal palace, at that time a recent marvel. Constructed of glass and steel for the exposition in London, representing the very latest in man's achievement, it became the symbol of perfection and attainment. Dostoevsky objects to its merely mechanical perfection. It satisfies man's physical needs, but not his spiritual ones. It is only an oversized anthill, a more imposing chicken coop.

Much wider implications lurk beyond these immediate explanations. They depend upon two antecedent theories. Hegel's formula "All that exists is rational, all that is rational exists" and the Hegelian World-Will provide the basis for scientific determinism, materialism, and the idea of historical progress. Rousseau, the *"homme de la nature et vérité"* who emphasized the individual and feelings, opened a whole new era. What had previously been considered as moral or religious transgression could now be examined as a psychological phenomenon—not the less disturbing, but explicable in other terms: those of individual reactions, of the individual's right and desire to assert his individuality in the face of society. It is but one further step, a step Rousseau frequently took in his own *Confessions,* to absolve the individual and place the blame on his environment. No two theories seem at first to be more antithetical. Yet they were ultimately combined in such sanguine utopias as Chernyshevsky's, not to mention the more real, short-lived attempts of Fourier and Saint-Simon. Dostoevsky combats both ideas. His author's footnote identifies the narrator as an historical phenomenon that had to spring up under particular circumstances, a peculiarly nineteenth-century phenomenon. The footnote marks the juncture of the two ideas; the text examines the resultant moral illness.

One cause of this illness, and some explanation for man's behavior, lies in urbanism. Dostoevsky, like Dickens and Balzac, is primarily a novelist of the city, and has fixed an image of Petersburg forever in the minds of readers. One of his earliest stories, *The Double*, is subtitled "A Petersburg Poem." It uses St. Petersburg, "the most fantastic and intentional city in the world," as an effective backdrop. Ever since it was founded by Peter the Great at the beginning of the eighteenth century, few other cities have so clearly symbolized impersonality, man's willful imposition of an artificial order on nature, and the toll it has exacted on man in return. Another of Dostoevsky's early stories, *White Nights*, emphasizes the eerie beauty of St. Petersburg's gigantic constructs, particularly in the summertime, when daylight lasts almost throughout the night. In this strange artificial setting, man loses touch with nature, distorts the meaning of natural phenomena, and ultimately distorts his own personality. Thus snow, a vital element in the *Notes*, becomes dingy, yellow, wet, and all its associations are unpleasant. It is never conceived neutrally, much less as though it were exhilarating. Similarly, the narrator of the *Notes* incarcerates himself in his quarters. His sallies into the open are infrequent and usually not very successful. Even opening a window is so rare an event that its occurrence in the *Notes* is highly revealing.

Dostoevsky considers the consequences of urbanism in an even broader sense. His vague political platform, formulated at that time and called *"Pochvenichestva"* (from *"pochva"*—soil), held that Russians were losing their identity and hindering their spontaneous development because they had lost touch with their native soil. They had substituted abstract, harmful ideas that originated in Western Europe for their native heritage, and these ideas are transmitted and find expression primarily in the large cities. The narrator conveniently groups them under the rubric "the sublime and the beautiful," and they range far beyond Hegel and Rousseau. They are modern, philosophical, pseudophilosophical and humanitarian ideas, primarily from Germany and France. While the specific reference seems to be to Kant, the "sublime and the beautiful" covers such notions as Schelling's *Naturphilosophie* and the literary productions of Schiller and German romantics that played an important role in the developments of Russian thought and literature in the second quarter of the nineteenth century. Striving for a vague ideal, surrendering oneself to pleasant meditations and feelings, seeking refuge in a supersensory realm resulted in the blunting of immediate reactions and responses to actual things, and escape into daydreaming, meditation, fancy. This plays an important function in Dostoevsky's early works and is clearly vital to an understanding of the narrator's personality. For man's increased consciousness of himself and the impingement of society on his individual life force him more and more persistently into daydreams, so much so that they interfere with the process of living. "We have almost reached the point of looking at actual 'real life' as an effort," writes the narrator, "almost as hard work, and we are all privately agreed that it is better in books."

Nevertheless, consciousness (or conscience, for the word in Russian carries two meanings, the cognitive and the ethical), through which man distinguishes himself from animals, arises from conflict with reality, not from abstraction. Consciousness leads, in the narrator's formulation, to "intensively developed individuality" and involves separation, loneliness, isolation. Such withdrawal, however, while desperately defending the validity of the individual, paradoxically recognizes his dependence on humanity at large. Insofar as consciousness is an act of ratiocination, it precludes action: "Every primary cause immediately indicates another, even more primary cause." If finite, scientific thought leads to unacceptable, deadly conclusions, then thought can only be considered relative and action must be denied, for all positive assertion indicates limitation. And so modern man must be characterless, "neither spiteful nor good, neither scoundrel nor noble, neither a hero nor an insect." Better to do nothing than to commit oneself to limitation. Still, such a life becomes boring. Out of his impasse and tragic isolation, the narrator begins to "create life," to lose himself in imaginary adventures. At the same time he stands apart and judges those adventures. In him the sublime and grotesque exist side by side; bookish fantasies of himself as noble and generous coexist with petty debauchery. The narrator's desperate solution is to refine the realization of one's despicability to such a pitch that the anguish it induces becomes an outright pleasure. Hyperconsciousness may be a disease, entailing suffering, but man prefers suffering, which is the token of his individuality, to a life devoid of suffering but also devoid of individuality, hence of humanity. This chain of thought, then, asserts the tragedy of modern man.

Suffering and the necessity for suffering become a mainstay of Dostoevsky's philosophy. In the *Notes* he introduces one of his most brilliant discoveries, that suffering can become an object rather than a result. Hyperconsciousness can only find pleasure in the refinements of suffering by substituting an aesthetic scheme for an ethical one. One no longer questions *what* is reflected—pleasure, pain, good or evil—but rather *how* it is reflected. If one can derive pleasure from the consciousness of one's pain, and at the same time invent situations giving rise to that pain, then one can do without real life. The narrator eventually feels that it would be a "superfluous luxury" to apply the emotions in his invented adventures to "real life." He even attempts to destroy his last refuge, aesthetic pleasure, by claiming to destroy the novel form, as all the traits of the anti-hero are gathered in this work on purpose. Yet the final note emphasizes that he continues to derive pleasure from committing his more painful experiences to paper.

The whole scheme is of course a barren treadmill. The narrator has a dim consciousness of that, too: "It is not at all underground that is better, but something different, entirely different, for which I long." Intellect alone cannot explain the essence of man. Dostoevsky saw that the answer to this paradox lay not in reason but in faith, in an acceptance of belief and Christ. We gather from the letter to his brother given in the appendix that this was clearly indicated in section ten of Part I, but that the censor mutilated the passage. There are only vague hints left in that chapter. The narrator now seeks a "crystal edifice" rather than a "crystal palace"—an acceptable ideal unlike any he has commented on so far. Strange as it may seem, Dostoevsky did not restore the cuts when he subsequently republished the *Notes,* and their omission makes the *Notes* one of the gloomiest works in world literature. Nevertheless, the omission is just and artistically justified: the narrator, the strange psychological personality displayed before us, must be left in limbo. No solution is possible for him.

One can assert this the more surely as the *Notes* is first and foremost a work of fiction, not a philosophical tract. While the narrator indubitably comes to symbolize modern man, he is primarily a narrator in a confession, a literary form particularly favored by Dostoevsky. The *Notes* were first announced under the title *A Confession.* They take the form of an extended monologue, but are full of suggestions of dialogue: "you say," "you laugh," "this is all that you say," "yes, gentlemen," and so on. Such locutions also appear sporadically in Dostoevsky's earlier critical work; they dominate his *Diary of a Writer,* since Dostoevsky's thought and the temper of his mind are dialectic to an extraordinary degree. In the *Notes,* however, their function is broader. The narrator, by his own admission, is writing a confession, and he maintains that the oratorical flourishes simply exist so that he may express himself more easily and clearly. But this in turn gives the work the illusion of dialogue and makes it seem like a sustained polemic with an opponent, as if the narrator were anticipating objections. Like all confessions, the narrator's confession postulates the existence of an auditor, but psychologically, the auditor here is never passive and cannot be passive for this is a confession to one's self—the auditor and the confessor are one. The *Notes* may even be considered as a parody of confession which, in religious terms, is ostensibly preceded by contrition, but here is replaced by proud (though ambivalent) self-defense. The confession is Rousseauistic rather than Augustinian, with the added temporal notation of Musset's title *Confessions d'un enfant du siècle*. The narrator approves Heine's criticism of Rousseau and of autobiography—that a man will lie about himself from sheer vanity—but he also adduces it as proof that his own confession is true, unexaggerated, since it is not meant for publication. The narrator is correct in his contention, but not in the manner he thinks. Dostoevsky's psychological insight permits him to trace a portrait which is, or can be, clear to the reader despite the narrator's evasions, repetitions, contradictions, self-lacerations. At their deepest level the narrator's analyses are honestly meant. That they appear not to be so, or to be incorrect, can be attributed to the distortion of these analyses and judgments by the narrator's personality. The reader must constantly discount the distorting prism, and assess the narrator's incorrect judgments about others and himself in terms of what they tell about the narrator. The narrator is portrayed twice. His own statements account for his actions at one level, but his statements are not trustworthy. Dostoevsky indicates the profounder psychological level which is manifest in the contradiction between the narrator's analyses and his behavior. Parenthetically, it should be pointed out that the narrator's knowledge is not emotional but rational; that although he claims about the *Notes* "it's hardly literature so much as corrective punishment," the *Notes*—unlike those of the *Adolescent*—have no ameliorative or therapeutic value to their ostensible author.

The confessional form also affects the structure of the *Notes*. So long as we consider the *Notes* as a psychological portrait, their main interest for the narrator lies in the symbolic re-enactment of his experiences in the second part. From that point of view, much of the first part is simply a false start, an attempt by the narrator to present himself to his imaginary audience—or even merely to a mirror—in a more attractive light, by parading before it the brilliance of his intellect. Still, the narrator's personality is equally evident in both parts. In the first, psychology is turned into a polemic against intellectual theories; in the second, it is externalized, projected onto characters and situations. But the relationship of the parts is far from mechanical. Part II is a continuation as well as a result of Part I, a reply as well as an illustration.

Part I falls into three main sections. The short introduction propounds a number of riddles whose meaning will be further developed. Sections two, three and four deal with suffering and the enjoyment of suffering; sections five and six with intellectual and moral vacillation and with conscious "inertia"—inaction; sections seven through nine with theories of reason and advantage; the last two sections are a summary and a transition to Part II. Similarly, Part II focuses on three incidents. The first, the incident with the officer on the Nevsky Prospect, illustrates the narrator's theories on insults and suffering; the second, the farewell dinner for Zverkov, is clearly connected with vacillation and "inertia"; the third and most crucial episode, that with the prostitute Liza, is the extension and embodiment of the narrator's theories on reason and advantage, and of his views on the nature of man. While each may start as an illustration of a previously stated idea, it rapidly assumes the richness and complexity of human behavior, involving other people, other ideas, giving substance to its subject. They show man in the throes of irrational impulses, working to his own detriment, purposely rejecting proffered solutions. Short of analyzing Part II in detail, we may still note that in the central episode with Liza, the narrator has tried with spectacular success to arouse an ignorant soul and has led it out of an acquiescence to, and involvement in, humanity's shoddier side to an appreciation of its individuality, value, and stature. The narrator has salvaged one life, and in his concern for an "insignificant" person has demonstrated the mainspring of his view of man. The success of his effort, both on Liza and on himself (for he becomes involved in his own eloquence and is moved by it), indicates that he has found and developed the basic issues to which man responds.

The continuation, at his own rooms, even provides the solution unsuccessfully sought in Part I. For Dostoevsky, only love in its Christian meaning made life bearable. The love Liza offers the narrator when she recognizes his unhappiness is the climax of the work. It is the highest level of relationship reached by the narrator. The officer in the first episode had completely ignored him; his former classmates had only tolerated him ungraciously; Liza accepts him completely, for she now recognizes him as an unhappy fellow creature. But for the narrator, petty motives of vanity, self-revenge, of psychological illness, coupled with the moral illness that, for all its rejection of reason, cannot in the final analysis accept non-rational theory or religion, all these now assert themselves and render Liza's offer unacceptable. He prefers his unhappy state to any solution, and his preference is perfectly characteristic in terms of the artistic work Dostoevsky has presented to the reader. Only a formal conclusion is necessary. Even here, however, the treadmill continues. The conclusion drives the reader back to Part I, the product of "forty years' thought in the underground," to a whole philosophy of tragedy: the tragedy of the individual and freedom, the tragedy of the historical process, the tragedy of universal evil.

A number of years after writing the *Notes* Dostoevsky is reported to have said that the attitudes of the *Notes* were rather too extreme and that it is a point of view he has long since passed. Readers of the work, however, have all too eagerly accepted the image of the narrator as the symbol of modern man, as a precursor of Existentialist thought, as themselves. Like the narrator they permit themselves a loophole—it is what the narrator represents, it is his plight, his intellectual temperament that are recognized as their own, but not, usually, his personality. In fact, however, the two necessarily complement each other. The narrator's figure has so impressed itself in the consciousness of readers that he has been made into an archetype: criticism rarely speaks of him as a "narrator"—an accepted literary convention—and has made him into "the underground man."

* * *

"The Grand Inquisitor" is narrated by another of Dostoevsky's brilliant and self-torturing rationalists at a crucial point in *The Brothers Karamazov*. To lift it from its context is to distort its meaning, for it too is a highly revealing confession by a character and is elsewhere in the novel balanced by other confessions, statements, attitudes and actions, both by the author of the legend and by other characters. Even the refutation of its own argument, contained within "The Grand Inquisitor," will primarily appear in logical terms rather than the solutions the novel's dramatic action offers. "The Grand Inquisitor" is a much richer and fuller episode when read in the novel than it can be here. On the other hand, juxtaposing it to the *Notes* more clearly illustrates the relationship of the two works.

The *Notes* had demonstrated that the laws of history and reason show nothing more than man's imperfection. Irrational man rejects a human society based only on external comfort and historical progress and asserts himself by acting against his best interests, merely to assert his individuality. In "The Grand Inquisitor" the problem is stated somewhat differently. As *The Brothers Karamazov* is a theodicy and the legend itself examines the meaning and existence of God and religion, human behavior is no longer considered in terms of rationality or irrationality, but rather as freedom of choice and its consequences. Suffering now is no longer considered in terms of a gnawing senseless toothache: it accompanies man's search for his essential meaning. It is no longer a goal but a necessary, if unfortunate, by-product.

V. V. Rozanov, a fervent admirer and disciple of Dostoevsky, first maintained that all Dostoevsky's work culminates in the philosophical and religious statement of "The Grand Inquisitor" and that the clue to all his subsequent fiction is contained in the *Notes from Underground*. Rozanov inaugurated modern criticism of Dostoevsky, and his views are both useful and essentially accurate, even though they emphasize the ideological, more specifically the religious, in a work, at the expense of its artistic fulfillment.

Rozanov claimed that "The Grand Inquisitor" presented three basic ideas: 1) "Man is weaker and baser by nature than You believed him to be"; 2) "How is the weak soul to blame that it is unable to receive such terrible gifts?"; 3) "Then we will give them the quiet humble happiness of weak creatures such as they are by nature." They may be considered as extensions of the triad—anthill, chicken coop and crystal palace. They also depend on a triad of man's fundamental traits—reason, feeling and will, and what Dostoevsky considered their manifestation in the world—man's search for truth, goodness and freedom. While "The Grand Inquisitor" is based on man's inner demands, it deals primarily with historical contradictions rather than with those demands. The Inquisitor shapes man's fate on earth by utilizing man's weaknesses. True freedom consists in the concord of inner impulse and outer action, but the Inquisitor's utopia denies the essence of man, for it denies him freedom. Christ's repudiation of the devil's three temptations is in turn repudiated by the Inquisitor. He gives man bread instead of freedom, miracles rather than true faith, and accepts temporal power to maintain the spiritual. Thereby he hopes to eliminate the suffering imposed on man in consequence of Christ's overestimate of man's capacities. And he will burn at the stake "heretics" who reject his order and assert their individuality. Dostoevsky, however, exalted freedom at any cost, including suffering: in the legend Christ will not even censure the Inquisitor. If the Inquisitor is to undo his work, the impulse must come from within.

The deepest meaning of "The Grand Inquisitor" is thus the metaphysical assertion of man's freedom. A more limited meaning lies in its defense of Russian Orthodoxy against Roman Catholicism. Dostoevsky felt that the doctrine of apostolic succession betrayed and denied Christianity, as it hindered man's free striving. In "The Grand Inquisitor," therefore, the Catholic Church serves a function similar to that of socialist utopias in the Notes, and indeed it must also be read as a criticism of those ideas. Further, the legend also recapitulates the historical development of political radicalism and of the church. It is the religious statement of the political principle discovered by Shigalev in Dostoevsky's *The Devils:* that starting with absolute freedom one necessarily reaches a position of absolute subjugation.

Even in excerpted form, however, the legend communicates considerably more than these ideas. The ardor of the legend, the persistent image of fire, counteract what Rozanov thought was the abstract and generalizing tendency of the mind (Ivan Karamazov's) that composed "The Grand Inquisitor." Surely a tragedy is inherent in the Inquisitor, who has exceeded by a score of years man's allotted span and who has reached his bitter realization after a lifetime of thought. In *The Brothers Karamazov* the reader may question whether the same qualities are inherent in the twenty-four-year-old Ivan. But there, as in "The Grand Inquisitor" and *Notes from Underground,* Dostoevsky ultimately confronts the reader with the tragic grandeur of man. The narrator from "underground" standing at the crossroads as the snow settles upon him and the Inquisitor carrying within him the burning kiss of Christ are the two facets displayed here.

RALPH E. MATLAW

Princeton University
December 1959

TRANSLATOR'S NOTE

The Constance Garnett versions of *Notes from Underground* and "The Grand Inquisitor" have been thoroughly revised. Some changes were made for accuracy and consistency; others so that the text might approximate Dostoevsky's idiosyncratic style. Certain key words or turns of speech have always been rendered in the same way, even when at times they might have been given more idiomatically. Thus "to be conscious" has been used where "to recognize" might have seemed more desirable stylistically; "after all" when "indeed," "surely," "however" and the like might have provided pleasing variety. I have changed "Thou" to "You" whenever Christ is addressed in "The Grand Inquisitor." It would have sounded too stilted to use "Thou," and, moreover, would have rendered the Inquisitor's colloquial Russian incorrectly. I have, however, retained the Biblical overtones and the use of "Thou" in direct quotations from Scripture. In revising, and in translating the other selections, I have refrained, where possible, from using the quaint locutions, the "little fathers" and "muzhiks" that, "complimenting and ducking each to other," occasionally populate English versions of Russian literature. On the other hand, I have not hesitated to translate into stilted English obvious stylistic infelicities or outright ineptitudes, particularly Chernyshevsky's prose and in the narrator's torturous monologue from "underground." The resulting errors and the odd hits are, of course, mine.

R. E. M.

Notes from Underground

PART ONE

Underground[1]

I

I am a sick man . . . I am a spiteful man. I am an unpleasant man. I think my liver is diseased. However, I don't know beans about my disease, and I am not sure what is bothering me. I don't treat it and never have, though I respect medicine and doctors. Besides, I am extremely superstitious, let's say sufficiently so to respect medicine. (I am educated enough not to be superstitious, but I am.) No, I refuse to treat it out of spite. You probably will not understand that. Well, but *I* understand it. Of course, I can't explain to you just whom I am annoying in this case by my spite. I am perfectly well aware that I cannot "get even" with the doctors by not consulting them. I know better than anyone that I thereby injure only myself and no one else. But still, if I don't treat it, it is out of spite. My liver is bad, well then—let it get even worse!

I have been living like that for a long time now—twenty years. I am forty now. I used to be in the civil service, but no

[1] The author of these notes and the "Notes" themselves are, of course, imaginary. Nevertheless, such persons as the writer of these notes, not only may, but positively must, exist in our society, considering those circumstances under which our society was in general formed. I wanted to expose to the public more clearly than it is done usually, one of the characters of the recent past. He is one of the representatives of the current generation. In this excerpt, entitled "Underground," this person introduces himself, his views, and, as it were, tries to explain the reasons why he appeared and was bound to appear in our midst. In the following excerpt, the actual notes of this person about several events in his life will appear. (*Fyodor Dostoevsky*)

shows serial nature

3

longer am. I was a spiteful official. I was rude and took pleasure in being so. After all, I did not accept bribes, so I was bound to find a compensation in that, at least. (A bad joke but I will not cross it out. I wrote it thinking it would sound very witty; but now that I see myself that I only wanted to show off in a despicable way, I will purposely not cross it out!) When petitioners would come to my desk for information I would gnash my teeth at them, and feel intense enjoyment when I succeeded in distressing someone. I was almost always successful. For the most part they were all timid people—of course, they were petitioners. But among the fops there was one officer in particular I could not endure. He simply would not be humble, and clanked his sword in a disgusting way. I carried on a war with him for eighteen months over that sword. At last I got the better of him. He left off clanking it. However, that happened when I was still young. But do you know, gentlemen, what the real point of my spite was? Why, the whole trick, the real vileness of it lay in the fact that continually, even in moments of the worst spleen, I was inwardly conscious with shame that I was not only not spiteful but not even an embittered man, that I was simply frightening sparrows at random and amusing myself by it. I might foam at the mouth, but bring me some kind of toy, give me a cup of tea with sugar, and I would be appeased. My heart might even be touched, though probably I would gnash my teeth at myself afterward and lie awake at night with shame for months after. That is the way I am.

I was lying when I said just now that I was a spiteful official. I was lying out of spite. I was simply indulging myself with the petitioners and with the officer, but I could never really become spiteful. Every moment I was conscious in myself of many, very many elements completely opposite to that. I felt them positively teeming in me, these opposite elements. I knew that they had been teeming in me all my life, begging to be let out, but I would not let them, would not let them, purposely would not let them out. They tormented me till I was ashamed; they drove me to convulsions, and finally, they bored me, how they bored me! Well, are you not imagining, gentlemen, that I am repenting for something now, that I am asking your forgiveness for something? I am sure you are imagining that. However, I assure you it does not matter to me if you are.

Not only could I not become spiteful, I could not even become anything: neither spiteful nor kind, neither a rascal nor an honest man, neither a hero nor an insect. Now, I am living out my life in my corner, taunting myself with the spiteful and useless consolation that an intelligent man cannot seriously become anything and that only a fool can become something. Yes, an intelligent man in the nineteenth century must and morally ought to be pre-eminently a characterless creature; a man of character, an active man, is pre-eminently a limited creature. That is the conviction of my forty years. I am forty years old now, and forty years, after all, is a whole lifetime; after all, that is extreme old age. To live longer than forty years is bad manners; it is vulgar, immoral. Who does live beyond forty? Answer that, sincerely and honestly. I will tell you who do: fools and worthless people do. I tell all old men that to their face, all those respectable old men, all those silver-haired and reverend old men! I tell the whole world that to its face. I have a right to say so, for I'll go on living to sixty myself. I'll live till seventy! Till eighty! Wait, let me catch my breath.

No doubt you think, gentlemen, that I want to amuse you. You are mistaken in that, too. I am not at all such a merry person as you imagine, or as you may imagine; however, if irritated by all this babble (and I can feel that you are irritated) you decide to ask me just who I am—then my answer is, I am a certain low-ranked civil servant. I was in the service in order to have something to eat (but only for that reason), and when last year a distant relation left me six thousand roubles in his will I immediately retired from the service and settled down in my corner. I used to live in this corner before, but now I have settled down in it. My room is a wretched, horrid one on the outskirts of town. My servant is an old country-woman, spiteful out of stupidity, and, moreover, she always smells bad. I am told that the Petersburg climate is bad for me, and that with my paltry means it is very expensive to live in Petersburg. I know all that better than all these sage and experienced counsellors and monitors. But I am going to stay in Petersburg. I will not leave Petersburg! I will not leave because . . . Bah, after all it does not matter in the least whether I leave or stay.

But incidentally, what can a decent man speak about with the greatest pleasure?

Answer: About himself.

Well, then, I will talk about myself.

II

Now I want to tell you, gentlemen, whether you care to hear it or not, why I could not even become an insect. I tell you solemnly that I wanted to become an insect many times. But I was not even worthy of that. I swear to you, gentlemen, that to be hyperconscious is a disease, a real positive disease. Ordinary human consciousness would be too much for man's everyday needs, that is, half or a quarter of the amount which falls to the lot of a cultivated man of our unfortunate nineteenth century, especially one who has the particular misfortune to inhabit Petersburg, the most abstract and intentional city in the whole world. (There are intentional and unintentional cities.) It would have been quite enough, for instance, to have the consciousness by which all so-called straightforward persons and men of action live. I'll bet you think I am writing all this to show off, to be witty at the expense of men of action; and what is more, that out of ill-bred showing-off, I am clanking a sword, like my officer. But, gentlemen, whoever can pride himself on his diseases and even show off with them?

However, what am I talking about? Everyone does that. They do pride themselves on their diseases, and I, perhaps, more than anyone. There is no doubt about it: my objection was absurd. Yet just the same, I am firmly convinced not only that a great deal of consciousness, but that any consciousness is a disease. I insist on it. Let us drop that, too, for a minute. Tell me this: why did it happen that at the very, yes, at the very moment when I was most capable of recognizing every refinement of "all the sublime and beautiful," as we used to say at one time, I would, as though purposely, not only feel but do such hideous things, such that—well, in short, such as everyone probably does but which, as though purposely, occurred to me at the very time when I was most conscious that they ought not to be done. The more conscious I was of goodness, and of all that "sublime and beautiful," the more deeply I sank into my mire and the more capable I became of sinking into it completely. But the main thing was that all this did not seem to occur in me accidentally, but as though it had to be so. As though it were my most normal condition, and not in the least disease or depravity, so that finally I even lost the desire to struggle against this depravity. It ended by my almost believing (perhaps actually believing) that probably this was really my normal condition. But at first, in the beginning, that is, what agonies I suffered in that struggle! I did not believe that others went through the same things, and therefore I hid this fact about myself as a secret all my life. I was ashamed (perhaps I am even ashamed now). I reached the point of feeling a sort of secret abnormal, despicable enjoyment in returning home to my corner on some disgusting Petersburg night, and being acutely conscious that that day I had again done something loathsome, that what was done could never be undone, and secretly, inwardly gnaw, gnaw at myself for it, nagging and consuming myself till at last the bitterness turned into a sort of shameful accursed sweetness, and finally into real positive enjoyment! Yes, into enjoyment, into enjoyment! I insist upon that. And that is why I have started to speak, because I keep wanting to know for a fact whether other people feel such an enjoyment. Let me explain: the enjoyment here consisted precisely in the hyperconsciousness of one's own degradation; it was from feeling oneself that one had reached the last barrier, that it was nasty, but that it could not be otherwise; that you no longer had an escape; that you could never become a different person; that even if there remained enough time and faith for you to change into something else you probably would not want to change; or if you did want to, even then you would do nothing; because perhaps in reality there was nothing for you to change into. And the worst of it, and the root of it all, was that it all proceeded according to the normal and fundamental laws of hyperconsciousness, and with the inertia that was the direct result of those laws, and that consequently one could not only not change but one could do absolutely nothing. Thus it would follow, as the result of hyperconsciousness, that one is not to blame for being a scoundrel, as though that were any consolation to the scoundrel once he himself has come to realize that he actually is a scoundrel. But enough. Bah, I have talked a lot of nonsense, but what have I explained? Can this enjoyment be explained? But I will explain it! I will get to the bottom of it! That is why I have taken up my pen.

To take an instance, I am terribly vain. I am as suspicious and touchy as a hunchback or a dwarf. But to tell the truth, there have been moments when if someone had happened to slap my face I would, perhaps, have even been glad of that. I say, very seriously, that I would probably have been able to discover a peculiar sort of enjoyment even in that—the enjoyment, of course, of despair; but in despair occur the most intense enjoyments, especially when one is very acutely conscious of one's hopeless position. As for the slap in the face—why then the consciousness of being beaten to a pulp would positively overwhelm one. The worst of it is, no matter how I tried, it still turned out that I was always the most to blame in everything, and what is most humiliating of all, to blame for no fault of my own but, so to say, through the laws of nature. In the first place, to blame because I am cleverer than any of the people surrounding me. (I have always considered myself cleverer than any of the people surrounding me, and sometimes, would you believe it, I have even been ashamed of that. At any rate, all my life, I have, as it were, looked away and I could never look people straight in the eye.) To blame, finally, because even if I were magnanimous, I would only have suffered more from the consciousness of all its uselessness. After all, I would probably never have been able to do anything with my magnanimity—neither to forgive, for my assailant may have slapped me because of the laws of nature, and one cannot forgive the laws of nature; nor to forget, for even if it were the laws of nature, it is insulting all the same. Finally, even if I had wanted to be anything but magnanimous, had desired on the contrary to revenge myself on the man who insulted me, I could not have revenged myself on anyone for anything because I would certainly never have made up my mind to do anything, even if I had been able to. Why would I not have made up my mind? I want to say a few words about that in particular.

III

After all, people who know how to revenge themselves and to take care of themselves in general, how do they do it? After all, when they are possessed, let us suppose, by the feeling of revenge, then for the time there is nothing else but that feeling left in their whole being. Such a man simply rushes straight toward his object like an infuriated bull with its horns down, and nothing but a wall will stop him. (By the way: facing the wall, such people—that is, the straightforward persons and men of action—are genuinely nonplussed. For them a wall is not an evasion, as for example for us people who think and consequently do nothing; it is not an excuse for turning aside, an excuse for which our kind is always very glad, though we scarcely believe in it ourselves, usually. No, they are nonplussed in all sincerity. The wall has for them something tranquilizing, morally soothing, final— maybe even something mysterious . . . but of the wall later.)

Well, such a direct person I regard as the real normal man, as his tender mother nature wished to see him when she graciously brought him into being on the earth. I envy such a man till I am green in the face. He is stupid. I am not disputing that, but perhaps the normal man should be stupid, how do you know? Perhaps it is very beautiful, in fact. And I am all the more convinced of that suspicion, if one can call it so, by the fact that if, for instance, you take the antithesis of the normal man, that is, the hyperconscious man, who has come, of course, not out of the lap of nature but out of a retort (this is almost mysticism, gentlemen, but I suspect this, too), this retort-made man is sometimes so nonplussed in the presence of his antithesis that with all his hyperconsciousness he genuinely thinks of himself as a mouse and not a man. It may be a hyperconscious mouse, yet it is a mouse, while the other is a man, and therefore, etc. And the worst is, he himself, his very own self, looks upon himself as a mouse. No one asks him to do so. And that is an important point. Now let us look at this mouse in action. Let us suppose, for instance, that it feels insulted, too (and it almost always does feel insulted), and wants to revenge itself too. There may even be a greater accumulation of spite in it than in *l'homme de la nature et de la vérité*. The base, nasty desire to repay with spite whoever has offended it, rankles perhaps even more nastily in it than in *l'homme de la nature et de la vérité*, because *l'homme de la nature et de la vérité* through his innate stupidity looks upon his revenge as justice pure and simple; while in consequence of his hyperconsciousness the mouse does not believe in the justice of it. To come at last to the deed itself, to the very act of revenge. Apart from the one fundamental nastiness the unfortunate mouse succeeds in creating around it so many other nastinesses in the form of doubts and questions, adds to the one question so many unsettled questions, that there inevitably works up around it a sort of fatal brew, a stinking mess, made up of its doubts, agitations and lastly of the contempt spat upon it by the straightforward men of action who stand solemnly about it as judges and arbitrators, laughing at it till their healthy sides ache. Of course the only thing left for it is to dismiss all that with a wave of its paw, and, with a smile of assumed contempt in which it does not even believe itself, creep ignominiously into its mouse-hole. There, in its nasty, stinking, underground home our insulted, crushed and ridiculed mouse promptly becomes absorbed in cold, malignant and, above all, everlasting spite. For forty years together it will remember its injury down to the smallest, most shameful detail, and every time will add, of itself, details still more shameful, spitefully teasing and irritating itself with its own imagination. It will be ashamed of its own fancies, but yet it will recall everything, it will go over it again and again, it will invent lies against itself pretending that those things might have happened, and will forgive nothing. Maybe it will begin to revenge itself, too, but, as it were, piecemeal, in trivial ways, from behind the stove, incognito, without believing either in its own right to vengeance, or in the success of its revenge, knowing beforehand that from all its efforts at revenge it will suffer a hundred times more than he on whom it revenges itself, while he, probably will not even feel it. On its deathbed it will recall it all over again, with interest accumulated over all the years. But it is just in that cold, abominable half-despair, half-belief, in that conscious burying oneself alive for grief in the underworld for forty years, in that hyperconsciousness and yet to some extent doubtful hopelessness of one's position, in that hell of unsatisfied desires turned inward, in that fever of oscillations, of resolutions taken for ever and regretted again a minute later—that the savor of that strange enjoyment of which I have spoken lies. It is so subtle, sometimes so difficult to analyze consciously, that somewhat limited people, or simply people with strong nerves, will not understand anything at all in it. "Possibly," you will add on your own account with a grin, "people who have never received a slap in the face will not understand it either," and in that way you will politely hint to me that I, too, perhaps, have been slapped in the face in my life, and so I speak as an expert.

another possible translation, instead of hyperconsciousness -heightened / acute acute

The Russian word for consciousness, itself, also connotes "conscience" → AWARENESS

I'll bet that you are thinking that. But set your minds at rest, gentlemen, I have not received a slap in the face, though it doesn't matter to me at all what you may think about it. Possibly, I even myself regret that I have given so few slaps in the face during my life. But enough, not another word on the subject of such extreme interest to you.

I will continue calmly about people with strong nerves who do not understand a certain refinement of enjoyment. Though in certain circumstances these gentlemen bellow their loudest like bulls, though this, let us suppose, does them the greatest honor, yet, as I have already said, confronted with the impossible they at once resign themselves. Does the impossible mean the stone wall? What stone wall? Why, of course, the laws of nature, the conclusions of natural science, of mathematics. As soon as they prove to you, for instance, that you are descended from a monkey, then it is no use scowling, accept it as a fact. When they prove to you that in reality one drop of your own fat must be dearer to you than a hundred thousand of your fellow creatures, and that this conclusion is the final solution of all so-called virtues and duties and all such ravings and prejudices, then you might as well accept it, you can't do anything about it, because two times two is a law of mathematics. Just try refuting it.

"But really," they will shout at you, "there is no use protesting; it is a case of two times two makes four! Nature does not ask your permission, your wishes, and whether you like or dislike her laws does not concern her. You are bound to accept her as she is, and consequently also all her conclusions. A wall, you see, is a wall—etc. etc." Good God! but what do I care about the laws of nature and arithmetic, when, for some reason, I dislike those laws and the fact that two times two makes four? Of course I cannot break through a wall by battering my head against it if I really do not have the strength to break through it, but I am not going to resign myself to it simply because it is a stone wall and I am not strong enough.

As though such a stone wall really were a consolation, and

really did contain some word of conciliation, if only because it is as true as two times two makes four. Oh, absurdity of absurdities! How much better it is to understand it all, to be conscious of it all, all the impossibilities and the stone walls, not to resign yourself to a single one of those impossibilities and stone walls if it disgusts you to resign yourself; to reach, through the most inevitable, logical combinations, the most revolting conclusions on the everlasting theme that you are yourself somehow to blame even for the stone wall, though again it is as clear as day you are not to blame in the least, and therefore grinding your teeth in silent impotence sensuously to sink into inertia, brooding on the fact that it turns out that there is even no one for you to feel vindictive against, that you have not, and perhaps never will have, an object for your spite, that it is a sleight-of-hand, a bit of juggling, a card-sharper's trick, that it is simply a mess, no knowing what and no knowing who, but in spite of all these uncertainties, and jugglings, still there is an ache in you, and the more you do not know, the worse the ache.

IV

"Ha, ha, ha! Next you will find enjoyment in a toothache," you cry with a laugh.

"Well? So what? There is enjoyment even in a toothache," I answer. I had a toothache for a whole month and I know there is. In that case, of course, people are not spiteful in silence, they moan; but these are not sincere moans, they are malicious moans, and the maliciousness is the whole point. The sufferer's enjoyment finds expression in those moans; if he did not feel enjoyment in them he would not moan. It is a good example, gentlemen, and I will develop it. The moans express in the first place all the aimlessness of your pain, which is so humiliating to your consciousness; the whole legal system of Nature on which you spit disdainfully, of course, but from which you suffer all the same while she does not. They express the consciousness that

you have no enemy, but that you do have a pain; the consciousness that in spite of all the dentists in the world you are in complete slavery to your teeth; that if someone wishes it, your teeth
will leave off aching, and if he does not, they will go on aching
another three months; and that finally if you still disagree and
still protest, all that is left you for your own gratification is to
thrash yourself or beat your wall with your fist as hard as you
can, and absolutely nothing more. Well then, these mortal insults, these jeers on the part of someone unknown, end at last in
an enjoyment which sometimes reaches the highest degree of
sensuality. I beg you, gentlemen, to listen sometimes to the
moans of an educated man of the nineteenth century who is suffering from a toothache, particularly on the second or third day
of the attack, when he has already begun to moan not as he
moaned on the first day, that is, not simply because he has a
toothache, not just as any coarse peasant might moan, but as a
man affected by progress and European civilization, a man who
is "divorced from the soil and the national principles," as they
call it these days. His moans become nasty, disgustingly spiteful,
and go on for whole days and nights. And, after all, he himself
knows that he does not benefit at all from his moans; he knows
better than anyone that he is only lacerating and irritating himself and others in vain; he knows that even the audience for
whom he is exerting himself and his whole family now listen to
him with loathing, do not believe him for a second, and that
deep down they understand that he could moan differently, more
simply, without trills and flourishes, and that he is only indulging himself like that out of spite, out of malice. Well, sensuality exists precisely in all these consciousnesses and infamies.
"It seems I am troubling you, I am lacerating your hearts, I am
keeping everyone in the house awake. Well, stay awake then,
you, too, feel every minute that I have a toothache. I am no
longer the hero to you now that I tried to appear before, but simply a nasty person, a scoundrel. Well, let it be that way, then! I
am very glad that you see through me. Is it nasty for you to hear

my foul moans? Well, let it be nasty. Here I will let you have an even nastier flourish in a minute. . . ." You still do not understand, gentlemen? No, it seems our development and our consciousness must go further to understand all the intricacies of this sensuality. You laugh? I am delighted. My jokes, gentlemen, are of course in bad taste, uneven, involved, lacking self-confidence. But of course that is because I do not respect myself. Can a man with consciousness respect himself at all?

V

Come, can a man who even attempts to find enjoyment in the very feeling of self-degradation really have any respect for himself at all? I am not saying this now from any insipid kind of remorse. And, indeed, I could never endure to say, "Forgive me, Daddy, I won't do it again," not because I was incapable of saying it, but, on the contrary, perhaps just because I was too capable of it, and in what a way, too! As though on purpose I used to get into trouble on occasions when I was not to blame in the faintest way. That was the nastiest part of it. At the same time I was genuinely touched and repentant, I used to shed tears and, of course, tricked even myself, though it was not acting in the least and there was a sick feeling in my heart at the time. For that one could not even blame the laws of nature, though the laws of nature have offended me continually all my life more than anything. It is loathsome to remember it all, but it was loathsome even then. Of course, in a minute or so I would realize with spite that it was all a lie, a lie, an affected, revolting lie, that is, all this repentance, all these emotions, these vows to reform. And if you ask why I worried and tortured myself that way, the answer is because it was very dull to twiddle one's thumbs, and so one began cutting capers. That is really it. Observe yourselves more carefully, gentlemen, then you will understand that that's right! I invented adventures for myself and made up a life, so as to live at least in some way. How many times it has happened to me—

well, for instance, to take offense at nothing, simply on purpose; and one knows oneself, of course, that one is offended at nothing, that one is pretending, but yet one brings oneself, at last, to the point of really being offended. All my life I have had an impulse to play such pranks, so that in the end, I could not control it in myself. Another time, twice, in fact, I tried to force myself to fall in love. I even suffered, gentlemen, I assure you. In the depth of my heart I did not believe in my suffering, there was a stir of mockery, but yet I did suffer, and in the real, regular way I was jealous, I was beside myself, and it was all out of boredom, gentlemen, all out of boredom; inertia overcame me. After all, the direct, legitimate, immediate fruit of consciousness is inertia, that is, conscious thumb twiddling. I have referred to it already, I repeat, I repeat it emphatically: all straightforward persons and men of action are active just because they are stupid and limited. How can that be explained? This way: as a result of their limitation they take immediate and secondary causes for primary ones, and in that way persuade themselves more quickly and easily than other people do that they have found an infallible basis for their activity, and their minds are at ease and that, you know, is the most important thing. To begin to act, you know, you must first have your mind completely at ease and without a trace of doubt left in it. Well, how am I, for example, to set my mind at rest? Where are the primary causes on which I am to build? Where are my bases? Where am I to get them from? I exercise myself in the process of thinking, and consequently with me every primary cause at once draws after itself another still more primary, and so on to infinity. That is precisely the essence of every sort of consciousness and thinking. It must be a case of the laws of nature again. In what does it finally result? Why, just the same. Remember I spoke just now of vengeance. (I am sure you did not grasp that.) I said that a man revenges himself because he finds justice in it. Therefore he has found a primary cause, found a basis, to wit, justice. And so he is completely set at rest, and consequently he carries out his revenge calmly and successfully, as he is convinced that he is doing a just and honest thing. But, after all, I see no justice in it, I find no sort of virtue in it either, and consequently if I attempt to revenge myself, it would only be out of spite. Spite, of course, might overcome everything, all my doubts, and could consequently serve quite successfully in a place of a primary cause, precisely because it is not a cause. But what can be done if I do not even have spite (after all, I began with that just now)? Again, in consequence of those accursed laws of consciousness, my spite is subject to chemical disintegration. You look into it, the object flies off into air, your reasons evaporate, the criminal is not to be found, the insult becomes fate rather than an insult, something like the toothache, for which no one is to blame, and consequently there is only the same outlet left again—that is, to beat the wall as hard as you can. So you give it up as hopeless because you have not found a fundamental cause. And try letting yourself be carried away by your feelings, blindly, without reflection, without a primary cause, repelling consciousness at least for a time; hate or love, if only not to sit and twiddle your thumbs. The day after tomorrow, at the latest, you will begin despising yourself for having knowingly deceived yourself. The result—a soap-bubble and inertia. Oh, gentlemen, after all, perhaps I consider myself an intelligent man only because all my life I have been able neither to begin nor to finish anything. Granted, granted I am a babbler, a harmless annoying babbler, like all of us. But what is to be done if the direct and sole vocation of every intelligent man is babble, that is, the intentional pouring of water through a sieve?

VI

Oh, if I had done nothing simply out of laziness! Heavens, how I would have respected myself then. I would have respected myself because I would at least have been capable of being lazy; there would at least have been in me one positive quality, as it were, in which I could have believed myself. Question: Who is he? Answer: A loafer. After all, it would have been pleasant to hear that about oneself! It would mean that I was positively defined, it would mean that there was something to be said about me. "Loafer"—why, after all, it is a calling and an appointment, it is a career, gentlemen. Do not joke, it is so. I would then, by rights, be a member of the best club, and would occupy myself only in continually respecting myself. I knew a gentleman who prided himself all his life on being a connoisseur of Lafitte. He considered this as his positive virtue, and never doubted himself. He died, not simply with a tranquil but with a triumphant conscience, and he was completely right. I should have chosen a career for myself then too: I would have been a loafer and a glutton, not a simple one, but, for instance, one in sympathy with everything good and beautiful. How do you like that? I have long had visions of it. That "sublime and beautiful" weighs heavily on my mind at forty. But that is when I am forty, while then—oh, then it would have been different! I would have found myself an appropriate occupation, namely, to drink to the health of everything sublime and beautiful. I would have seized every opportunity to drop a tear into my glass and then to drain it to all that is sublime and beautiful. I would then have turned everything into the sublime and the beautiful; I would have sought out the sublime and the beautiful in the nastiest, most unquestionable trash. I would have become as tearful as a wet sponge. An artist, for instance, paints Ge's picture.[2] At once I drink to the health of the artist who painted Ge's picture, because I love all that is "sublime and beautiful." An author writes "Whatever You Like"[3]; at once I drink to the health of "Whatever You Like" because I love all that is "sublime and beautiful." I would demand respect for doing so, I would persecute anyone who would not

[2] N. N. Ge exhibited his "Last Supper" in 1863. Dostoevsky thought it a faulty conception. The sentence makes no grammatical sense and may refer to Shchedrin's article on the painting, wherein its meaning is further distorted so that, in a sense, "a new picture" is created.

[3] An article on improving man written by Shchedrin, in 1863. See Appendix.

show me respect. I would live at ease, I would die triumphantly—
why, after all, it is charming, perfectly charming! And what a belly
I would have grown, what a triple chin I would have established,
what a red nose I would have produced for myself, so that every
passer-by would have said, looking at me: "Here is an asset!
Here is something really positive!" And, after all, say what you
like, it is very pleasant to hear such remarks about oneself in this
negative age, gentlemen.

VII

But these are all golden dreams. Oh, tell me, who first declared,
who first proclaimed, that man only does nasty things because
he does not know his own real interests; and that if he were enlightened, if his eyes were opened to his real normal interests,
man would at once cease to do nasty things, would at once become good and noble because, being enlightened and understanding his real advantage, he would see his own advantage in
the good and nothing else, and we all know that not a single
man can knowingly act to his own disadvantage. Consequently,
so to say, he would begin doing good through necessity. Oh, the
babe! Oh, the pure, innocent child! Why, in the first place, when
in all these thousands of years has there ever been a time when
man has acted only for his own advantage? What is to be done
with the millions of facts that bear witness that men, *knowingly*,
that is, fully understanding their real advantages, have left them
in the background and have rushed headlong on another path,
to risk, to chance, compelled to this course by nobody and by
nothing, but, as it were, precisely because they did not want the
beaten track, and stubbornly, wilfully, went off on another difficult, absurd way seeking it almost in the darkness. After all, it
means that this stubbornness and willfulness were more pleasant
to them than any advantage. Advantage! What is advantage?
And will you take it upon yourself to define with perfect accuracy in exactly what the advantage of man consists of? And

what if it so happens that a man's advantage *sometimes* not only may, but even must, consist exactly in his desiring under certain conditions what is harmful to himself and not what is advantageous. And if so, if there can be such a condition then the whole principle becomes worthless. What do you think—are there such cases? You laugh; laugh away, gentlemen, so long as you answer me: have man's advantages been calculated with perfect certainty? Are there not some which not only have been included but cannot possibly be included under any classification? After all, you, gentlemen, so far as I know, have taken your whole register of human advantages from the average of statistical figures and scientific-economic formulas. After all, your advantages are prosperity, wealth, freedom, peace—and so on, and so on. So that a man who, for instance, would openly and knowingly oppose that whole list would, to your thinking, and indeed to mine too, of course, be an obscurantist or an absolute madman, would he not? But, after all, here is something amazing: why does it happen that all these statisticians, sages and lovers of humanity, when they calculate human advantages invariably leave one out? They don't even take it into their calculation in the form in which it should be taken, and the whole reckoning depends upon that. There would be no great harm to take it, this advantage, and to add it to the list. But the trouble is, that this strange advantage does not fall under any classification and does not figure in any list. For instance, I have a friend. Bah, gentlemen! But after all he is your friend, too; and indeed there is no one, no one, to whom he is not a friend! When he prepares for any undertaking this gentleman immediately explains to you, pompously and dearly, exactly how he must act in accordance with the laws of reason and truth. What is more, he will talk to you with excitement and passion of the real normal interests of man; with irony he will reproach the short-sighted fools who do not understand their own advantage, for the true significance of virtue; and, within a quarter of an hour, without any sudden outside provocation, but precisely through that something internal which is stronger than all his advantages, he will go off on quite a different tack—that is, act directly opposite to what he has just been saying himself, in opposition to the laws of reason, in opposition to his own advantage—in fact, in opposition to everything. I warn you that my friend is a compound personality, and therefore it is somehow difficult to blame him as an individual. The fact is, gentlemen, it seems that something that is dearer to almost every man than his greatest advantages must really exist, or (not to be illogical) there is one most advantageous advantage (the very one omitted of which we spoke just now) which is more important and more advantageous than all other advantages, for which, if necessary, a man is ready to act in opposition to all laws, that is, in opposition to reason, honor, peace, prosperity—in short, in opposition to all those wonderful and useful things if only he can attain that fundamental, most advantageous advantage which is dearer to him than all.

"Well, but it is still advantage just the same," you will retort. But excuse me, I'll make the point clear, and it is not a case of a play on words, but what really matters is that this advantage is remarkable from the very fact that it breaks down all our classifications, and continually shatters all the systems evolved by lovers of mankind for the happiness of mankind. In short, it interferes with everything. But before I mention this advantage to you, I want to compromise myself personally, and therefore I boldly declare that all these fine systems—all these theories for explaining to mankind its real normal interests, so that inevitably striving to obtain these interests, it may at once become good and noble—are, in my opinion, so far, mere logical exercises. Yes, logical exercises. After all, to maintain even this theory of the regeneration of mankind by means of its own advantage, is, after all, to my mind almost the same thing as—as to claim, for instance, with Buckle, that through civilization mankind becomes softer, and consequently less bloodthirsty, and less fitted for warfare. Logically it does not seem to follow from his arguments. But man is so fond of systems and abstract deductions that he is ready to distort the truth intentionally, he is ready to deny what he can see and hear just to justify his logic. I take this example because it is the most glaring instance of it. Only look about you: blood is being spilled in streams, and in the merriest way, as though it were champagne. Take the whole of the nineteenth century in which Buckle lived. Take Napoleon—both the Great and the present one. Take North America—the eternal union. Take farcical Schleswig-Holstein. And what is it that civilization softens in us? Civilization only produces a greater variety of sensations in man—and absolutely nothing more. And through the development of this variety, man may even come to find enjoyment in bloodshed. After all, it has already happened to him. Have you noticed that the subtlest slaughterers have almost always been the most civilized gentlemen, to whom the various Attilas and Stenka Razins could never hold a candle, and if they are not so conspicuous as the Attilas and Stenka Razins it is precisely because they are so often met with, are so ordinary and have become so familiar to us. In any case if civilization has not made man more bloodthirsty, it has at least made him more abominably, more loathsomely bloodthirsty than before. Formerly he saw justice in bloodshed and with his conscience at peace exterminated whomever he thought he should. And now while we consider bloodshed an abomination, we nevertheless engage in this abomination and even more than ever before. Which is worse? Decide that for yourselves. It is said that Cleopatra (pardon the example from Roman history) was fond of sticking gold pins into her slave-girls' breasts and derived enjoyment from their screams and writhing. You will say that that occurred in comparatively barbarous times; that these are barbarous times too, because (also comparatively speaking) pins are stuck in even now; that even though man has now learned to see more clearly occasionally than in barbarous times, he is still far from having *accustomed* himself to act as reason and science would dictate. But all the same you are fully convinced that he will inevitably accustom himself to it when he gets

completely rid of certain old bad habits, and when common sense and science have completely re-educated human nature and turned it in a normal direction. You are confident that man will then refrain from erring *intentionally*, and will, so to say, willy-nilly, not want to set his will against his normal interests. More than that: then, you say, science itself will teach man (though to my mind that is a luxury) that he does not really have either caprice or will of his own and that he has never had it, and that he himself is something like a piano key or an organ stop, and that, moreover, laws of nature exist in this world, so that everything he does is not done by his will at all, but is done by itself, according to the laws of nature. Consequently we have only to discover these laws of nature, and man will no longer be responsible for his actions and life will become exceedingly easy for him. All human actions will then, of course, be tabulated according to these laws, mathematically, like tables of logarithms up to 108,000, and entered in a table; or, better still, there would be published certain edifying works like the present encyclopedic lexicons, in which everything will be so clearly calculated and designated that there will be no more incidents or adventures in the world.

determinism   utilitarianism   utopianism

Then—it is still you speaking—new economic relations will be established, all ready-made and computed with mathematical exactitude, so that every possible question will vanish in a twinkling, simply because every possible answer to it will be provided. Then the crystal palace will be built. Then—well, in short, those will be halcyon days. Of course there is no guaranteeing (this is my comment now) that it will not be, for instance, terribly boring then (for what will one have to do when everything is calculated according to the table?) but on the other hand everything will be extraordinarily rational. Of course boredom may lead you to anything. After all, boredom even sets one to sticking gold pins into people, but all that would not matter. What is bad (this is my comment again) is that for all I know people will be thankful for the gold pins then. After all, man is

❢ (not a gold pin)

stupid, phenomenally stupid. Or rather he is not stupid at all, but he is so ungrateful that you could not find another like him in all creation. After all, it would not surprise me in the least, if, for instance, suddenly for no reason at all, general rationalism in the midst of the future, a gentleman with an ignoble, or rather with a reactionary and ironical, countenance were to arise and, putting his arms akimbo, say to us all: "What do you think, gentlemen, hadn't we better kick over all that rationalism at one blow, scatter it to the winds, just to send these logarithms to the devil, and to let us live once more according to our own foolish will!" That again would not matter; but what is annoying is that after all he would be sure to find followers—such is the nature of man. And all that for the most foolish reason, which, one would think, was hardly worth mentioning: that is, that man everywhere and always, whoever he may be, has preferred to act as he wished and not in the least as his reason and advantage dictated. Why, one may choose what is contrary to one's own interests, and sometimes one *positively ought* (that is my idea). One's own free unfettered choice, one's own fancy, however wild it may be, one's own fancy worked up at times to frenzy—why that is that very "most advantageous advantage" which we have overlooked, which comes under no classification and through which all systems and theories are continually being sent to the devil. And how do these sages know that man must necessarily need a rationally advantageous choice? What man needs is simply *independent* choice, whatever that independence may cost and wherever it may lead. Well, choice, after all, the devil only knows . . .

VIII

"Ha! ha! ha! But after all, if you like, in reality, there is no such thing as choice," you will interrupt with a laugh. "Science has even now succeeded in analyzing man to such an extent that we know already that choice and what is called freedom of will are nothing other than—"

Wait, gentlemen, I meant to begin with that myself. I admit that I was even frightened. I was just going to shout that after all the devil only knows what choice depends on, and that perhaps that was a very good thing, but I remembered the teaching of science—and pulled myself up. And here you have begun to speak. After all, really, well, if some day they truly discover a formula for all our desires and caprices—that is, an explanation of what they depend upon, by what laws they arise, just how they develop, what they are aiming at in one case or another and so on, and so on, that is, a real mathematical formula—then, after all, man would most likely at once stop to feel desire, indeed, he will be certain to. For who would want to choose by rule? Besides, he will at once be transformed from a human being into an organ stop or something of the sort; for what is a man without desire, without free will and without choice, if not a stop in an organ? What do you think? Let us consider the probability—can such a thing happen or not?

"H'm!" you decide. "Our choice is usually mistaken through a mistaken notion of our advantage. We sometimes choose absolute nonsense because in our stupidity we see in that nonsense the easiest means for attaining an advantage assumed beforehand. But when all that is explained and worked out on paper (which is perfectly possible, for it is contemptible and senseless to assume in advance that man will never understand some laws of nature), then, of course, so-called desires will not exist. After all, if desire should at any time come to terms completely with reason, we shall then, of course, reason and not desire, simply because, after all, it will be impossible to retain reason and *desire* something senseless, and in that way knowingly act against reason and desire to injure ourselves. And as all choice and reasoning can really be calculated, because some day they will discover the laws of our so-called free will—so joking aside, there may one day probably be something like a table of desires so that we really shall choose in accordance with it. After all, if, for instance, some day they calculate and prove to me that I stuck my tongue out at someone because I could not help sticking my tongue out at him and that I had to do it in that particular way, what sort of *freedom* is left me, especially if I am a learned man and have taken my degree somewhere? After all, then I would be able to calculate my whole life for thirty years in advance. In short, if that comes about, then, after all, we could do nothing about it. We would have to accept it just the same. And, in fact, we ought to repeat to ourselves incessantly that at such and such a time and under such and such circumstances, Nature does not ask our leave; that we must accept her as she is and not as we imagine her to be, and if we really aspire to tables and indices and well, even—well, let us say to the chemical retort, then it cannot be helped. We must accept the retort, too, or else it will be accepted without our consent."

Yes, but here I come to a stop! Gentlemen, you must excuse me for philosophizing; it's the result of forty years underground! Allow me to indulge my fancy for a minute. You see, gentlemen, reason, gentlemen, is an excellent thing, there is no disputing that, but reason is only reason and can only satisfy man's rational faculty, while will is a manifestation of all life, that is, of all human life including reason as well as all impulses. And although our life, in this manifestation of it, is often worthless, yet it is life nevertheless and not simply extracting square roots. After all, here I, for instance, quite naturally want to live, in order to satisfy all my faculties for life, and not simply my rational faculty, that is, not simply one-twentieth of all my faculties for life. What does reason know? Reason only knows what it has succeeded in learning (some things it will perhaps never learn; while this is nevertheless no comfort, why not say so frankly?) and human nature acts as a whole, with everything that is in it, consciously or unconsciously, and, even if it goes wrong, it lives. I suspect, gentlemen, that you are looking at me with compassion; you repeat to me that an enlightened and developed man, such, in short, as the future man will be, cannot knowingly desire anything disadvantageous to himself, that this can be proved mathematically. I thoroughly agree, it really can—by mathematics. But I repeat for the hundredth time, there is one case, one only, when man may purposely, consciously, desire what is injurious to himself, what is stupid, very stupid—simply in order *to have the right* to desire for himself even what is very stupid and not to be bound by an obligation to desire only what is rational. After all, this very stupid thing, after all, this caprice of ours, may really be more advantageous for us, gentlemen, than anything else on earth, especially in some cases. And in particular it may be more advantageous than any advantages even when it does us obvious harm, and contradicts the soundest conclusions of our reason about our advantage—because in any case it preserves for us what is most precious and most important—that is, our personality, our individuality. Some, you see, maintain that this really is the most precious thing for man; desire can, of course, if it desires, be in agreement with reason; particularly if it does not abuse this practice but does so in moderation, it is both useful and sometimes even praiseworthy. But very often, and even most often, desire completely and stubbornly opposes reason, and . . . and . . . and do you know that that, too, is useful and sometimes even praiseworthy? Gentlemen, let us suppose that man is not stupid. (Indeed, after all, one cannot say that about him anyway, if only for the one consideration that, if man is stupid, then, after all, who is wise?) But if he is not stupid, he is just the same monstrously ungrateful! Phenomenally ungrateful. I even believe that the best definition of man is—a creature that walks on two legs and is ungrateful. But that is not all, that is not his worst defect; his worst defect is his perpetual immorality, perpetual—from the days of the Flood to the Schleswig-Holstein period of human destiny. Immorality, and consequently lack of good sense; for it has long been accepted that lack of good sense is due to no other cause than immorality. Try it, and cast a look upon the history of mankind. Well, what will you see? Is it a grand spectacle? All right, grand, if

you like. The Colossus of Rhodes, for instance, that is worth
something. Mr. Anaevsky may well testify that some say it is the
work of human hands, while others maintain that it was created
by Nature herself. Is it variegated? Very well, it may be variegated too. If one only took the dress uniforms, military and
civilian, of all peoples in all ages—that alone is worth something, and if you take the undress uniforms you will never get
to the end of it; no historian could keep up with it. Is it monotonous? Very well. It may be monotonous, too; they fight and
fight; they are fighting now, they fought first and they fought
last—you will admit that it is almost too monotonous. In short,
one may say anything about the history of the world—anything
that might enter the most disordered imagination. The only
thing one cannot say is that it is rational. The very word sticks
in one's throat. And, indeed, this is even the kind of thing that
continually happens. After all, there are continually turning up
in life moral and rational people, sages, and lovers of humanity,
who make it their goal for life to live as morally and rationally
as possible, to be, so to speak, a light to their neighbors, simply
in order to show them that it is really possible to live morally
and rationally in this world. And so what? We all know that
those very people sooner or later toward the end of their lives
have been false to themselves, playing some trick, often a most
indecent one. Now I ask you: What can one expect from man
since he is a creature endowed with such strange qualities?
Shower upon him every earthly blessing, drown him in bliss so
that nothing but bubbles would dance on the surface of his
bliss, as on a sea; give him such economic prosperity that he
would have nothing else to do but sleep, eat cakes and busy
himself with ensuring the continuation of world history and
even then man, out of sheer ingratitude, sheer libel, would play
you some loathsome trick. He would even risk his cakes and
would deliberately desire the most fatal rubbish, the most un-
economical absurdity, simply to introduce into all this positive
rationality his fatal fantastic element. It is just his fantastic

dreams, his vulgar folly, that he will desire to retain, simply in order to prove to himself (as though that were so necessary) that men still are men and not piano keys, which even if played by the laws of nature themselves threaten to be controlled so completely that soon one will be able to desire nothing but by the calendar. And, after all, that is not all: even if man really were nothing but a piano key, even if this were proved to him by natural science and mathematics, even then he would not become reasonable, but would purposely do something perverse out of sheer ingratitude, simply to have his own way. And if he does not find any means he will devise destruction and chaos, will devise sufferings of all sorts, and will thereby have his own way. He will launch a curse upon the world, and, as only man can curse (it is his privilege, the primary distinction between him and other animals), then, after all, perhaps only by his curse will he attain his object, that is, really convince himself that he is a man and not a piano key! If you say that all this, too, can be calculated and tabulated, chaos and darkness and curses, so that the mere possibility of calculating it all beforehand would stop it all, and reason would reassert itself—then man would purposely go mad in order to be rid of reason and have his own way! I believe in that, I vouch for it, because, after all, the whole work of man seems really to consist in nothing but proving to himself continually that he is a man and not an organ stop. It may be at the cost of his skin! But he has proved it; he may become a caveman, but he will have proved it. And after that can one help sinning, rejoicing that it has not yet come, and that desire still depends on the devil knows what!

You will shout at me (that is, if you will still favor me with your shout) that, after all, no one is depriving me of my will, that all they are concerned with is that my will should somehow of itself, of its own free will, coincide with my own normal interests, with the laws of nature and arithmetic.

Bah, gentlemen, what sort of free will is left when we come to tables and arithmetic, when it will all be a case of two times two makes four? Two times two makes four even without my will. As if free will meant that!

IX

Gentlemen, I am joking, of course, and I know myself that I'm joking badly, but after all you know, one can't take everything as a joke. I am, perhaps, joking with a heavy heart. Gentlemen, I am tormented by questions; answer them for me. Now you, for instance, want to cure men of their old habits and reform their will in accordance with science and common sense. But how do you know, not only that it is possible, but also that it is *desirable,* to reform man in that way? And what leads you to the conclusion that it is so *necessary* to reform man's desires? In short, how do you know that such a reformation will really be advantageous to man? And to go to the heart of the matter, why are you *so sure* of your conviction that not to act against his real normal advantages guaranteed by the conclusions of reason and arithmetic is always advantageous for man and must be a law for all mankind? After all, up to now it is only your supposition. Let us assume it to be a law of logic, but perhaps not a law of humanity at all. You gentlemen perhaps think that I am mad? Allow me to defend myself. I agree that man is pre-eminently a creative animal, predestined to strive consciously toward a goal, and to engage in engineering; that is, eternally and incessantly, to build new roads, *wherever they may lead.* But the reason why he sometimes wants to swerve aside may be precisely that he is *forced* to make that road, and perhaps, too, because however stupid the straightforward practical man may be in general, the thought nevertheless will sometimes occur to him that the road, it would seem, almost always does lead *somewhere,* and that the destination it leads to is less important than the process of making it, and that the chief thing is to save the well-behaved child from despising engineering, and so giving way to the fatal idleness, which, as we all know, is the mother of all vices. Man likes to create and build roads, that is beyond dispute. But why does he also have such a passionate love for destruction and chaos? Now tell me that! But on that point I want to say a few special words myself. May it not be that he loves chaos and destruction (after all, he sometimes unquestionably likes it very much, that is surely so) because he is instinctively afraid of attaining his goal and completing the edifice he is constructing? How do you know, perhaps he only likes that edifice from a distance, and not at all at close range, perhaps he only likes to build it and does not want to live in it, but will leave it, when completed, *aux animaux domestiques*—such as the ants, the sheep, and so on, and so on. Now the ants have quite a different taste. They have an amazing edifice of that type, that endures forever—the anthill.

With the anthill, the respectable race of ants began and with the anthill they will probably end, which does the greatest credit to their perseverance and staidness. But man is a frivolous and incongruous creature, and perhaps, like a chessplayer, loves only the process of the game, not the end of it. And who knows (one cannot swear to it), perhaps the only goal on earth to which mankind is striving lies in this incessant process of attaining, or in other words, in life itself, and not particularly in the goal which of course must always be two times two makes four, that is a formula, and after all, two times two makes four is no longer life, gentlemen, but is the beginning of death. Anyway, man has always been somehow afraid of this two times two makes four, and I am afraid of it even now. Granted that man does nothing but seek that two times two makes four, that he sails the oceans, sacrifices his life in the quest, but to succeed, really to find it— he is somehow afraid, I assure you. He feels that as soon as he has found it there will be nothing for him to look for. When workmen have finished their work they at least receive their pay, they go to the tavern, then they wind up at the police station— and there is an occupation for a week. But where can man go? Anyway, one can observe a certain awkwardness about him every time he attains such goals. He likes the process of attaining, but does not quite like to have attained, and that, of course, is terribly funny. In short, man is a comical creature; there seems to be a kind of pun in it all. But two times two makes four is, after all, something insufferable. Two times two makes four seems to me simply a piece of insolence. Two times two makes four is a fop standing with arms akimbo barring your path and spitting. I admit that two times two makes four is an excellent thing, but if we are going to praise everything, two times two makes five is sometimes also a very charming little thing.

And why are you so firmly, so triumphantly convinced that only the normal and the positive—in short, only prosperity—is to the advantage of man? Is not reason mistaken about advantage? After all, perhaps man likes something besides prosperity? Perhaps he likes suffering just as much? Perhaps suffering is just as great an advantage to him as prosperity? Man is sometimes fearfully, passionately in love with suffering and that is a fact. There is no need to appeal to universal history to prove that; only ask yourself, if only you are a man and have lived at all. As far as my own personal opinion is concerned, to care only for prosperity seems to me somehow even ill-bred. Whether it's good or bad, it is sometimes very pleasant to smash things, too. After all, I do not really insist on suffering or on prosperity either. I insist on my caprice, and its being guaranteed to me when necessary. Suffering would be out of place in vaudevilles, for instance; I know that. In the crystal palace it is even unthinkable; suffering means doubt, means negation, and what would be the good of a crystal palace if there could be any doubt about it? And yet I am sure man will never renounce real suffering, that is, destruction and chaos. Why, after all, suffering is the sole origin of consciousness. Though I stated at the beginning that consciousness, in my opinion, is the greatest misfortune for man, yet I know man loves it and would not give it up for any satisfaction. Consciousness, for instance, is infinitely superior to two times two makes four. Once you have two times two makes four, there is nothing left to do or to understand. There will be noth-

ing left but to bottle up your five senses and plunge into contemplation. While if you stick to consciousness, even though you
attain the same result, you can at least flog yourself at times, and
that will, at any rate, liven you up. It may be reactionary, but
corporal punishment is still better than nothing.

X

You believe in a crystal edifice that can never be destroyed; that
is, an edifice at which one would neither be able to stick out
one's tongue nor thumb one's nose on the sly. And perhaps I am
afraid of this edifice just because it is of crystal and can never be
destroyed and that one could not even put one's tongue out at it
even on the sly.

You see, if it were not a palace but a chicken coop and rain
started, I might creep into the chicken coop to avoid getting wet,
and yet I would not call the chicken coop a palace out of gratitude to it for sheltering me from the rain. You laugh, you even say
that in such circumstances a chicken coop is as good as a mansion. Yes, I answer, if one had to live simply to avoid getting wet.

But what is to be done if I have taken it into my head that this
is not the only object in life, and that if one must live one may
as well live in a mansion. That is my choice, my desire. You will
only eradicate it when you have changed my desire. Well, do
change it, tempt me with something else, give me another ideal.
But in the meantime, I will not take a chicken coop for a palace.
Let the crystal edifice even be an idle dream, say it is inconsis-
tent with the laws of nature and that I have invented it only
through my own stupidity, through some old-fashioned irrational habits of my generation. But what do I care if it is incon-
sistent? Does it matter at all, since it exists in my desires, or
rather exists as long as my desires exist? Perhaps you are laughing again? Laugh away; I will put up with all your laughter
rather than pretend that I am satisfied when I am hungry. I
know, anyway, that I will not be appeased with a compromise,

with an endlessly recurring zero, simply because it is consistent with the laws of nature and *really* exists. I will not accept as the crown of my desires a block of buildings with apartments for the poor on a lease of a thousand years and, to take care of any contingency, a dentist's shingle hanging out. Destroy my desires, eradicate my ideals, show me something better, and I will follow you. You may say, perhaps, that it is not worth your getting involved in it; but in that case, after all, I can give you the same answer. We are discussing things seriously; but if you won't deign to give me your attention, then, after all, I won't speak to you, I do have my underground.

But while I am still alive and have desires I would rather my hand were withered than to let it bring one brick to such a building! Don't remind me that I have just rejected the crystal edifice for the sole reason that one cannot put out one's tongue at it. I did not say it at all because I am so fond of putting my tongue out. Perhaps the only thing I resented was that of all your edifices up to now, there has not been a single one at which one could not put out one's tongue. On the contrary, I would let my tongue be cut off out of sheer gratitude if things could be so arranged that I myself would lose all desire to put it out. What do I care that things cannot be so arranged, and that one must be satisfied with model apartments? Why then am I made with such desires? Can I have been made simply in order to come to the conclusion that the whole way I am made is a swindle? Can this be my whole purpose? I do not believe it.

But do you know what? I am convinced that we underground folk ought to be kept in tow. Though we may be able to sit underground forty years without speaking, when we do come out into the light of day and break out we talk and talk and talk.

XI

The long and the short of it is, gentlemen, that it is better to do nothing! Better conscious inertia! And so hurrah for underground!

Though I have said that I envy the normal man to the point
of exasperation, yet I would not care to be in his place as he is
now (though I will not stop envying him. No, no; anyway the
underground life is more advantageous!). There, at any rate, one
can—Bah! But after all, even now I am lying! I am lying because
I know myself as surely as two times two makes four, that it is
not at all underground that is better, but something different,
quite different, for which I long but which I cannot find! Damn
underground!

I will tell you another thing that would be better, and that is,
if I myself believed even an iota of what I have just written. I
swear to you, gentlemen, that I do not really believe one thing,
not even one word, of what I have just written. That is, I believe
it, perhaps, but at the same time, I feel and suspect that I am
lying myself blue in the face.

"Then why have you written all this?" you will say to me.

"I ought to put you underground for forty years without anything to do and then come to you to find out what stage you
have reached! How can a man be left alone with nothing to do
for forty years?"

"Isn't that shameful, isn't that humiliating?" you will say,
perhaps, shaking your heads contemptuously. "You long for life
and try to settle the problems of life by a logical tangle. And how
tiresome, how insolent your outbursts are, and at the same time,
how scared you are! You talk nonsense and are pleased with it;
you say impudent things and are constantly afraid of them and
apologizing for them. You declare that you are afraid of nothing
and at the same time try to ingratiate yourself with us. You declare that you are gnashing your teeth and at the same time you
try to be witty so as to amuse us. You know that your witticisms
are not witty, but you are evidently well satisfied with their literary value. You may perhaps really have suffered, but you have
no respect whatsoever for your own suffering. You may be
truthful in what you have said but you have no modesty; out of
the pettiest vanity you bring your truth to public exposure, to

the market place, to ignominy. You doubtlessly mean to say something, but hide your real meaning for fear, because you lack the resolution to say it, and only have a cowardly impudence. You boast of consciousness, but you are unsure of your ground, for though your mind works, yet your heart is corrupted by depravity, and you cannot have a full, genuine consciousness without a pure heart. And how tiresome you are, how you thrust yourself on people and grimace! Lies, lies, lies!"

Of course I myself have made up just now all the things you say. That, too, is from underground. For forty years I have been listening to your words there through a crack under the floor. I have invented them myself. After all there was nothing else I could invent. It is no wonder that I have learned them by heart and that it has taken a literary form.

But can you really be so credulous as to think that I will print all this and give it to you to read too? And another problem; why do I really call you "gentlemen," why do I address you as though you really were my readers? Such declarations as I intend to make are never printed nor given to other people to read. Anyway, I am not strong-minded enough for that, and I don't see why I should be. But you see a fancy has occurred to me and I want to fulfill it at all costs. Let me explain.

Every man has some reminiscences which he would not tell to everyone, but only to his friends. He has others which he would not reveal even to his friends, but only to himself, and that in secret. But finally there are still others which a man is even afraid to tell himself, and every decent man has a considerable number of such things stored away. That is, one can even say that the more decent he is, the greater the number of such things in his mind. Anyway, I have only lately decided to remember some of my early adventures. Till now I have always avoided them, even with a certain uneasiness. Now, however, when I am not only recalling them, but have actually decided to write them down, I want to try the experiment whether one can be perfectly frank, even with oneself, and not take fright at the whole truth. I will observe, parenthetically, that Heine maintains that a true auto-biography is almost an impossibility, and that man is bound to lie about himself. He considers that Rousseau certainly told lies about himself in his confessions, and even intentionally lied, out of vanity. I am convinced that Heine is right; I understand very well that sometimes one may, just out of sheer vanity, attribute regular crimes to oneself, and indeed I can very well conceive that kind of vanity. But Heine judged people who made their confessions to the public. I, however, am writing for myself, and wish to declare once and for all that if I write as though I were addressing readers, that is simply because it is easier for me to write in that way. It is merely a question of form, only an empty form—I shall never have readers. I have made this plain already.

I don't wish to be hampered by any restrictions in compiling my notes. I shall not attempt any system or method. I will jot things down as I remember them.

But here, perhaps, someone will take me at my word and ask me: if you really don't count on readers, why do you make such compacts with yourself—and on paper too—that is, that you won't attempt any system or method, that you will jot things down as you remember them, etc., etc? Why do you keep ex-plaining? Why do you keep apologizing?

Well, there it is, I answer.

Incidentally, there is a whole psychological system in this. Or, perhaps, I am simply a coward. And perhaps also, that I pur-posely imagine an audience before me in order to conduct my-self in a more dignified manner while I am jotting things down. There are perhaps thousands of reasons.

And here is still something else. What precisely is my object in writing? If it is not for the public, then after all, why should I not simply recall these incidents in my own mind without put-ting them down on paper?

Quite so; but yet it is somehow more dignified on paper. There is something more impressive in it; I will be able to criti-cize myself better and improve my style. Besides, perhaps I will really get relief from writing. Today, for instance, I am particularly oppressed by a certain memory from the distant past. It came back to my mind vividly a few days ago, and since then, has remained with me like an annoying tune that one cannot get rid of. And yet I must get rid of it. I have hundreds of such memories, but at times some single one stands out from the hundreds and oppresses me. For some reason I believe that if I write it down I will get rid of it. Why not try?

Besides, I am bored, and I never do anything. Writing will really be a sort of work. They say work makes man kindhearted and honest. Well, here is a chance for me, anyway.

It is snowing today. A wet, yellow, dingy snow. It fell yesterday too and a few days ago. I rather think that I remembered that incident which I cannot shake off now, apropos of the wet snow. And so let it be a story apropos of the wet snow.

PART TWO

Apropos of the Wet Snow

When from the gloom of corruption
I delivered your fallen soul
With the ardent speech of conviction;
And, full of profound torment,
Wringing your hands, you cursed
The vice that ensnared you;
When, with memories punishing
Forgetful conscience
You told me the tale
Of all that happened before me,
And suddenly, covering your face,
Full of shame and horror,
You tearfully resolved,
Outraged, shocked. . . .
Etc., etc,, etc.

From the poetry of N. A. Nekrasov

I

At that time I was only twenty-four. My life was even then
gloomy, disorganized, and solitary to the point of savagery. I
made friends with no one and even avoided talking, and hid myself in my corner more and more. At work in the office I even
tried never to look at anyone, and I was very well aware that my
colleagues looked upon me, not only as a crank, but looked
upon me—so I always thought—seemed to look upon me with a
sort of loathing. I sometimes wondered why no one except me

thought that he was looked upon with loathing. One of our clerks had a repulsive, pock-marked face, which even looked villainous. I believe I would not have dared to look at anyone with such an unsightly face. Another had a uniform so worn that there was an unpleasant smell near him. Yet not one of these gentlemen was disconcerted either by his clothes or his face or in some moral sense. Neither of them imagined that he was looked at with loathing, and even if he had imagined it, it would not have mattered to him, so long as his superiors did not look at him in that way. It is perfectly clear to me now that, owing to my unbounded vanity and, probably, to the high standard I set for myself, I very often looked at myself with furious discontent, which verged on loathing, and so I inwardly attributed the same view to everyone. For instance, I hated my face; I thought it disgusting, and even suspected that there was something base in its expression and therefore every time I turned up at the office I painfully tried to behave as independently as possible so that I might not be suspected of being base, and to give my face as noble an expression as possible. "Let my face even be ugly," I thought, "but let it be noble, expressive, and, above all, *extremely* intelligent." But I was absolutely and painfully certain that my face could never express those perfections; but what was worst of all, I thought it positively stupid-looking. And I would have been quite satisfied if I could have looked intelligent. In fact, I would even have put up with looking base if, at the same time, my face could have been thought terribly intelligent.

Of course, I hated all my fellow-clerks, one and all, and I despised them all, yet at the same time I was, as it were, afraid of them. It happened at times that I even thought more highly of them than of myself. It somehow happened quite suddenly then that I alternated between despising them and thinking them superior to myself. A cultivated and decent man cannot be vain without setting an inordinately high standard for himself, and without despising himself at certain moments to the point of hatred. But whether I despised them or thought them superior I dropped my eyes almost every time I met anyone. I even made experiments whether I could face So and-So's looking at me, and I was always the first to drop my eyes. This tormented me to the point of frenzy. I was also morbidly afraid of being ridiculous, and so I slavishly worshiped the conventional in everything external. I loved to fall into the common rut, and had a whole-hearted terror of any kind of eccentricity in myself. But how could I live up to it? I was morbidly cultivated as a cultivated man of our age should be. They were all dull, and as like one another as so many sheep. Perhaps I was the only one in the office who constantly thought that I was a coward and a slave, and I thought it precisely because I was cultivated. But I did not only think it, in actuality it was really so. I was a coward and a slave. I say this without the slightest embarrassment. Every decent man in our age must be a coward and a slave. That is his normal condition. I am profoundly convinced of that. He is made that way and is constructed for that very purpose. And not only at the present time owing to some casual circumstances, but always, at all times, a decent man must be a coward and a slave. That is the law of nature for all decent people on the earth. If any one of them happens to be brave about something, he need not be comforted or carried away by that; he will funk out just the same before something else. That is how it invariably and inevitably ends. Only asses and mules are brave, and even they are so only until they come up against the wall. It is not even worth while to pay attention to them. Because they don't mean anything at all.

Still another circumstance tormented me in those days: that no one resembled me and that I resembled no one else. "I am alone and they are *every one*," I thought—and pondered.

From that it can be seen that I was still an absolute child.

The very opposite sometimes happened. After all, how vile it sometimes seemed to have to go to the office; things reached such a point that I often came home ill. But all at once, for no rhyme or reason, there would come a phase of skepticism and indifference (everything happened to me in phases), and I would myself laugh at my intolerance and fastidiousness. I would reproach myself with being *romantic*. Sometimes I was unwilling to speak to anyone, while at other times I would not only talk, but even think of forming a friendship with them. All my fastidiousness would suddenly vanish for no rhyme or reason. Who knows, perhaps I never had really had it, and it had simply been affected, and gotten out of books. I have still not decided that question even now. Once I quite made friends with them, visited their homes, played preference, drank vodka, talked of promotions . . . But here let me make a digression.

We Russians, speaking generally, have never had those foolish transcendental German, and still more, French, romantics on whom nothing produces any effect; if there were an earthquake, if all France perished at the barricades, they would still be the same, they would not even change for decency's sake, but would still go on singing their transcendental songs, so to speak, to the hour of their death, because they are fools. We, in Russia, have no fools; that is well known. That is what distinguishes us from foreign lands. Consequently those transcendental natures do not exist among us in their pure form. We only think they do because our "positivistic" journalists and critics of that time, always on the hunt for Kostanzhoglos and Uncle Peter Ivaniches[1] and foolishly accepting them as our ideal, slandered our romantics, taking them for the same transcendental sort that exists in Germany or France. On the contrary, the characteristics of our romantics are absolutely and directly opposed to the transcendental European type, and not a single European standard can be applied to them. (Allow me to make use of this word "romantic"—an oldfashioned and much-respected word which has done good service and is familiar to all.) The characteristics of our romantics are to understand everything, *to see everything and often to see it incomparably more clearly than our most positivistic minds see it*;

---

[1] Characters in Part II of Gogol's *Dead Souls* and Goncharov's *The Same Old Story,* respectively.

to refuse to accept anyone or anything, but at the same time not to despise anything; to give way, to yield, from policy; never to lose sight of a useful practical goal (such as rent-free government quarters, pensions, decorations), to keep their eye on that object through all the enthusiasms and volumes of lyrical poems, and at the same time to preserve "the sublime and the beautiful" inviolate within them to the hour of their death, and also, incidentally, to preserve themselves wrapped in cotton, like some precious jewel if only for the benefit of "the sublime and the beautiful." Our romantic is a man of great breadth and the greatest rogue of all our rogues, I assure you. I can even assure you from experience. Of course all that occurs if he is intelligent. But what am I saying! The romantic is always intelligent, and I only meant to observe that although we have had foolish romantics they don't count, and they were only so because in the flower of their youth they degenerated completely into Germans, and to preserve their precious jewel more comfortably, settled somewhere out there— by preference in Weimar or the Black Forest. I, for instance, genuinely despised my official work and did not openly abuse it simply through necessity because I was in it myself and got a salary for it. And, as a result, take note, I did not openly abuse it. Our romantic would rather go out of his mind (which incidentally happened very rarely) than abuse it, unless he had some other career in view; and he is never kicked out, unless, of course, he is taken to the lunatic asylum as "the King of Spain" and then only if he went very mad. But after all, it is only the thin, fair people who go out of their minds in Russia. Innumerable romantics later in life rise to considerable rank in the service. Their versatility is remarkable! And what a faculty they have for the most contradictory sensations! I was comforted by those thoughts even in those days, and I am so still. That is why there are so many "broad natures" among us who never lose their ideal even in the depths of degradation; and though they never lift a finger for their ideal, though they are arrant thieves and robbers, yet they tearfully cherish their first ideal and are extraordinarily honest at heart. Yes, only among us can the most arrant rogue be absolutely and even loftily honest at heart without in the least ceasing to be a rogue. I repeat, our romantics, after all, frequently become such accomplished rascals (I use the term "rascals" affectionately), suddenly display such a sense of reality and practical knowledge, that their bewildered superiors and the public can only gape in amazement at them.

Their many-sidedness is really astounding, and goodness knows what it may turn itself into under future circumstances, and what lies in store for us later on. They are good stuff! I do not say this out of any foolish or boastful patriotism. But I feel sure that you are again imagining that I am joking. Or perhaps it's just the contrary, and you are convinced that I really think so. Anyway, gentlemen, I shall welcome both views as an honor and a special favor. And do forgive my digression.

I did not, of course, maintain a friendship with my comrades and soon was at loggerheads with them, and in my youthful inexperience I even gave up bowing to them, as though I had cut off all relations. That, however, only happened to me once. As a rule, I was always alone.

In the first place, at home, I spent most of my time reading. I tried to stifle all that was continually seething within me by means of external sensations. And the only source of external sensation possible for me was reading. Reading was a great help, of course, it excited, delighted and tormented me. But at times it bored me terribly. One longed for movement just the same, and I plunged all at once into dark, subterranean, loathsome—not vice but petty vice. My petty passions were acute, smarting, from my continual sickly irritability. I had hysterical fits, with tears and convulsions. I had no resource except reading—that is, there was then nothing in my surroundings which I could respect and which attracted me. I was overwhelmed with depression, too; I had an hysterical craving for contradictions and for contrast, and so I took to vice. I have not said all this to justify myself, after all—but no, I am lying. I did want to justify myself. I make that little observation for my own benefit, gentlemen. I don't want to lie. I vowed to myself I would not.

I indulged my vice in solitude at night, furtively, timidly, filthily, with a feeling of shame which never deserted me, even at the most loathsome moments, and which at such moments drove me to curses. Even then I already had the underground in my soul. I was terribly afraid of being seen, of being met, of being recognized. I visited various completely obscure places.

One night as I was passing a tavern, I saw through a lighted window some gentlemen fighting with billiard cues, and saw one of them thrown out of the window. At another time I would have felt very much disgusted, but then I was suddenly in such a mood that I actually envied the gentleman thrown out of the window, and I envied him so much that I even went into the tavern and into the billiard-room. "Perhaps," I thought, "I'll have a fight, too, and they'll throw me out of the window."

I was not drunk, but what is one to do—after all, depression will drive a man to such a pitch of hysteria. But nothing happened. It seemed that I was not even equal to being thrown out of the window and I went away without having fought.

An officer put me in my place from the very first moment.

I was standing by the billiard-table and in my ignorance blocking up the way, and he wanted to pass; he took me by the shoulders and without a word—without a warning or an explanation—moved me from where I was standing to another spot and passed by as though he had not noticed me. I could even have forgiven blows, but I absolutely could not forgive his having moved me and so completely failing to notice me.

Devil knows what I would then have given for a real regular quarrel—a more decent, a more *literary* one, so to speak. I had been treated like a fly. This officer was over six feet, while I am short and thin. But the quarrel was in my hands. I had only to protest and I certainly would have been thrown out of the window. But I changed my mind and preferred to beat a resentful retreat.

I went out of the tavern straight home, confused and troubled, and the next night I continued with my petty vices, still
more furtively, abjectly and miserably than before, as it were,
with tears in my eyes—but still I did continue them. Don't imagine, though, that I funked out on the officer through cowardice.
I have never been a coward at heart, though I have always been
a coward in action. Don't be in a hurry to laugh. There is an explanation for it. I have an explanation for everything, you may
be sure.

Oh, if only that officer had been one of the sort who would
consent to fight a duel! But no, he was one of those gentlemen
(alas, long extinct!) who preferred fighting with cues, or, like
Gogol's Lieutenant Pirogov, appealing to the police. They did
not fight duels and would have thought a duel with a civilian
like me an utterly unseemly procedure in any case—and they
looked upon the duel altogether as something impossible, something free-thinking and French, but they were quite ready to insult people, especially when they were over six feet.

I did not funk out through cowardice here but through unbounded vanity. I was not afraid of his six feet, not of getting a
sound thrashing and being thrown out of the window; I would
probably have had sufficient physical courage; but I lacked sufficient moral courage. What I was afraid of was that everyone
present, from the insolent marker down to the lowest little stinking pimply clerk hanging around in a greasy collar, would jeer at
me and fail to understand when I began to protest and to address them in literary language. For even now we cannot, after
all, speak of the point of honor—not of honor, but of the point
of honor (point d'honneur)—except in literary language. You
cannot allude to the "point of honor" in ordinary language. I
was fully convinced (the sense of reality, in spite of all romanticism!) that they would all simply split then: sides with laughter
and that the officer would not simply, that is, not uninsultingly,
beat me, but would certainly prod me in the back with his knee,
kick me round the billiard-table that way and only then perhaps

have pity and throw me out of the window. Of course, this trivial incident could not have ended like that with me. I often met that officer afterward in the street and observed him very carefully. I am not quite sure whether he recognized me, I imagine not; I judge from certain signs. But I—I stared at him with spite and hatred and so it went on—for several years! My resentment even grew deeper with the years. At first I began making stealthy inquiries about this officer. It was difficult for me to do so, for I knew no one. But one day I heard someone call him by his name in the street when I was following him at a distance, just as though I were tied to him—and so I learned his surname. Another time I followed him to his flat, and for a few pennies learned from the porter where he lived, on which floor, whether he lived alone or with others, and so on—in fact, everything one could learn from a porter. One morning, though I had never tried to write anything before, it suddenly occurred to me to describe this officer in the form of an exposé, in a satire, in a tale. I wrote the tale with relish. I did expose him. I slandered him; at first I so altered his name that it could easily be recognized but on second thought I changed it, and sent the story to the *Annals of the Fatherland*. But at that tune such exposés were not yet the fashion and my story was not printed. That was a great vexation to me. Sometimes I was positively choked with resentment. At last I decided to challenge my enemy to a duel. I composed a splendid, charming letter to him, imploring him to apologize to me, and hinting rather plainly at a duel in case of refusal. The letter was so composed that if the officer had had the least understanding of the "sublime and the beautiful" he would certainly have rushed to me to fling himself on my neck and to offer me his friendship. And how fine that would have been! How we would have gotten along! How we would have gotten along! "He could have shielded me with his higher rank, while I could have improved his mind with my culture, and, well—my ideas, and all sorts of things might have happened." Just think, this was two years after his insult to me, and my challenge was the most ridiculous anachronism, in spite of all the ingenuity of my letter in disguising and explaining away the anachronism. But, thank God (to this day I thank the Almighty with tears in my eyes), I did not send the letter to him. Cold shivers run down my back when I think of what might have happened if I had sent it. And all at once I revenged myself in the simplest way, by a stroke of genius! A brilliant thought suddenly dawned upon me. Sometimes on holidays I used to stroll along the sunny side of the Nevsky between three and four in the afternoon. That is, I did not stroll so much as experience innumerable torments, humiliations and resentments; but no doubt that was just what I wanted. I used to wriggle like an eel among the passers-by in the most unbecoming fashion, continually moving aside to make way for generals, for officers of the Guards and the Hussars, or for ladies. In those minutes I used to feel a convulsive twinge at my heart, and hot all the way down my back at the mere thought of the wretchedness of my dress, of the wretchedness and vulgarity of my little wriggling figure. This was a regular martyrdom, a continual, intolerable humiliation at the thought, which passed into an incessant and direct sensation, that I was a fly in the eyes of this whole world, a nasty, disgusting fly—more intelligent, more cultured, more noble than any of them, of course, but a fly that was continually making way for everyone, insulted and humiliated by everyone. Why I inflicted this torment upon myself, why I went to the Nevsky, I don't know. I felt simply *drawn* there at every possible opportunity.

Already then I began to experience a rush of the enjoyment of which I spoke in the first chapter. After my affair with the officer I felt even more drawn there than before: it was on the Nevsky that I met him most frequently, it was *there* that I could admire him. He, too, went there chiefly on holidays. He, too, made way for generals and persons of high rank, and he, too, shifted among them like an eel; but people like me, or even neater than I, he simply walked over; he made straight for them as though there was nothing but empty space before him, and never, under any circumstances, moved aside. I gloated over my resentment watching him and—resentfully made way for him every time. It tormented me that even in the street I could not be on an even footing with him. "Why must you invariably be the first to move aside?" I kept asking myself in hysterical rage, waking up sometimes at three o'clock in the morning. "Why precisely you and not he? After all, there's no regulation about it; after all, there's no written law about it. Let the making way be equal as it usually is when refined people meet; he moves halfway and you move halfway; you pass with mutual respect." But that never happened, and I always made way, while he did not even notice I moved aside for him. And lo and behold the most astounding idea dawned upon me! "What," I thought, "if I meet him and—don't move aside? What if I don't move aside on purpose, even if I were to bump into him? How would that be?" This audacious idea little by little took such a hold on me that it gave me no peace. I dreamt of it continually, terribly, and I purposely went to the Nevsky more frequently in order to picture more vividly how I would do it when I did do it I was delighted. This plan seemed to me more and more practical and possible. "Of course I will not really bump him," I thought, already more good-natured in my joy. I will simply not turn aside, will bump against him, not very violently, but just shouldering each other—just as much as decency permits. I will bump him just as much as he bumps me. At last I made up my mind completely. But my preparations took a great deal of time. To begin with, when I carried out my plan I would have to look rather more decent, and I had to think of my clothes. "In any case, if, for instance, there were any sort of public scandal (and the public there is of the most *superflu:* the Countess walks there; Prince D. walks there; the whole literary world is there), I would have to be well dressed; that inspires respect and of itself puts us in some way on equal footing in the eyes of high society." With that in mind I asked for my salary in advance, and bought at Churkin's a pair of black gloves and a decent hat. Black gloves seemed to me both more dignified and *bon ton* than the lemon-colored ones which I had contemplated at first. "The color is too gaudy, it looks as though one were trying to be conspicuous," and I did not take the lemon-colored ones. I had gotten ready a good shirt, with the bone studs, long beforehand; but my overcoat very much delayed me. The coat in itself was a very good one, it kept me warm; but it was wadded and it had a raccoon collar which was the height of vulgarity. I had to change the collar at any sacrifice, and to have a beaver one like an officer's. For this purpose I began visiting the Gostiny Dvor and after several attempts I lit on a piece of cheap German beaver. Though these German beavers very soon wear out and look shabby, at first, when new, they look exceedingly well, and after all, I only needed it for one occasion. I asked the price; even so, it was too expensive. After thinking it over thoroughly I decided to sell my raccoon collar. The rest of the money—a considerable sum for me, I decided to borrow from Anton Antonich Syetochkin, my superior, an unassuming person, but grave and dependable. He never lent money to anyone, but I had, on entering the service, been specially recommended to him by an important personage who had got me my job. I was terribly worried. To borrow from Anton Antonich seemed to me monstrous and shameful. I did not sleep for two or three nights, and indeed I did not sleep well in general at that time, I was in a fever; I had a vague sinking at my heart or suddenly it would start to throb, throb, throb! Anton Antonich was at first surprised, then he frowned, then he reflected, and did after all lend me the money, receiving from me a written authorization to take from my salary a fortnight later the sum that he had lent me. In this way everything was at last ready. The handsome beaver was established in place of the mean-looking raccoon, and I began by degrees to get to work. It would never have done to act offhand, at random; the plan had to be carried out skillfully, by degrees. But I must confess that after many efforts I almost even began to despair; we could not run into each other and that is all there was to it. I made every preparation, I was quite determined—it seemed as though we would run into one another directly—and before I knew what I was doing I had stepped aside for him again and he had passed without noticing me. I even prayed as I approached him that God would grant me determination. One time I had made up my mind thoroughly, but it ended in my stumbling and falling at his feet because at the very last instant when I was only some six inches from him my courage failed me. He very calmly stepped over me, while I flew to one side like a ball. That night I was ill again, feverish and delirious. And suddenly it ended most happily. The night before I had made up my mind not to carry out my fatal plan and to abandon it all, and with that goal in mind I went to the Nevsky for the last time, just to see how I would abandon it all. Suddenly, three paces from my enemy, I unexpectedly made up my mind—I closed my eyes, and we ran full tilt, shoulder to shoulder, into each other! I did not budge an inch and passed him on a perfectly equal footing! He did not even look round and pretended not to notice it; but he was only pretending, I am convinced of that. I am convinced of that to this day! Of course, I got the worst of it—he was stronger, but that was not the point. The point was that I had attained my goal, I had kept up my dignity. I had not yielded a step, and had put myself publicly on an equal social footing with him. I returned home feeling that I was perfectly avenged for everything. I was delighted. I was triumphant and sang Italian arias. Of course, I will not describe to you what happened to me three days later; if you have read my first chapter "Underground," you can guess for yourself. The officer was afterward transferred; I have not seen him now for fourteen years. What is the dear fellow doing now? Whom is he walking over?

II

But the period of my dissipation would end and I always felt terribly sick afterward. It was followed by remorse—I tried to drive it away; I felt too sick. By degrees, however, I grew used to that, too. I grew used to everything, that is, I did not really grow used to it, but rather I voluntarily resigned myself to enduring it But I had a means of escape that reconciled everything—that was to find refuge in "the sublime and the beautiful," in dreams. Of course I was a terrible dreamer. I would dream for three months on end, tucked away in my corner, and you may believe me that at those moments I had no resemblance to the gentleman who, in his chicken-hearted anxiety, put a German beaver collar on his greatcoat. I suddenly became a hero. I would not have received my six-foot lieutenant even if he had called on me. I could not even picture him before me then. What were my dreams and how I could satisfy myself with them, it is hard to say now, but at the time I did satisfy myself with them, to some extent. Dreams were particularly sweet and vivid after a little vice; they came with remorse and with tears, with curses and transports. There were moments of such positive intoxication, of such happiness, that there was not the faintest trace of irony within me, on my honor. I had faith, hope, love. That is just it. I believed blindly at such times that by some miracle, through some external circumstance, all this would suddenly open out, expand; that suddenly a vista of suitable activity—beneficial, good, and above all, *ready-made* (what sort of activity I had no idea, but the great thing was that it should be all ready for me)—would rise up before me, and I should come out into the light of day, almost riding a white horse and crowned with laurel. I could not conceive of a secondary role for myself, and for that reason I quite contentedly played the lowest one in reality. Either to be a hero or to grovel in the mud—there was nothing between. That was my ruin, for when I was in the mud I comforted myself with the thought that at other times I was a hero, and I took refuge in this hero for the mud: for an ordinary man, say, it is shameful to defile himself, but a hero is too noble to be utterly defiled, and so he might defile himself. It is worth noting that these attacks of "the sublime and the beautiful" visited me even during the pe-

NOTES FROM UNDERGROUND   53

riod of vice and just at the times when I had sunk to the very bottom. They came in separate spurts, as though reminding me of themselves, but did not banish the vice by their appearance. On the contrary, they seemed to add a zest to it by contrast, and were only sufficiently present to serve as an appetizing sauce. That sauce was made up of contradictions and sufferings, of agonizing inward analysis, and all these torments and pin-pricks lent my vice a certain piquancy, even a significance—in short, completely fulfilled the function of a good sauce. There was even a certain depth of meaning in it. And I could hardly have restrained myself to the simple, vulgar, direct clerk-like vice and have endured all the filthiness of it. What could have attracted me about it then and have driven me at night into the street? No, I had a noble loophole for everything.

And what love, oh Lord, what love I felt at times in those dreams of mine! In those "flights into the sublime and the beautiful"; though it was fantastic love, though it was never applied to anything human in reality, yet there was so much of this love that afterward one did not even feel the impulse to apply it in reality; that would have been a superfluous luxury. Everything, however, always passed satisfactorily by a lazy and fascinating transition into the sphere of art; that is, into the beautiful forms of life, ready-made, violently stolen from the poets and novelists and adapted to all sorts of needs and uses. I, for instance, was triumphant over everyone; everyone, of course, lay in the dust and was forced to recognize my superiority spontaneously, and I forgave them all. I, a famous poet, and a courtier, fell in love; I inherited countless millions and immediately devoted them to humanity, and at the same time I confessed before all the people my shameful deeds, which, of course, were not merely shameful, but contained an enormous amount of "the sublime and the beautiful," something in the Manfred style. Everyone would weep and kiss me (what idiots they would be if they did not), while I would go barefoot and hungry preaching new ideas and fighting a victorious Austerlitz against the reactionaries. Then a march would sound, an amnesty would be declared, the Pope would agree to retire from Rome to Brazil; then there would be a ball for the whole of Italy at the Villa Borghese on the shores of Lake Como, Lake Como being for that purpose transferred to the neighborhood of Rome; then would come a scene in the bushes, etc., etc.—as though you did not know all about it! You will say that it is vulgar and base to drag all this into public after all the tears and raptures I have myself admitted. But why is it base? Can you imagine that I am ashamed of it all, and that is was stupider than anything in your life, gentlemen? And I can assure you that some of these fancies were by no means badly composed. Not everything took place on the shores of Lake Como. And yet you are right—it really is vulgar and base. And what is most base of all is that I have now started to justify myself to you. And even more base than that is my making this remark now. But that's enough, or, after all, there will be no end to it; each step will be more base than the last.

I could never stand more than three months of dreaming at a time without feeling an irresistible desire to plunge into society. To plunge into society meant to visit my superior, Anton Antonich Syetochkin. He was the only permanent acquaintance I have had in my life, and I even wonder at the fact myself now. But I even went to see him only when that phase came over me, and when my dreams had reached such a point of bliss that it became essential to embrace my fellows and all mankind immediately. And for that purpose I needed at least one human being at hand who actually existed. I had to call on Anton Antonich, however, on Tuesday—his at-home day; so I always had to adjust my passionate desire to embrace humanity so that it might fall on a Tuesday. This Anton Antonich lived on the fourth floor in a house in Five Corners, in four low-pitched rooms of a particularly frugal and sallow appearance, one smaller than the next. He had two daughters and their aunt, who used to pour out the tea. Of the daughters one was thirteen and another fourteen, they both had snub noses, and I was terribly embarrassed

by them because they were always whispering and giggling together. The master of the house usually sat in his study on a
leather couch in front of the table, with some gray-headed gentleman, usually a colleague from our office or even some other
department. I never saw more than two or three visitors there,
and those always the same. They talked about the excise duty,
about business in the senate, about salaries, about promotions,
about His Excellency, and the best means of pleasing him, and
so on, and so on. I had the patience to sit like a fool beside these
people for four hours at a stretch, listening to them without
knowing what to say to them or venturing to say a word. I became stupefied; several times I felt myself perspiring. I was overcome by a sort of paralysis; but that was pleasant and useful for
me. On returning home I deferred for a time my desire to embrace all mankind.

I had, however, one other acquaintence of a sort, Simonov,
who was an old schoolfellow. Indeed I had a number of
schoolfellows in Petersburg, but I did not associate with them
and had even given up nodding to them in the street. Perhaps I
even transferred into the department I was in simply to avoid
their company and to cut off at one stroke all connection with
my hateful childhood. Curses on that school and all those terrible years of penal servitude! In short, I parted from my schoolfellows as soon as I got out into the world. There were two or
three left to whom I nodded in the street. One of them was Simonov, who had been in no way distinguished at school, was of
a quiet and even disposition; but I discovered in him a certain independence of character and even honesty. I don't even suppose
that he was particularly limited. I had at one time spent some
rather soulful moments with him, but these had not lasted long
and had somehow been suddenly clouded over. He was evidently
uncomfortable at these reminiscences, and was, it seemed, always afraid that I might take up the same tone again. I suspected
that he had an aversion for me, but I still went on going to see
him, not being completely certain of it.

And so on one occasion, on a Thursday, unable to endure my solitude and knowing that it was Thursday Anton Antonich's door would be closed, I thought of Simonov. Climbing up four floors to his place, I was thinking that I made the man uncomfortable and that it was a mistake to go to see him. But as it always happened that such reflections impelled me even more strongly, as though purposely, to put myself into a false position, I went in. It was almost a year since I had last seen Simonov.

III

I found two more of my old schoolfellows with him. They seemed to be discussing an important matter. All of them scarcely took any notice of my entrance, which was strange, for I had not seen them for years. Evidently they looked upon me as something on the level of a common fly. I had not been treated like that even at school, although everybody hated me there. I knew, of course, that they must despise me now for my lack of success in the service, and for having let myself sink so low, going about badly dressed and so on which seemed to them a sign of my inaptitude and insignificance. But nevertheless I had not expected such contempt. Simonov even seemed surprised at my turning up. Even in the old days he had always seemed surprised at my coming. All this disconcerted me; I sat down, feeling rather miserable, and began listening to what they were saying.

They were engaged in an earnest and even heated discussion about a farewell dinner these gentlemen wanted to arrange together the very next day for their friend Zverkov, an officer in the army, who was going away to a distant province. Monsieur Zverkov had been all the time at school with me too. I had begun to hate him particularly in the upper classes. In the lower classes he had simply been a pretty, playful boy whom everybody liked. I had hated him, however, even in the lower classes, just because he was a pretty and playful boy. He was always consistently poor in his work, and got worse and worse as he went on; nevertheless he was successfully graduated as influence was exerted on his behalf. During his last year at school he inherited an estate of two hundred serfs, and as almost all of us were poor he even started to boast before us. He was vulgar to the worst degree, but nevertheless he was a good-natured fellow, even when he boasted. In spite of superficial, fantastic and rhetorical notions of honor and dignity, all but a very few of us positively grovelled before Zverkov, and the more so the more he boasted. And they did not grovel for any advantage, but simply because he had been favored by the gifts of nature. Moreover, we came somehow to accept the idea that Zverkov was a specialist in regard to tact and good manners. That particularly infuriated me. I hated the sharp, self-confident tone of his voice, his admiration for his own witticisms, which were terribly stupid, though he was bold in his expressions; I hated his handsome but stupid face (for which I would, however, have gladly exchanged my *intelligent* one), and the free-and-easy military manners in fashion in the forties. I hated the way in which he used to talk of his future conquests of women (he did not venture to begin with women until he had officer's epaulettes and was looking forward to them with impatience), and boasted of the duels he would constantly be fighting. I remember how I, invariably so taciturn, suddenly attacked Zverkov, when one day he talked at a leisure moment with his schoolfellows of the affairs he would have in the future and growing as sportive as a puppy in the sun, he all at once declared that he would not leave a single village girl on his estate unnoticed, that that was his *droit de seigneur,* and that if the peasants dared to protest he would have them all flogged and double their taxes, the bearded rascals. Our servile rabble applauded, but I attacked him, not at all out of compassion for the girls and their fathers, but simply because they were applauding such a beetle. I got the better of him on that occasion, but though Zverkov was stupid he was lively and impudent, and so laughed it off, and even in such a way that my victory was not really complete: the laugh was on his side. He got the better of me on several occasions afterward, but without malice, somehow just in jest, casually, in fun. I remained maliciously and contemptuously silent. When we left school he made advances to me; I did not rebuff them much, for I was flattered, but we soon parted naturally. Afterward I heard of his barrack-room success as a lieutenant, and of the *fast life* he was leading. Then there came other rumors—of his *successes* in the service. By then he no longer greeted me in the street, and I suspected that he was afraid of compromising himself by greeting a person as insignificant as I. I also saw him once in the theater, in the third tier of boxes. By then he was a staff officer. He was twisting and twirling about, ingratiating himself with the daughters of an ancient general. In three years his looks had gotten considerably worse, though he was still rather handsome and smart. He had somehow swelled, started to put on weight. One could see that by the time he was thirty he would be completely fat. So it was, finally, to this Zverkov that my schoolfellows were going to give a dinner on his departure. They had kept up with him for those three years, though privately they did not consider themselves on an equal footing with him, I am convinced of that.

Of Simonov's two visitors, one was Ferfichkin, a Russianized German—a little fellow with the face of a monkey, a blockhead who was always deriding everyone, a very bitter enemy of mine from our days in the lower classes—a vulgar, impudent, boastful fellow, who affected a most sensitive feeling of personal honor, though, of course, he was a wretched little coward at heart. He was one of those admirers of Zverkov who made up to the latter out of calculation, and often borrowed money from him. Simonov's other visitor, Trudolyubov, was a person in no way remarkable—a military lad, tall with a cold face, quite honest. But he worshipped success of every sort, and was only capable of thinking of promotion. He was some distant relation of Zverkov and this, foolish as it seems, gave him a certain importance among us. He never thought me of any consequence whatever; while his behavior to me was not quite courteous, it was tolerable.

"Well then, with seven roubles each," said Trudolyubov, "twenty-one *roups* from the three of us, we can dine well. Zverkov, of course, won't pay."

"Of course not, since we are inviting him," Simonov decided.

"Can you imagine," Ferfichkin interrupted hotly and conceitedly, like some insolent flunky boasting of his master the general's decorations, "can you imagine that Zverkov will let us pay alone? He will accept from delicacy, but he will order *a half case* on his own."

"Why do we need half a case for the four of us?" observed Trudolyubov, taking notice only of the half case.

"So the three of us, with Zverkov for the fourth, twenty-one roubles, at the Hôtel de Paris at five o'clock tomorrow," Simonov, who had been asked to make the arrangements, concluded finally.

"How about twenty-one roubles?" I asked in some agitation, even offended, apparently; "if you count me it will be twenty-eight, not twenty-one roubles."

It seemed to me that to invite myself so suddenly and unexpectedly would be positively graceful, and that they would all be conquered at once and would look at me with respect.

"Do you want to join, too?" Simonov observed, with displeasure, and seemed to avoid looking at me. He knew me inside out.

It infuriated me that he knew me inside out.

"Why not? After all, I am an old schoolfellow of his too, I believe, and I must admit I feel offended that you have left me out," I said, boiling over again.

"And where were we to find you?" Ferfichkin put in roughly.

"You were never on good terms with Zverkov," Trudolyubov added, frowning. But I had already clutched at the idea and would not let go.

"I do not think that anyone has a right to judge that," I retorted in a shaking voice, as though God only knows what had happened. "Perhaps that is just my reason for wishing it now, that I have not always been on good terms with him."

"Oh, there's no making you out—with these refinements," Trudolyubov jeered.

"We'll put your name down," Simonov decided, addressing me. "Tomorrow at five o'clock at the Hôtel de Paris."

"What about the money?" Ferfichkin began in an undertone, indicating me to Simonov, but he broke off, for even Simonov was embarrassed.

"That will do," said Trudolyubov, getting up. "If he wants to come so much, let him."

"But after all it's a private thing, between us friends," Ferfichkin said crossly, as he too picked up his hat. "It's not an official meeting. Perhaps we do not want you at all—"

They went away. Ferfichkin did not salute me in any way as he went out. Trudolyubov barely nodded. Simonov, with whom I remained alone, was in some state of vexed perplexity, and looked at me strangely. He did not sit down and did not ask me to.

"H'm—yes—tomorrow, then. Will you pay your share now? I just ask so as to know," he muttered in embarrassment.

I blazed up in anger but as I did so I remembered that I had owed Simonov fifteen roubles for ages—which I had, indeed, never forgotten, though I had not paid it.

"You will understand, Simonov, that I could have had no idea when I came here—I am very much vexed that I have forgotten—"

"All right, all right, it doesn't matter. You can pay tomorrow after the dinner. After all, I simply wanted to know—Please don't—"

He broke off and began pacing the room still more vexed. As he walked he began to thump with his heels and stomped even louder.

"Am I keeping you?" I asked, after two minutes of silence.

"Oh, no!" he said, starting, "that is—to be truthful—yes. I

have to go and see someone—not far from here," he added in a sort of apologetic voice, somewhat ashamed.

"My goodness, but why didn't you say so?" I cried, seizing my cap with, incidentally, an astonishingly free-and-easy air, which was the last thing I would have expected of myself.

"After all, it's close by—not two paces away," Simonov repeated, accompanying me to the front door with a fussy air which did not suit him at all. "So five o'clock, punctually, tomorrow," he called down the stairs after me. He was very glad to get rid of me. I was in a fury.

"What possessed me, what possessed me to force myself upon them?" I gnashed my teeth, as I strode along the street. "For a scoundrel, a pig like that Zverkov! Of course, I had better not go; of course, I can just snap my fingers at them. I am not bound in any way. I'll send Simonov a note by tomorrow's post—"

But what made me furious was that I knew for certain that I would go, that I would purposely go; and the more tactless, the more ill-mannered my going would be, the more certainly I would go.

And there was even a positive obstacle to my going: I had no money. All I had altogether was nine roubles. But I had to give seven of that to my servant, Apollon, for his monthly wages. That was all I paid him—he had to keep himself.

Not to pay him was impossible, considering his character. But I will talk about that fellow, about that plague of mine, another time.

However, I knew I would go after all and would not pay him his wages.

That night I had the most hideous dreams. No wonder; the whole evening I had been oppressed by memories of my days of penal servitude at school, and I could not shake them off. I was sent to the school by distant relations, upon whom I was dependent and of whom I have heard nothing since—they sent me there, a lonely, silent boy, already crushed by their reproaches, already troubled by doubt, and looking savagely at everything around him. My schoolfellows met me with spiteful and merciless jibes because I was not like any of them. But I could not endure their taunts; I could not give in to them as cheaply as they gave in to one another. I hated them from the first, and shut myself away from everyone in timid, wounded and disproportionate pride. Their coarseness revolted me. They laughed cynically at my face, at my clumsy figure; and yet what stupid faces they themselves had. In our school the boys' faces somehow degenerated and grew stupider particularly. How many fine-looking boys came to us? In a few years they became repulsive looking. Even at sixteen I wondered at them morosely; even then I was struck by the pettiness of their thoughts, the stupidity of their pursuits, their games, their conversations. They had no understanding of such essential things, they took no interest in such striking, impressive subjects that I could not help considering them inferior to myself. It was not wounded vanity that drove me to it, and for God's sake do not thrust upon me your hackneyed remarks, repeated to nausea, that "I was only a dreamer, while they even then understood real life." They understood nothing, they had no idea of real life, and I swear that that was what made me most indignant with them. On the contrary, the most obvious, striking reality they accepted with fantastic stupidity and even then had already begun to respect only success. Everything that was just, but oppressed and looked down upon, they laughed at cruelly and shamefully. They took rank for intelligence; even at sixteen they were already talking about a snug berth. Of course a great deal of it was due to their stupidity, to the bad examples that constantly surrounded them in their childhood and boyhood. They were monstrously depraved. Of course much of that, too, was superficial and much was only affected cynicism; of course there were glimpses of youth and freshness in them even beneath their depravity; but even that freshness was not attractive in them, and showed itself in a certain rakishness. I hated them terribly, though perhaps I was worse than any of them. They repaid me in kind, and did not conceal their aversion for me. But by then I did not want them to like me; on the contrary, I continually longed for them to humiliate me. To escape from their derision I purposely began to make all the progress I could with my studies and forced my way to the very top. This impressed them. Moreover, they all began to grasp slowly that I was already reading books none of them could read, and understood things (not forming part of our school curriculum) of which they had not even heard. They took a savage and sarcastic view of it, but were morally impressed, especially as the teachers began to notice me on those grounds. The mockery ceased but the hostility remained, and cold and strained relations were formed between us. In the end I could not stand it myself; with years a craving for society, for friends, developed in me. I attempted to get on friendly terms with some of my schoolfellows; but somehow or other my intimacy with them was always strained and soon ended of itself. Once, indeed, I did have a friend. But I was already a tyrant at heart; I wanted to exercise unlimited power over him; I tried to instill into him a contempt for his surroundings; I required of him a disdainful and complete break with those surroundings. I frightened him with my passionate affection; I reduced him to tears, to convulsions. He was a simple and devoted soul; but when he submitted to me completely I began to hate him immediately and rejected him—as though all I needed him for was to win a victory over him, to subjugate him and nothing else. But I could not subjugate all of them; my friend was not at all like them either, he was, in fact, a rare exception. The first thing I did on leaving school was to give up the special job for which I had been destined so as to break all ties, to curse my past and scatter it to the winds— And goodness knows why, after all that, I should drag myself to that Simonov!

Early next morning I roused myself and jumped out of bed with excitement, as though it were all about to happen at once. But I believed that some radical change in my life was coming, and would inevitably come that day. Owing to its rarity, per-

haps, any external event, however trivial, always made me feel
as though some radical change in my life would occur immediately. I went to the office as usual, however, but slipped away
home two hours early to get ready. The important thing, I
thought, is not to be the first to arrive, or they will think I was
overjoyed at coming. But there were thousands of such important points to consider, and they all agitated me to the point of
impotence. I polished my boots a second time with my own
hands; nothing in the world would have induced Apollon to
clean them twice a day, as he considered that it was more than
his duties required of him. I stole the brushes to clean them
from the passage, so that he would not detect it and then start
to despise me. Then I minutely examined my clothes, and found
that everything looked old, worn and threadbare. I had let myself get too slovenly. My uniform, perhaps, was in good shape,
but I could hardly go out to dinner in my uniform. And the
worst thing was that on the knee of my trousers was a big yellow stain. I had a foreboding that that stain would in itself deprive me of nine-tenths of my personal dignity. I knew, too, that
it was stooping very low to think so. "But this is no time for
thinking: now the real thing is beginning," I thought, and my
heart sank. I knew, too, perfectly well even then, that I was
monstrously exaggerating the facts. But how could I help it? I
could not control myself and I was already shaking with fever.
With despair I pictured to myself how coldly and disdainfully
that "scoundrel" Zverkov would greet me; with what dull-witted,
absolutely profound contempt the blockhead Trudolyubov
would look at me; with what nasty insolence the beetle Ferfichkin would snigger at me in order to curry favor with
Zverkov; how completely Simonov would take it all in, and
how he would despise me for the abjectness of my vanity and
faint-heartedness, and worst of all how paltry, *unliterary,* commonplace it would all be. Of course the best thing would be not
to go at all. But that was the most impossible of all: once I feel
impelled to do anything, I am completely drawn into it, head

first. I would have jeered at myself ever afterward: "So you funked it, you funked the *real thing,* you funked it!" On the contrary, I passionately longed to show all that "rabble" that I was not at all such a coward as I pictured myself. What is more, even in the acutest paroxysm of this cowardly fever, I dreamed of getting the upper hand, of overcoming them, carrying them away, making them like me—if only for my "elevation of thought and unmistakable wit." They would abandon Zverkov, he would sit on one side, silent and ashamed, while I would crush Zverkov. Then, perhaps, I would be reconciled to him and toast our camaraderie; but what was most spiteful and insulting for me was that I knew even then, knew completely and for certain, that I needed nothing of all this really, that I did not really want to crush, to subdue, to attract them, and that I would be the first not to care a straw, really, for the result, even if I did achieve it. Oh, how I prayed to God for the day to pass quickly! In inexpressible anguish I went to the window, opened a pane and looked out into the turbid darkness of the thickly failing wet snow.

At last my wretched little wall clock hissed out five. I seized my hat trying not to look at Apollon, who had been all day expecting his month's wages, but in his pride was unwilling to be the first to speak about it. I slipped past him and out the door, and jumping into a high-class sledge, on which I spent my last half-rouble, I drove up in grand style to the Hôtel de Paris.

IV

I had already known the day before that I would be the first to arrive. But it was no longer a question of precedence.

Not only were they not there, but I even had difficulty finding our room. The table had still not been completely set. What did it mean? After a good many questions I finally ascertained from the waiters that the dinner had been ordered not for five, but for six o'clock. This was confirmed at the buffet too. I even felt ashamed to go on questioning them. It was still only twenty-five minutes past five. If they changed the dinner hour they ought in any case to have let me know—that is what the post is for, and not to have subjected me to "shame" both in my own eyes and—well, before the waiters. I sat down: the servant began to set the table; I felt even more insulted when he was present. Toward six o'clock they brought in candles, though there were lamps burning in the room. It had not occurred to the waiter, however, to bring them in at once when I arrived. In the next room, two gloomy, angry-looking persons were eating their dinners in silence at two different tables. There was a great deal of noise, even shouting, in a room farther away; one could hear the laughter of a crowd of people, and nasty little shrieks in French; there were ladies at the dinner. In short, it was sickening. I rarely passed a more unpleasant time, so much so that when they did arrive all together punctually at six I was for the first moment overjoyed to see them, as though they were my deliverers, and almost forgot it was incumbent upon me to look insulted.

Zverkov walked in at the head of them; evidently he was the leading spirit. He and all of them were laughing; but, seeing me, Zverkov drew himself up, walked up to me unhurriedly with a slight, rather jaunty bend from the waist, and shook hands with me in a friendly but not over-friendly fashion, with a sort of circumspect courtesy almost like a general's as though in giving me his hand he were warding off something. I had imagined, on the contrary, that as soon as he came in he would immediately break into his former thin, shrieking laugh and fall to making his insipid jokes and witticisms. I had been preparing for them ever since the previous day, but I had never expected such condescension, such high-official courtesy. So, then, he felt himself immeasurably superior to me in every respect! If he had only meant to insult me by that high-official tone, it would still not have mattered, I thought—I could pay him back for it one way or another. But what if, in reality, without the least desire to be offensive, that sheep's-head had seriously acquired the notion that he was immeasurably superior to me and could only look at me in a patronizing way? The very supposition made me gasp.

"I was surprised to hear of your desire to join us," he began, lisping and drawling, which was something new. "You and I seem to have seen nothing of one another. You fight shy of us. You shouldn't. We are not such terrible people as you think. Well, anyway, I am glad to renew our acquaintance."

And he turned carelessly to put down his hat on the window sill.

"Have you been waiting long?" Trudolyubov inquired.

"I arrived punctually at five o'clock as I was informed yesterday," I answered aloud, with an irritability that promised an imminent explosion.

"Didn't you let him know that we had changed the hour?" said Trudolyubov to Simonov.

"No, I didn't, I forgot," the latter replied, with no sign of regret, and without even apologizing to me he went off to order the *hors d'ouevres*.

"So you've been here a whole hour? Oh, you poor fellow!" Zverkov cried ironically, for according to his notions this was bound to be extremely funny. That scoundrel Ferfichkin followed with his nasty little snigger like a puppy yapping. My position struck him, too, as extremely ludicrous and embarrassing.

"It isn't funny at all!" I cried to Ferfichkin, more and more irritated. "It wasn't my fault, but other people's. They neglected to let me know. It was—it was—it was simply absurd."

"It's not only absurd, but something else as well," muttered Trudolyubov, naïvely taking my part. "You are too complacent about it. It was simply rudeness—unintentional, of course. And how could Simonov—h'm!"

"If a trick like that had been played on me," observed Ferfichkin, "I would—"

"But you should have ordered yourself something," Zverkov interrupted, "or simply asked for dinner without waiting for us."

"You will allow-that I might have done that without your permission," I rapped out. "If I waited, it was—"

"Let us sit down, gentlemen," cried Simonov, coming in. "Everything is ready; I can answer for the champagne; it is capitally chilled.—After all, I did not know your address. Where was I to look for you?" He suddenly turned to me, but again he seemed to avoid looking at me. Evidently he had something against me. He must have made up his mind after what happened yesterday.

Everybody sat down: I did the same. It was a round table. Trudolyubov was on my left, Simonov on my right. Zverkov was sitting opposite, Ferfichkin next to him, between him and Trudolyubov.

"Te-e-ell me, are you—in a government agency?" Zverkov went on, attending to me. Seeing that I was embarrassed, he seriously thought that he ought to be friendly to me, and, so to speak, cheer me up. "Does he want me to throw a bottle at his head or something?" I thought, in a fury. In my unaccustomed surroundings I was unnaturally quick to be irritated.

"In the N——office," I answered jerkily, with my eyes on my plate.

"And—ha-ave you a go-od berth? Te-e-ll me, what ma-a-de you leave your former job?"

"What ma-a-de me was that I wanted to leave my original job," I drawled twice as much as he, hardly able to control myself. Ferfichkin snorted. Simonov looked at me ironically. Trudolyubov stopped eating and began looking at me with curiosity.

Zverkov was jarred but he pretended not to notice it.

"A-a-and the remuneration?"

"What remuneration?"

"I mean, your sa-a-lary?"

"Why are you cross-examining me?"

However, I told him at once what my salary was. I blushed terribly.

"It is not very handsome," Zverkov observed majestically.

"Yes, you can't afford to dine in restaurants on that," Ferfichkin added insolently.

"I think it's very low," Trudolyubov observed gravely.

"And how thin you have grown! How you have changed!" added Zverkov, with a shade of venom in his voice, scanning me and my attire with a sort of insolent compassion.

"Oh, spare his blushes," cried Ferfichkin, sniggering.

"My dear sir, permit me to tell you I am not blushing," I broke out at last; "Do you hear? I am dining here, at this restaurant, at my own expense, at mine, not at other people's—note that, Monsieur Ferfichkin."

"Wha-at do you mean? Isn't everyone here dining at his own expense? You seem to be—" Ferfichkin let fly at me, turning as red as a lobster, and looking me in the face with fury.

"Tha-at's what I mean," I answered, feeling I had gone too far, "and I imagine it would be better to talk of something more intelligent."

"You intend to show off your intelligence, I suppose?"

"Don't disturb yourself, that would be quite out of place here."

"What are you clacking away like that for, my good sir, eh? Have you gone out of your wits in your *dumb*partment?"

"Enough, gentlemen, enough!" Zverkov cried, authoritatively.

"How stupid it is," muttered Simonov.

"It really is stupid. We have met here, a company of friends, for a farewell dinner to a good comrade and you are settling old scores," said Trudolyubov, rudely addressing himself to me alone. "Yesterday you invited yourself to join us, so don't disturb the general harmony."

"Enough, enough!" cried Zverkov. "Stop it, gentlemen, it's out of place. Better let me tell you how I nearly got married the day before yesterday . . ."

And then followed a burlesque narrative of how this gentleman had almost been married two days before. There was not a word about marriage, however, but the story was adorned with generals, colonels and high courtiers while Zverkov practically took the lead among them. It was greeted with approving laughter; Ferfichkin even squealed.

No one paid any attention to me, and I sat crushed and humiliated.

"Good heavens, these are not the people for me!" I thought. "And what a fool I have made of myself before them! I let Ferfichkin go too far, though. The brutes imagine that it is an honor for me to sit down with them. They don't understand that I do them an honor. I to them and not they to me! I've grown thinner! My clothes! Oh, damn my trousers! Zverkov long ago noticed the yellow stain on the knee . . . But what's the use! I must get up at once, this very minute, take my hat and simply go without a word—out of contempt! And tomorrow I can send a challenge. The scoundrels! After all, I don't care about the seven roubles. They may think . . . Damn it! I don't care about the seven roubles. I'll go this minute!"

Of course I remained.

I drank sherry and Lafitte by the glassful in my distress. Being unaccustomed to it, I quickly became intoxicated and my annoyance increased with the intoxication. I longed all at once to insult them all in a most flagrant manner and then go away. To seize the moment and show what I could do, so that they would say, "Though he is absurd, he's clever," and—and—in short, damn them all!

I scanned them all insolently with my dulled eyes. But they seemed to have forgotten me altogether. *They* were noisy, vociferous, cheerful. Zverkov kept talking. I began to listen. Zverkov was talking about some sumptuous lady whom he had at last led on to declaring her love (of course, he was lying like a horse), and how he had been helped in this affair by an intimate friend of his, a Prince Kolya, an officer in the Hussars, who had three thousand serfs.

"And yet, this Kolya, who has three thousand serfs, has not

put in an appearance here tonight at all to see you off," I cut in
suddenly. For a minute everyone was silent.

"You are drunk already." Trudolyubov deigned to notice me
at last, glancing contemptuously in my direction. Zverkov, without a word, examined me as though I were a little beetle. I
dropped my eyes. Simonov made haste to fill up the glasses with
champagne.

Trudolyubov raised his glass, as did everyone else but me.

"Your health and good luck on the journey!" he cried to
Zverkov. "To old times, gentlemen, to our future, hurrah!"

They all tossed off their glasses, and crowded round Zverkov
to kiss him. I did not move; my full glass stood untouched before me.

"Why, aren't you going to drink it?" roared Trudolyubov,
losing patience and turning menacingly to me.

"I want to make a toast separately, on my own account . . . and then I'll drink it, Mr. Trudolyubov."

"Disgusting crank!" muttered Simonov.

I drew myself up in my chair and feverishly seized my glass,
prepared for something extraordinary, though I did not know
myself precisely what I was going to say.

"*Silence!*" cried Ferfichkin, in French. "Now for a display
of wit!"

Zverkov waited very gravely, knowing what was coming.

"Lieutenant Zverkov," I began, "let me tell you that I hate
phrases, phrasemongers and corseted waists—that's the first
point, and there is a second one to follow it."

There was a general stir.

"The second point is: I hate dirty stories and people who tell
dirty stories. Especially people who tell dirty stories!

"The third point: I love truth, sincerity and honesty," I went
on almost mechanically, for I was beginning to shiver with horror and had no idea how I came to be talking like this. "I love
thought, Monsieur Zverkov; I love true comradeship, on an
equal footing and not—h'm—I love—but, however, why not? I

will drink to your health, too, Monsieur Zverkov. Seduce the Circassian girls, shoot the enemies of the fatherland and—and—to your health, Monsieur Zverkov!"

Zverkov got up from his seat, bowed to me and said:

"I am very much obliged to you."

He was frightfully offended and even turned pale.

"Damn the fellow!" roared Trudolyubov, bringing his fist down on the table.

"Well, he ought to be punched in the nose for that," squealed Ferfichkin.

"We ought to turn him out," muttered Simonov.

"Not a word, gentlemen, not a movement!" cried Zverkov solemnly, checking the general indignation. "I thank you all, but I can show him for myself how much value I attach to his words."

"Mr. Ferfichkin, you will give me satisfaction tomorrow at the latest for your words just now!" I said aloud, turning with dignity to Ferfichkin.

"A duel, you mean? Certainly," he answered. But probably I was so ridiculous as I challenged him and it was so out of keeping with my appearance that everyone, including Ferfichkin, roared with laughter.

"Yes, let him alone, of course! After all, he is completely drunk," Trudolyubov said with disgust.

"I will never forgive myself for letting him join us," Simonov muttered again.

"Now is the time to throw a bottle at their heads," I thought to myself. I picked up the bottle . . . and poured myself a full glass.

"No, I had better sit on to the end," I went on thinking; "you would be pleased, my friends, if I left. Nothing will induce me to go. I'll go on sitting here, and drinking to the end, on purpose, as a sign that I don't attach the slightest importance to you. I will go on sitting and drinking, because this is a public-house and I paid my entrance money. I'll sit here and drink, for I look upon you as so many pawns, as inanimate pawns. I'll sit here and drink—and sing if I want to, yes, sing, for I have the right to—to sing—h'm!"

But I did not sing. I simply tried not to look at any of them. I assumed most unconcerned attitudes and waited with impatience for them to speak *first,* of their own accord. But alas, they did not speak! And oh, how I wished, how I wished at that moment to be reconciled to them! It struck eight, at last nine. They moved from the table to the sofa. Zverkov stretched himself on a couch and put one foot on a round table. The wine was brought there. He did, as a matter of fact, order three bottles on his own account. He didn't, of course, invite me to join them. They all sat round him on the sofa. They listened to him, almost with reverence. It was evident that they were fond of him. "For what? For what?" I wondered. From time to time they were moved to drunken enthusiasm and kissed each other. They talked of the Caucasus, of the nature of true passion, of advantageous jobs in the service, of the income of a Hussar called Podkharzhevsky, whom none of them knew personally and rejoiced that he had a large income; of the extraordinary grace and beauty of a Princess D., whom none of them had ever seen; then it came to Shakespeare's being immortal.

I smiled contemptuously and walked up and down the other side of the room, opposite the sofa, along the wall, from the table to the stove and back again. I tried my very utmost to show them that I could do without them, and yet I purposely stomped with my boots, thumping with my heels. But it was all in vain. They paid no attention at all. I had the patience to walk up and down in front of them that way from eight o'clock till eleven, in one and the same place, from the table to the stove and from the stove back again to the table. "I walk up and down to please myself and no one can prevent me." The waiter who came into the room several times stopped to look at me. I was somewhat giddy from turning round so often; at moments it seemed to me that I was in delirium. During those three hours I was three times soaked with sweat, and then dry again. At times, with an intense, acute pang, I was stabbed to the heart by the thought that ten years, twenty years, forty years would pass, and that even in forty years I would remember with loathing and humiliation those filthiest, most ludicrous, and most terrible moments of my life. No one could have gone out of his way to degrade himself more shamelessly and voluntarily, and I fully realized it, fully, and yet I went on pacing up and down from the table to the stove. "Oh, if you only knew what thoughts and feelings I am capable of, how cultured I am!" I thought at moments, mentally addressing the sofa on which my enemies were sitting. But my enemies behaved as though I did not exist in the room. Once—only once—they turned toward me, just when Zverkov was talking about Shakespeare, and I suddenly gave a contemptuous laugh. I snorted in such an affected and nasty way that they all at once broke off their conversation, and silently and gravely for two minutes watched me walking up and down from the table to the stove, *paying no attention whatsoever to them*. But nothing came of it; they said nothing, and two minutes later they ceased to notice me again. It struck eleven.

"Gentlemen," cried Zverkov, getting up from the sofa, "let us all go there *now!*"

"Of course, of course," the others said.

I turned sharply to Zverkov. I was so exhausted, so broken, that I would have cut my throat to put an end to it. I was in a fever; my hair, soaked with perspiration, stuck to my forehead and temples.

"Zverkov, I beg your pardon," I said abruptly and resolutely. "Ferfichkin, yours too, and everyone's, everyone's; I have insulted you all!"

"Aha! A duel is not in your line, old man," Ferfichkin hissed venomously.

It sent a deep pang to my heart.

"No, it's not the duel I am afraid of, Ferfichkin! I am ready to fight you tomorrow, after we are reconciled. I insist upon it, in fact, and you cannot refuse. I want to show you that I am not afraid of a duel. You will fire first and I will fire into the air."

"He is comforting himself," remarked Simonov.

"He's simply raving," declared Trudolyubov.

"But let us pass. Why are you barring our way? Well, what do you want?" Zverkov answered disdainfully. They were all flushed; their eyes were bright; they had been drinking heavily.

"I asked for your friendship, Zverkov; I insulted you, but—"

"Insulted? You-u insulted me-e-e! Permit me to tell you, sir, that you never, under any circumstances, could possibly insult *me*."

"And that's enough of you. Out of the way!" concluded Trudolyubov. "Let's go."

"Olympia is mine, gentlemen, that's agreed!" cried Zverkov.

"We won't dispute your right, we won't dispute your right," the others answered, laughing.

I stood as though spat upon. The party went noisily out of the room. Trudolyubov struck up some stupid song. Simonov remained behind for a moment to tip the waiters. I suddenly went up to him.

"Simonov! give me six roubles!" I said, decisively and desperately.

He looked at me in extreme amazement, with dulled eyes. He, too, was drunk.

"You don't mean you are even coming with us *there?*"

"Yes."

"I've no money," he snapped out, and with a scornful laugh he went out of the room.

I clutched at his overcoat. It was a nightmare.

"Simonov! I saw you had money, why do you refuse me? Am I a scoundrel? Beware of refusing me; if you knew, if you knew why I am asking! Everything depends upon it! My whole future, my whole plans!"

Simonov pulled out the money and almost flung it at me.

"Take it, if you have no sense of shame!" he pronounced pitilessly, and ran to overtake them.

I was left alone for a moment. Disorder, the remains of dinner, a broken wineglass on the floor, spilt wine, cigarette butts, intoxication and delirium in my brain, an agonizing misery in my heart and finally the waiter, who had seen and heard all and was looking inquisitively into my face.

"I am going *there!*" I shouted. "Either they will all fall down on their knees to beg for my friendship—or I will give Zverkov a slap in the face!"

V

"So this is it, so this is it at last, a clash with reality," I muttered as I ran headlong downstairs. "This, it seems, is very different from the Pope's leaving Rome and going to Brazil; this, it seems, is very different from the ball on the shores of Lake Como!"

"You are a scoundrel," flashed through my mind, "if you laugh at this now."

"No matter!" I cried, answering myself. "Now everything is lost!"

There was no trace of them left, but that made no difference—I knew where they had gone.

At the steps was standing a solitary night sledge-driver in a rough peasant coat, powdered over with the wet, and, as it were, warm snow mat was still falling thickly. It was sultry and warm. The little shaggy piebald horse was also powdered with snow and was coughing, I remember that very well. I made a rush for the roughly made sledge; but as soon as I raised my foot to get into it, the recollection of how Simonov had just given me six roubles seemed to double me up and I tumbled into the sledge like a sack.

"No, I must do a great deal to make up for all that," I cried. "But I will make up for it or perish on the spot this very night. Start!"

We set off. There was an absolute whirl in my head.

"They won't go down on their knees to beg for my friendship. That is a mirage, a cheap mirage, revolting, romantic and fantastical—that is another ball at Lake Como. And so I have to slap Zverkov's face! It is my duty to. And so it is settled; I am flying to give him a slap in the face. Hurry up!"

The cabby tugged at the reins.

"As soon as I go in I'll give it to him. Ought I to say a few words by way of preface before giving him the slap? No, I'll simply go in and give it to him. They will all be sitting in the drawing-room, and he with Olympia on the sofa. That damned Olympia! She laughed at my looks on one occasion and refused me. I'll pull Olympia's hair, pull Zverkov's ears! No, better one ear, and pull him by it round the room. Maybe they will all begin beating me and will kick me out. That is even very likely. No matter! Anyway, I will slap him first; the initiative will be mine; and according to the code of honor that is everything: he will be branded and no blows can wipe off the slap, nothing but a duel can. He will be forced to fight. And let them beat me then. Let them, the ungrateful wretches! Trudolyubov will beat me hardest, he is so strong; Ferfichkin is sure to catch hold from the side and tug at my hair. But no matter, no matter! That's what I am going for. The blockheads will be forced at last to see the tragedy of it all! When they drag me to the door I shall call out to them that in reality they are not worth my little finger." "Get on, driver, get on!" I cried to the driver. He started and flicked his whip, I shouted so savagely.

"We shall fight at daybreak, that's a settled thing. I am through with the Department Ferfichkin called the Department 'Dumbpartment' before. But where can I get pistols? Nonsense! I'll call my salary in advance and buy them. And powder, and bullets? That's the second's business. And how can it all be done by daybreak? And where am I to get a second? I have no friends. Nonsense!" I cried, lashing myself more and more into a fury. "Nonsense! the first person I meet in the street is bound to be my second, just as he would be bound to pull a drowning man out of water. The strangest things may happen. Even if I were to ask the Director himself to be my second tomorrow, even he would be bound to consent, if only from a feeling of chivalry, and to keep the secret! Anton Antonich—"

The fact is that at that very minute the disgusting absurdity of my plans and the other side of the question were clearer and more vivid to my imagination than they could be to anyone on earth, but—

"Get on, driver, get on, you rascal, get on!"

"Ugh, sir!" said the son of toil.

Cold shivers suddenly ran down me.

"Wouldn't it be better . . . wouldn't it be better . . . to go straight home now? Oh, my God! Why, why did I invite myself to this dinner yesterday? But no, it's impossible. And my three hours' walk from the table to the stove? No, they, they and no one else must pay for my walking up and down! They must wipe out this dishonor! Drive on!"

"And what if they hand me over to the police? They won't dare! They'll be afraid of the scandal. And what if Zverkov is so contemptuous that he refuses to fight a duel? That is even sure to happen, but in that case I'll show them—I will turn up at the posting station when he is setting off tomorrow—I'll catch him by the leg, I'll pull off his coat when he gets into the carriage. I'll get my teeth into his hand, I'll bite him. See to what lengths you can drive a desperate man! He may hit me on the head and they may pummel me from behind. I will shout to the whole crowd of spectators: 'Look at this young puppy who is driving off to captivate the Circassian girls after letting me spit in his face!'

"Of course, after that everything will be over! The Department will have vanished off the face of the earth. I will be arrested. I will be tried, I will be dismissed from the service, thrown in prison, sent to Siberia, deported. Never mind! In fifteen years when they let me out of prison I will trudge off to him, a begger in rags, I shall find him in some provincial city.

He will be married and happy. He will have a grown-up daughter . . . I will say to him: 'Look, monster, at my hollow cheeks
and my rags! I've lost everything—my career, my happiness, art,
science, *the woman I loved,* and all through you. Here are pistols. I have come to discharge my pistol and—and I . . . forgive
you.' Then I will fire into the air and he will hear nothing more
of me."

I was actually on the point of tears, though I knew perfectly
well at that very moment that all this was out of Pushkin's *Silvio*
and Lermontov's *Masquerade.* And all at once I felt terribly
ashamed, so ashamed that I stopped the sledge, stepped out of it
and stood still in the snow in the middle of the street. The driver
sighed and gazed at me in astonishment.

What was I to do? I could not go on there—that was clearly
absurd, and I could not leave things as they were, because that
would seem as though— "Heavens, how could I leave things! And
after such insults!" "No!" I cried, throwing myself into the sledge
again. "It is ordained! It is fate! Drive on, drive on to that place!"

And in my impatience I punched the sledge-driver on the
back of the neck.

"What are you up to? What are you hitting me for?" the
poor man shouted, but he whipped up his nag so that it began
to kick out.

The wet snow was falling in big flakes; I unbuttoned myself.
I did not care about it. I forgot everything else, for I had finally
decided on the slap, and felt with horror that after all it was
going to happen *now, at once,* that it would happen immediately and that *no force could stop it.* The deserted street lamps
gleamed sullenly in the snowy darkness like torches at a funeral.
The snow drifted under my greatcoat, under my coat, under my
necktie, and melted there. I did not cover myself up—after all,
all was already lost, anyway. At last we arrived. I jumped out,
almost fainting, ran up the steps and began knocking and kick-
ing at the door. My legs, particularly at the knee, felt terribly
weak. The door was opened quickly as though they knew I was

coming. As a matter of fact, Simonov had warned them that perhaps another would arrive, and this was a place in which one had to give notice and to observe certain precautions. It was one of the "millinery establishments" which were abolished by the police a long time ago. By day it really was a shop; but at night, if one had an introduction, one might visit it for other purposes.

I walked rapidly through the dark shop into the familiar drawing-room, where there was only one candle burning, and stopped in amazement; there was no one there.

"Where are they?" I asked somebody.

But by now, of course, they had separated.

Before me stood a person with a stupid smile, the "madam" herself, who had seen me before. A minute later a door opened and another person came in.

Paying no attention to anything, I strode about the room, and, I believe, I talked to myself. I felt as though I had been saved from death and was conscious of it, joyfully, all over: after all, I would have given that slap. I would certainly, certainly have given it! But now they were not here and—everything had vanished and changed! I looked round. I could not realize my condition yet. I looked mechanically at the girl who had come in and had a glimpse of a fresh, young, rather pale face, with straight, dark eyebrows, and with a grave, as it were, amazed glance, eyes that attracted me at once. I would have hated her if she had been smiling. I began looking at her more intently and, as it were, with effort. I had a not fully collected my thoughts. There was something simple and good-natured in her face, but something strangely serious. I am sure that this stood in her way here, and that not one of those fools had noticed her. She could not, however, have been called a beauty, though she was tall, strong-looking, and well built. She was very simply dressed. Something loathsome stirred within me. I went straight up to her—

I happened to look at myself in the mirror. My harassed face struck me as extremely revolting, pale, spiteful, nasty, with disheveled hair. "No matter, I am glad of it," I thought; "I am glad that I shall seem revolting to her; I like that."

VI

. . . Somewhere behind a screen a clock began wheezing, as though under some great pressure, as though someone were strangling it. After an unnaturally prolonged wheezing there followed a shrill, nasty and, as it were, unexpectedly rapid chime—as though someone were suddenly jumping forward. It struck two. I woke up, though I had not really been asleep but only lay semi-conscious.

It was almost completely dark in the narrow, cramped, low-pitched room, cluttered up with an enormous wardrobe and piles of cardboard boxes and all sorts of frippery and litter. The candle stump that had been burning on the table was going out and it gave a faint flicker from tune to time. In a few minutes it would be completely dark.

I was not long in coming to myself; everything came back to my mind at once, without an effort, as though it had been in ambush to pounce upon me again. And, indeed, even while I was unconscious, a point continually seemed to remain in my memory that could not ever be forgotten, and around it my dreams moved drearily. But strange to say, everything that had happened to me during that day seemed to me now, on waking, to be in the far, far-away distant past, as though I had long, long ago lived all that down.

My head was heavy. Something seemed to be hovering over me, provoking me, rousing me and making me restless. Misery and gall seemed to surge up in me again and to seek an outlet. Suddenly I saw beside me two wide-open eyes scrutinizing me curiously and persistently. The look in those eyes was coldly detached, sullen, utterly detached, as it were; it weighed heavily on me.

A grim idea came into my brain and passed all over my body,

like some nasty sensation, such as one feels when one goes into a damp and moldy cellar. It was somehow unnatural that those two eyes only now thought of beginning to examine me. I recalled, too, that during those two hours I had not said a single word to this creature, and had, in fact, considered it entirely unnecessary; it had even for some reason gratified me before. Now I suddenly realized vividly how absurd, revolting as a spider, was the idea of vice which, without love, grossly and shamelessly begins directly with that in which true love finds its consummation. For a long time we gazed at each other like that, but she did not drop her eyes before mine and did not change her expression, so that at last, somehow, I felt uncomfortable.

"What is your name?" I asked abruptly, to put an end to it quickly.

"Liza," she answered almost in a whisper, but somehow without any friendliness; she turned her eyes away.

I was silent.

"What weather today—the snow—it's abominable!" I said, almost to myself, putting my arm under my head despondently, and gazing at the ceiling.

She made no answer. This was all outrageous.

"Are you a local girl?" I asked a minute later, almost angrily, turning my head slightly toward her.

"No."

"Where do you come from?"

"From Riga," she answered reluctantly.

"Are you a German?"

"No, Russian."

"Have you been here long?"

"Where?"

"In this house?"

"A fortnight."

She spoke more and more jerkily. The candle went out: I could no longer distinguish her face.

"Have you a father and mother?"

"Yes—no—I have."

"Where are they?"

"There—in Riga."

"What are they?"

"Oh, nothing."

"Nothing? Why, what do they do?"

"Tradespeople."

"Have you always lived with them?"

"Yes."

"How old are you?"

"Twenty."

"Why did you leave them?"

"Oh, for no reason."

That answer meant "Let me alone; I feel wretched." We were silent.

God knows why I did not go away. I felt myself more and more wretched and dreary. The images of the previous day started to flit through my mind in confusion independently of my will. I suddenly recalled something I had seen that morning when, full of anxious thoughts, I was hurrying to the office.

"I saw them carrying a coffin out yesterday and they nearly dropped it," I suddenly said aloud with no desire at all to start a conversation, but just so, almost by accident.

"A coffin?"

"Yes, in the Haymarket; they were bringing it up out of a cellar."

"From a cellar?"

"Not from a cellar, but from a basement. Oh, you know—down below—from a house of ill-fame. It was filthy all round—eggshells, litter—a stench. It was loathsome."

Silence.

"A nasty day to be buried," I began, simply to avoid being silent.

"Nasty, in what way?"

"The snow, the wet." (I yawned.)

"It doesn't matter," she said suddenly, after a brief silence.

"No, it's abominable." (I yawned again.) "The grave-diggers must have sworn at getting drenched by the snow. And there must have been water m the grave."

"Why would there be water in the grave?" she asked, with a sort of curiosity, but speaking even more harshly and abruptly than before. I suddenly began to feel provoked.

"Why, there must have been water at the bottom a foot deep. You can't dig a dry grave in Volkovo Cemetery?"

"Why?"

"Why, the place is waterlogged. It's a regular marsh. So they bury them in water. I've seen it myself—many times."

(I had never seen it at all, and I had never even been in Volkovo, but had only heard stories of it.)

"Do you mean to say it doesn't matter to you whether you die?"

"But why should I die?" she answered, as though defending herself.

"Why, some day you will die, and you will die just the same as that dead woman. She was—a girl like you. She died of consumption."

"The wench would have died in a hospital, too . . . (She knows all about it already; she said "wench," not "girl.")

"She was in debt to her madam," I retorted, more and more provoked by the discussion; "and went on earning money for her almost up to the very end, though she was in consumption. Some coachmen standing by were talking about her to some soldiers and telling them so. No doubt her former acquaintances. They were laughing. They were going to meet in a pot-house to drink to her memory." (I lied a great deal here.)

Silence followed, profound silence. She did not even stir.

"And is it better to die in a hospital?"

"Isn't it just the same? Besides, why should I die?" she added irritably.

"If not now, a little later."

"Why a little later?"

"Why, indeed? Now you are young, pretty, fresh, you fetch a high price. But after another year of this life you will be very different—you will fade."

"In a year?"

"Anyway, in a year you will be worth less," I continued malignantly. "You will go from here to something lower, another house; a year later—to a third, lower and lower, and in seven years you will come to a basement in the Haymarket. And that's if you are lucky. But it would be much worse if you got some disease, consumption, say—and caught a chill, or something or other. It's not easy to get over an illness in your way of life. If you catch anything you may not get rid of it. And so you would die."

"Oh, well, then I will die," she answered, quite vindictively, and she made a quick movement.

"But after all, it's a pity."

"For whom?"

"Pity for life."

Silence.

"Were you engaged? Eh?"

"What's that to you?"

"Oh, I am not cross-examining you. It's nothing to me. Why are you so cross? Of course you may have had your own troubles. What is it to me? I simply felt sorry."

"For whom?"

"Sorry for you."

"No need," she whispered hardly audibly, and again made a faint movement.

That incensed me at once. What! I was so gentle with her, and she—

"Why, what do you think? Are you on the right path, ah?"

"I don't think anything."

"That's what's wrong, that you don't think. Wake up while there is still time. And there is still time. You are still young, good-looking; you might love, be married, be happy—"

"Not all married women are happy," she snapped out in the rude, fast way she had spoken before.

"Not all, of course, but anyway it is much better than the life here. Infinitely better. Besides, with love one can live even without happiness. Even in sorrow life is sweet; life is sweet, however one lives. But here you have nothing except foulness. Phew!"

I turned away with disgust; I was no longer reasoning coldly. I began to feel myself what I was saying and warmed to the subject. I was already longing to expound the cherished *little ideas* I had brooded over in my corner. Something suddenly flared up in me. An object had "appeared" before me.

"Never mind my being here. I am not an example for you. I am, perhaps, even worse than you are. I was drunk when I came here, though," I hastened, however, to say in self-defense. "Besides, a man is no example for a woman. It's a different thing. I may degrade and defile myself, but I am not anyone's slave. I come and go, and there's an end to it. I shake it off, and I am a different man. But you are a slave from the start. Yes, a slave! You give up everything, your whole freedom. If you want to break your chains afterward, you won't be able to; you will be caught more and more in the snares. It is an accursed bondage. I know it. I won't mention anything else, maybe you won't understand it, but tell me: after all, surely you are in debt to your madam already? There, you see," I added, though she made no answer, but only listened in silence, entirely absorbed, "that's bondage for you! You will never buy your freedom. They will see to that. It's like selling your soul to the devil—

"And besides—perhaps I, too, am just as unfortunate, how do you know—and wallow in the mud on purpose, also out of misery? After all, men take to drink out of grief; well, maybe I am here out of grief. Come, tell me, what good is there here? Here you and I—were intimate—just now and did not say one word to one another all the time, and it was only afterward you began staring at me like a wild creature, and I at you. Is that loving? Is that how human beings are intimate? It's hideous, that's what it is!"

"Yes!" she assented sharply and hurriedly.

I was even amazed by the eagerness of this "yes." So the same thought may have been straying through her mind when she was staring at me just before. So she, too, was capable of certain thoughts? "Damn it all, this was curious, this was *kinship*?" I thought, almost rubbing my hands. And indeed how can one fail to manage a young soul like that?

The sport in it attracted me most.

She turned her head nearer to me, and it seemed to me in the darkness that she propped herself on her arm. Perhaps she was scrutinizing me. How I regretted that I could not see her eyes. I heard her deep breathing.

"Why did you come here?" I asked her, with a note of authority already in my voice.

"Oh, I don't know."

"But after all how nice it would be to be living in your own father's house! It's warm and free; you have a nest of your own."

"But what if it's worse than this?"

"I must take the right tone," flashed through my mind. "I may not get far with sentimentality."

But it was only a momentary thought. I swear she really did interest me. Besides, I was exhausted and moody. And after all, cunning so easily goes hand in hand with feeling.

"Who denies it?" I hastened to answer. "Anything may happen. I am, after all, convinced that someone has wronged you and is guiltier toward you than you toward them. After all, I know nothing of your story, but it's not likely a girl like you has come here of her own inclination—"

"What kind of girl am I?" she whispered, hardly audible, but I heard it.

Damn it all, I was flattering her. That was abominable. But perhaps it was a good thing— She was silent.

"See, Liza, I will tell you about myself. If I had had a home

He's making a power play (handwritten marginal note)

from childhood, I shouldn't be what I am now. I often think about that. After all, no matter how bad it may be at home, at least they are your father and mother, and not enemies, strangers. Once a year, at least, they'll show their love for you. Anyway, you know you are at home. I grew up without a home; and perhaps that's why I've turned so—unfeeling."

I waited again.

"Perhaps she doesn't understand," I thought, "and, indeed, it is absurd, this moralizing."

"If I were a father and had a daughter, I believe I should love my daughter more than my sons, really," I began indirectly, as though talking of something else, in order to distract her attention. I confess I blushed.

"Why so?" she asked.

Ah! so she was listening!

"I don't know, Liza. I knew a father who was a stern, strict man, but he used to go down on his knees to his daughter, used to kiss her hands and feet, he couldn't make enough of her, really. When she danced at parties he used to stand for five hours at a stretch without taking his eyes off her. He was mad about her; I understand that! She would fall asleep tired at night, and he would get up to kiss her in her sleep and make the sign of the cross over her. He would go about in a dirty old coat, he was stingy to everyone else, but would spend his last penny for her, giving her expensive presents, and it was a delight to him when she was pleased with what he gave her. Fathers always love their daughters more than mothers do. Some girls live happily at home! And I believe I would never let my daughter marry."

"What next?" she said with a faint smile.

"I would be jealous, I really would. To think that she should kiss anyone else! That she should love a stranger more than her father! It's painful to imagine it. Of course, that's all nonsense, of course every father would be reasonable at last. But I believe before I would let her marry, I would worry myself to death; I would find fault with all her suitors. But I would end by letting her marry whom she herself loved. After all, the one whom the daughter loves always seems the worst to the father. That is always so. So many families get into trouble with that."

"Some are glad to sell their daughters, rather than to marry them honorably."

Ah! So that was it!

"Such a thing, Liza, happens in those accursed families in which there is neither love nor God," I retorted warmly, "and where there is no love, there is no sense either. There are such families, it's true, but I am not speaking of them. You must have seen wickedness in your own family, if you talk like that. You must have been genuinely unlucky. H'm!—that sort of thing mostly comes about through poverty."

"And is it any better among the rich? Even among the poor, honest people live happily."

"H'm—yes. Perhaps. Another thing, Liza, man only likes to count his troubles, but he does not count his joys. If he counted them up as he ought, he would see that every lot has enough happiness provided for it. And what if all goes well with the family, if the blessing of God is upon it, if the husband is a good one, loves you, cherishes you, never leaves you! There is happiness in such a family! Sometimes there is happiness even in the midst of sorrow; and indeed sorrow is everywhere. If you marry *you will find out for yourself.* But think of the first years of married life with one you love: what happiness, what happiness there sometimes is in it! And indeed it's the ordinary thing. In those early days even quarrels with one's husband end happily. Some women get up more quarrels with their husbands the more they love them. Indeed, I knew a woman like that: she seemed to say that because she loved him deeply, she would torment him out of love so that he'd feel it. Did you know that you may torment a man on purpose out of love? Women are particularly given to that, thinking to themselves, 'I will love him so much afterward, I will make so much of him, that it's no sin to torment him a little now.' And everyone in the house rejoices in the sight

of you, and you are happy and gay and peaceful and honorable.
Then there are some women who are jealous. If the husband
goes off someplace—I knew one such woman, she couldn't restrain herself, but would jump up at night and would run off on
the sly to find out where he was, whether he was with some
other woman. That's already bad. And the woman knows herself it's wrong, and her heart fails her and she suffers, but, after
all, she loves—it's all through love. And how sweet it is to make
up after quarrels, to admit she was wrong, or to forgive him!
And they are both so happy, all at once they become so happy,
as though they had met anew, been married over again; as
though their love had begun anew. And no one, no one should
know what passes between husband and wife if they love one
another. And no matter how their quarrels ended they ought not
to call in even their own mothers to judge between them and tell
tales of one another. They are their own judges. Love is a holy
mystery and ought to be hidden from all other eyes, no matter
what happens. That makes it holier and better. They respect one
another more, and much is built on respect. And if once there
has been love, if they have been married for love, why should
love pass away? Surely one can keep it! It is rare that one cannot keep it. And if the husband is kind and straightforward, why
should not love last? The first phase of married love will pass, it
is true, but then there will come a love that is better still. Then
there will be the union of souls, they will have everything in
common, there will be no secrets between them. And once they
have children, the most difficult times will seem to them happy,
so long as there is love and courage. Even toil will be a joy, you
may deny yourself bread for your children and even that will be
a joy. After all, they will love you for it afterward; so you are laying by for your future. As the children grow up you feel that you
are an example, a support for them; that even after you die your
children will always cherish your thoughts and feelings, because
they have received them from you, they will take on your semblance and likeness. So you see it is a great duty. How can it fail

to draw the father and mother closer? People say it's a trial to have children. Who says that? It is heavenly joy! Are you fond of little children, Liza? I am awfully fond of them. You know— a little rosy baby boy at your bosom, and what husband's heart is not touched, seeing his wife nursing his child! A plump little rosy baby, sprawling and snuggling, chubby little hands and feet, clean tiny little nails, so tiny that it makes one laugh to look at them; eyes that look as if they understand everything. And while it sucks it clutches at your bosom with its little hand, plays. When its father comes up, the child tears itself away from the bosom, flings itself back, looks at its father, laughs, as though it were God knows how funny, and falls to sucking again. Or it will bite its mother's breast when it is cutting its little teeth while it looks sideways at her with its little eyes as though to say, 'Look, I am biting!' Is not all that a joy when they are all three together, husband, wife and child? One can forgive a great deal for the sake of such moments. Yes, Liza, one must first learn to live oneself before one blames others!"

"It's by pictures, pictures like that one must get at you," I thought to myself, though I did not speak with real feeling, and all at once I flushed crimson. "What if she were suddenly to burst out laughing, what would I do then?" That idea drove me to fury. Toward the end of my speech I really was excited, and now my vanity was somehow wounded. The silence continued. I almost wanted to nudge her.

"Why are you . . ." she began, and stopped. But I understood: there was a quiver of something different in her voice, not abrupt, harsh and unyielding as before, but something soft and shamefaced, so shamefaced that I suddenly felt ashamed and guilty.

"What?" I asked with tender curiosity.

"Why, you . . ."

"What?"

"Why you—speak exactly like a book," she said, and something sarcastic was heard in her voice.

That remark sent a pang to my heart. It was not what I was expecting.

I did not understand that she was hiding her feelings by sarcasm and that this is usually the last refuge of modest and chaste-souled people when the privacy of their soul is coarsely and intrusively invaded, and that their pride makes them refuse to surrender till the last moment and shrink from expressing their feelings to you. I ought to have guessed the truth for the timidity with which she had a number of times attempted her sarcasm, only bringing herself to utter it at last with an effort. But I did not guess, and a spiteful feeling took possession of me.

"Wait a bit!" I thought.

VII

"Oh, hush, Liza! How can you talk about my speaking like a book when it makes even me, an outsider, feel sick? Though I don't look at it as an outsider, for, indeed, all that has touched me to the heart. Is it possible, is it possible that you do not feel sick at being here yourself? Evidently habit does wonders! God knows what habit can do with anyone. Can you really and seriously think that you will never grow old, that you will always be good-looking, and that they will keep you here forever and ever? I say nothing of the filth here. Though let me tell you this about it; about your present life, I mean; even though you are young now, attractive, nice, with soul and feeling, yet you know, as soon as I came to myself just now, I felt at once sick at being here with you! After all, one can only come here when one is drunk. But if you were anywhere else, living as decent people live, I would perhaps be more than attracted by you, I would fall in love with you, would be glad of a look from you, let alone a word. I would hang about your door, would go down on my knees to you, we would become engaged and I would even consider it an honor to do so. I would not dare to have an impure thought about you. But here, after all, I know that I have only to whistle and you have to come with me whether you like it or not. I don't consult your wishes, but you mine. The lowest laborer hires himself as a workman but he doesn't make a slave of himself altogether; besides, he knows that he will be free again. But when will you be free? Only think what you are giving up here! What is it you are making a slave of? It is your soul, together with your body; you are selling your soul which you have no right to dispose of! You give your love to be outraged by every drunkard! Love! But after all, that's everything, but after all, it's a jewel, it's a maiden's treasure, love—why, after all a man would be ready to give his soul, to face death to gain that love. But how much is your love worth now? You can be bought, all of you, body and soul, and there is no need to strive for love when you can have everything without love. And after all, there is no greater insult for a girl than that, do you understand? To be sure, I have heard that they comfort you, poor fools, they let you have lovers of your own here. But after all, that is simply a farce, that's simply a sham, it's just laughing at you, and you are taken in by it! Why, do you suppose he really loves you, that lover of yours? I don't believe it. How can he love you when he knows that you may be called away from him any minute? He would be a vile fellow if he did! Would he have a grain of respect for you? What have you in common with him? He laughs at you and robs you—that is all his love amounts to! You are lucky if he does not beat you. Very likely he does beat you, too. Ask him, if you have one, whether he will marry you. He will laugh in your face, if he doesn't spit in it or give you a blow—yet he may not be worth a plugged nickel himself. And for what have you ruined your life, if you come to think of it? For the coffee they give you to drink and the plentiful meals? But after all, why do they feed you? An honest girl couldn't swallow the food, she would know why she was being fed. You are in debt here, and, of course, you will always be in debt, and you will go on in debt to the end, till the visitors here begin to scorn you. And that will soon happen, don't rely upon your youth—all that flies by, like an express train here, after all. You will be kicked out. And not simply kicked out; long before that they will begin to nag you, scold you, abuse you, as though you had not sacrificed your health for her, had not ruined your youth and your soul for her benefit, but as though you had ruined her, ravaged her, robbed her. And don't expect anyone to take your part; the others, your companions, will attack you, too, to win her favor, for all are in slavery here, and have lost all conscience and pity long ago. They have become utterly vile, and nothing on earth is viler, more loathsome and more insulting than their abuse. And you are laying down everything here, everything unconditionally, youth and health and beauty and hope, and at twenty-two you will look like a woman of thirty-five, and you will be lucky if you are not diseased, pray to God for that! No doubt you are thinking now after all that you have a lark and no work to do! Yet there is no harder or more dreadful work in the world or ever has been. One would think that the heart alone would be worn out with tears. And you won't dare to say a word, not half a word, when they drive you away from here: you will go away as though you were to blame. You will change to another house, then to a third, then somewhere else, till you come down at last to the Haymarket. There you will be beaten at every turn; that is a courtesy there, the visitors there don't know how to be friendly without beating you. You don't believe that it is so hateful there? Go and look for yourself some time, you can see with your own eyes. Once, one New Year's Day, I saw a woman at a door. Her own kind had turned her out as a joke, to give her a taste of the frost because she had been howling too much, and they shut the door behind her. At nine o'clock in the morning she was already completely drunk, dishevelled, half-naked, covered with bruises, her face was powdered, but she had a black eye, blood was trickling from her nose and her teeth; some cabman had just beaten her. She was sitting on the stone steps, a salt fish of some sort was in her hand; she was howling, wailing something about her 'fate' and beating with the fish on the steps, and cabmen and drunken soldiers were crowding in the doorway taunting her. You don't believe that you will ever be like that? I would not like to believe it, either, but how do you know, maybe ten years, eight years ago that very woman with that salt fish came here fresh as a little cherub, innocent, pure, knowing no evil, blushing at every word. Perhaps she was like you, proud, ready to take offence, not like the others; perhaps she looked like a queen, and knew what happiness was in store for the man who would love her and whom she would love. Do you see how it ended? And what if at that very minute when she was beating on the filthy steps with that fish, drunken and dishevelled—what if at that very minute she recalled the pure early days in her father's house, when she used to go to school and the neighbor's son watched for her on the way, declaring that he would love her as long as he lived, that he would devote his life to her, and when they vowed to love one another for ever and be married as soon as they were grown up! No, Liza, it would be a joy for you, a joy if you were to die soon of consumption in some corner, in some cellar like that woman just now. In the hospital, do you say? You will be lucky if they take you, but what if you are still of use to the madam here? Consumption is a queer disease, it is not like fever. The patient goes on hoping till the last minute and says he is all right. He deludes himself. And that's just advantageous for your madam. Don't doubt it, that's how it is; you have sold your soul, and what is more you owe money, so you don't even dare to say a word. But when you are dying, everyone will abandon you, everyone will turn away from you, for then there will be nothing to get from you. What's more, they will reproach you for taking up space, for taking so long to die. You won't even be able to beg for a drink of water without getting abuse. 'Aren't you going to die, you foul wench; you won't let us sleep with your moaning, you make the gentlemen sick.' That's true. I have heard such things said myself. When you are really dying they will push you into the filthiest corner in the cellar; in the damp and darkness; what will your thoughts be, lying there alone? When you die, strange hands will lay you out, with grumbling and impatience; no one will bless you, no one will sigh for you, they will only want to get rid of you as soon as possible; they will buy a coffin, take you to the grave as they did that poor woman today, and celebrate your memory at the tavern. There is slush, filth, wet snow in the grave—no need to put themselves out for you: 'Let her down, Vanyukha; it's just like her "fate" after all, here she goes in, head first, the wench. Shorten the cord, you rascal.' 'It's all right as it is.' 'All right, is it? Why, she's on her side! Wasn't she a human being, too? Well, never mind, cover her up.' And they won't care to waste much time quarreling over you. They will scatter the wet blue day as quickly as they can and go off to the tavern—and there your memory on earth will end; other women have children who visit their graves, fathers, husbands. While for you there will be neither tear, nor sigh, nor remembrance; no one, no one in the whole wide world will ever come to you; your name will vanish from the face of the earth as though you had never existed, had never been born at all! Nothing but filth and mud, no matter how much you knock on your coffin lid at night, when the dead arise, however you cry: 'Let me out, kind people, to live in the light of day! My life was no life at all; my life has been thrown away like a dirty rag; it was drunk away in the tavern at the Haymarket; let me out, kind people, to live in the world again!' "

And I worked myself up to such a pitch that I began to have a lump in my throat myself and—and suddenly I stopped, sat up in dismay, and bending over apprehensively, began to listen with a beating heart. I had reason to be worried.

I felt for some time that I was turning her soul upside down and breaking her heart, and the more I was convinced of it, the more I wanted to gain my end as quickly and as effectively as possible. The sport, the sport attracted me; yet it was not merely the sport.

I knew I was speaking stiffly, artificially, even bookishly, in short I did not know how to speak except "just like a book." But that did not bother me: after all I knew, I felt, that I would be understood and that this very bookishness would perhaps even be a help. But now, having achieved my effect, I was suddenly panic-stricken. No, I had never, never before witnessed such despair! She was lying face down, pressing her face deep into the pillow and clutching it in both hands. Her heart was being torn. Her youthful body was shuddering all over as though in convulsions. Suppressed sobs rent her bosom and suddenly burst out in weeping and wailing, then she pressed even deeper into the pillow: she did not want anyone here, not a single living soul, to know of her anguish and her tears. She bit the pillow, bit her hand till it bled (I saw that afterward), or, thrusting her fingers into her dishevelled hair, seemed rigid with the effort to restrain herself, holding her breath and clenching her teeth. I began to say something to her, to beg her to calm herself, but felt that I did not dare; and suddenly, all in a sort of chill, almost in terror, began fumbling in the dark, trying hurriedly to get dressed to go. It was dark: try as I would, I could not finish dressing quickly. Suddenly I felt a box of matches and a candlestick with a whole new candle in it. As soon as the room was lighted up, Liza sprang up, sat up in bed, and with a contorted face, with a half-insane smile, looked at me almost senselessly. I sat down beside her and took her hands; she came to herself, made a movement toward me, would have clasped me, but did not dare, and slowly bowed her head before me.

"Liza, my dear, I was wrong to— Forgive me," I began but she squeezed my hand in her fingers so tightly that I felt I was saying the wrong thing and stopped. "This is my address, Liza, come to me."

"I will come," she whispered resolutely, her head still bowed.

"But now I am going, good-bye—till we meet again."

I got up; she, too, stood up and suddenly flushed all over, shuddered, snatched up a shawl that was lying on a chair and muffled herself in it to her chin. As she did this she gave another sickly smile, blushed and looked at me strangely. I felt wretched; I was in haste to get away—to disappear.

"Wait a minute," she said suddenly, in the passage just at the doorway, stopping me with her hand on my overcoat. She put down the candle hastily and ran off; evidently she had thought of something or wanted to show me something. As she ran away she flushed, her eyes shone, and a smile appeared on her lips—what was the meaning of it? Against my will I waited; she came back a minute later with an expression that seemed to ask forgiveness for something. In fact, it was not the same face, nor the same look it had been before: sullen, mistrustful and obstinate. Her look was now imploring, soft, and at the same time trustful, caressing, timid. Children look that way at people they are very fond of, of whom they are asking a favor. Her eyes were a light hazel, they were lovely eyes, full of life, capable of expressing love as well as sullen hatred.

Making no explanation, as though I, as a sort of higher being, must understand everything without explanations, she held out a piece of paper to me. Her whole face was positively beaming at that instant with naïve, almost childish, triumph. I unfolded it. It was a letter to her from a medical student or someone of that sort—a very high-flown and flowery, but extremely respectful, declaration of love. I don't recall the words now, but I remember well enough that through the high-flown phrases there was apparent a genuine feeling, which cannot be feigned. When I had finished reading it I met her glowing, questioning, and childishly impatient eyes fixed upon me. She fastened her eyes upon my face and waited impatiently for what I would say. In a few words, hurriedly, but with a sort of joy and pride, she explained to me that she had been to a dance somewhere, in a private house, at some "very, very nice people's house, a *family* who *still know nothing*, absolutely nothing," for she had only come here so lately and it had all happened—and she hadn't made up her mind to stay and was certainly going away as soon as she had paid her debt—"and at that party there had been that student who had danced with her the whole evening, had talked to her, and it turned out that he had known her in the old days at Riga when he was a child, they had played together, but a very long time ago—and he knew her parents, but *about this* he knew nothing, nothing, nothing whatever, and had no suspicion! And the day after the dance (three days ago) he had sent her that letter through the friend with whom she had gone to the party—and—well, that was all."

She dropped her shining eyes with a sort of bashfulness as she finished.

The poor girl was keeping that student's letter as a treasure and had run to fetch it, her only treasure, because she did not want me to go away without knowing that she, too, was honestly and genuinely loved; that she, too, was addressed respectfully. No doubt that letter was destined to lie in her box and lead to nothing. But it doesn't matter, I am certain that she would guard it as a treasure all her life, as her pride and justification, and now at such a minute she had thought of that letter and brought it with naïve pride to raise herself in my eyes that I might see, that I, too, might think well of her. I said nothing, pressed her hand and went out. I so longed to get away. I walked home all the way in spite of the fact that the wet snow was still falling in large flakes. I was exhausted, shattered, in bewilderment. But behind the bewilderment the truth was already gleaming. The loathsome truth!

VIII

It was some time, however, before I consented to recognize that truth. Waking up in the morning after some hours of heavy, leaden sleep, and immediately realizing all that had happened on the previous day, I was positively amazed at my last night's *sentimentality* with Liza, at all those "horrors and pity of yesterday." After all, to have such an attack of womanish hysteria, pah! I concluded. "And why did I force my address upon her? What if she comes? Let her come, though; it is all right—" But *obviously* that was not now the chief and the most important matter: I had to make haste and at all costs save my reputation in the eyes of Zverkov and Simonov as quickly as possible; that was the chief business. And I was so taken up that morning that I actually forgot all about Liza.

First of all I had to repay at once what I had borrowed the day before from Simonov. I resolved on a desperate course: to borrow fifteen roubles from Anton Antonich. As luck would have it he was in the best of humors that morning, and gave it to me at once, as soon as I asked. I was so delighted at this that, as I signed the IOU with a swaggering air, I told him *casually* that the night before "I had been making merry with some friends at the Hôtel de Paris; we were giving a farewell party to a comrade, in fact, I might say a friend of my childhood, and you know—a desperate rake, spoilt—of course, he belongs to a good family, and has considerable means, a brilliant career; he is witty, charming, carries on affairs with certain ladies, you understand; we drank an extra 'half-a-case' and—" And after all it went off all right; all this was said very lightly, unconstrainedly and complacently.

On reaching home I promptly wrote to Simonov.

To this hour I am lost in admiration when I recall the truly gentlemanly, good-humored, candid tone of my letter. With tact and good taste, and, above all, entirely without superfluous words, I blamed myself for all that had happened. I defended myself, "if only I may still be allowed to defend myself," by alleging that being utterly unaccustomed to wine, I had been intoxicated by the first glass which (I claimed) I had drunk before they arrived, while I was waiting for them at the Hôtel de Paris between five and six o'clock. I particularly begged Simonov's pardon; I asked him also to convey my explanations to all the others, especially to Zverkov whom "I remember as though in a dream" I seem to have insulted. I added that I would have called upon all of them myself, but that my head ached, and that besides, I was rather ashamed. I was especially pleased with that "certain lightness," almost carelessness (strictly within the bounds of politeness, however), which was suddenly reflected in my style, and better than any possible arguments, gave them at once to understand that I took rather an independent view of "all that unpleasantness last night"; that I was by no means so utterly crushed as you, gentlemen, probably imagine; but on the contrary that I looked at it as a gentleman serenely respecting himself should. "On a young hero's past no censure is cast!"

"There is, after all, even an aristocratic playfulness about it!" I thought admiringly, as I read over the letter. "And it's all because I am a cultured and educated man! Others in my place would not have known how to extricate themselves, but here I have gotten out of it and am as gay as ever again, and all because I am a cultured and educated man of our day." And, indeed, perhaps, everything really was due to the wine yesterday. H'm!— well, no, it was not the wine. I drank nothing at all between five and six while I was waiting for them. I had lied to Simonov; lied shamelessly; and even now I wasn't ashamed—

Hang it all, though! The important thing was that I was rid of it.

I put six roubles in the letter, sealed it up, and asked Apollon to take it to Simonov. When he learned that there was money in the letter, Apollon became more respectful and agreed to take it. Toward evening I went out for a walk. My head was still aching and giddy, after yesterday. But as evening came on and the twilight grew thicker, my impressions changed and grew more and more confused and, after them, my thoughts. Something was not dead within me, in the depths of my heart and conscience it would not die, and it expressed itself as a burning anguish. For the most part I jostled my way through the most crowded business streets, along Meshchansky Street, along Sadovy Street and in the Yusupov Garden. I always particularly liked to stroll along these streets at dusk just when they become more crowded with people of all sorts, merchants and artisans going home from their day's work, with faces looking malicious out of anxiety. What I liked was just that cheap bustle, that bare, humdrum prosaic quality. On this occasion all that bustling in the streets irritated me more than ever. I could not make out what was wrong with me, I could not find the clue. Something was rising up, rising up continually in my soul, painfully, and refusing to be appeased. I returned home completely upset; it was just as though some crime were lying on my conscience.

The thought that Liza was coming worried me continually. It seemed queer to me that of all yesterday's memories, the memory of her tormented me as it were, particularly, quite separately, as it were. I had succeeded in forgetting everything else by evening time. I dismissed it all and was still perfectly satisfied with my letter to Simonov. But on this point I was not satisfied at all. It was as though I were worried only by Liza. "What if she comes," I thought incessantly. "Well, so what, it's all right, let her come! H'm! it's horrid that she should see how I live for instance. Yesterday I seemed such a—hero to her, while now, h'm! It's horrid, though, that I have let myself sink so low, the room looks like a beggar's. And I brought myself to go out to dinner in such a suit! And my oilcloth sofa with the stuffing sticking out. And my robe, which will not cover me! What tatters. And she will see all this and she will see Apollon. That beast is certain to insult her. He will fasten upon her in order to be rude to me. And I, of course, will be panic-stricken as usual. I will begin to bow and scrape before her and to pull my robe around me, I will begin to smile, to lie. Oh, how foul! And it isn't the foulness of it that matters most! There is something more important, more loathsome, viler! Yes, viler! And to put on that dishonest lying mask again!"

When I reached that thought I flared up all at once.

"Why dishonest? How dishonest? I was speaking sincerely last night. I remember there was real feeling in me, too. What I wanted was to awake noble feelings in her. Her crying was a good thing, it will have a good effect."

Yet I could not feel at ease.

All that evening, even when I had come back home, even after nine o'clock, when I calculated that Liza could not possibly come, she still haunted me, and what was worse, she always came back to my mind in the same position. One moment out of all that had happened last night presented itself before me vividly: the moment when I struck a match and saw her pale, distorted face, with its tortured look. And what a pitiful, what an unnatural, what a distorted smile she had at that moment! But I did not know then that even fifteen years later I would still always picture Liza to myself with that pitiful, distorted, inappropriate smile which was on her face at that minute.

Next day I was ready again to look upon it all as nonsense, due to over-excited nerves, and, above all, as *exaggerated*. I always recognized that as a weak point of mine, and was sometimes very much afraid of it. "I exaggerate everything, that is where I go wrong," I repeated to myself every hour. But, nevertheless, Liza will very likely come still, nevertheless, was the refrain with which all my reflections ended then. I was so uneasy that I sometimes flew into a fury. "She'll come, she is certain to come!" I cried, running about the room, "if not today, she will come tomorrow; she'll seek me out! The damnable romanticism of these *pure hearts!* Oh, the vileness—oh, the silliness—oh, the stupidity of these 'wretched sentimental souls'! Why, how could one fail to understand? How could one possibly fail to understand?"

But at this point I stopped short, and even in great confusion.

"And how few, how few words," I thought, in passing, "were needed; how little of the idyllic (and affectedly, bookishly, artificially idyllic too) had sufficed to turn a whole human life at once according to my will. That's innocence for you! That's virgin soil for you!"

At times the thought occurred to me to go to her, "to tell her all" and beg her not to come to me. But this thought stirred such wrath in me that I believed I would have crushed that "damned" Liza if she had happened to be near me at the time. I would have insulted her, have spat at her, have turned her out, have struck her!

One day passed, however, a second and a third; she did not

come and I began to grow calmer, I felt particularly bold and
cheerful after nine o'clock, I even began sometimes to dream,
and rather sweetly: I, for instance, became the salvation of Liza,
simply through her coming to me and my talking to her. I develop her, educate her. Finally, I notice that she loves me, loves
me passionately. I pretend not to understand (I don't know, however, why I pretend, just for effect, perhaps). At last all confusion, beautiful, trembling and sobbing, she flings herself at my
feet and tells me that I am her savior, and that she loves me better than anything in the world. I am amazed, but—"Liza," I say,
"can you really believe that I have noticed your love? I saw it all,
I divined it, but I did not dare to approach you first, because I
had an influence over you and was afraid that you would force
yourself, out of gratitude, to respond to my love, would try to
rouse in your heart a feeling which was perhaps absent, and I did
not wish that because it would be—tyranny. It would be indeli-
cate (in short, I launch off at that point into European, inexpli-
cably lofty subtleties, à la George Sand), but now, now you are
mine, you are my creation, you are pure, you are beautiful, you
are my beautiful wife.

> "And into my house come bold and free,
> Its rightful mistress there to be."

Then we begin to live together happily, go abroad, etc., etc.
In short, in the end it seemed vulgar to me myself, and I began
to put out my tongue at myself.

Besides, they won't let her out, "the hussy!" I thought. After
all, they don't let them go out very readily, especially in the
evening (for some reason I fancied she would have to come in
the evening, and precisely at seven o'clock). Though she did say
she was not altogether a slave there yet, and had certain rights;
so, h'm! Damn it all, she will come, she is sure to come!

It was a good thing, in fact, that Apollon distracted my attention at that time by his rudeness. He drove me beyond all pa-

tience! He was the bane of my life, the curse laid upon me by Providence. We had been squabbling continually for years, and I hated him. My God, how I hated him! I believe I had never hated anyone in my life as I hated him, especially at some moments. He was an elderly, dignified man, who worked part of his time as a tailor. But for some unknown reason, he despised me beyond all measure, and looked down upon me insufferably. Though indeed, he looked down upon everyone. Simply to glance at that flaxen, smoothly brushed head, at the tuft of hair he combed up on his forehead and oiled with sunflower oil, at that dignified mouth, always pursed, made one feel one was confronting a man who never doubted himself. He was an insufferable pedant, the greatest pedant I had met on earth, and with that had a vanity only befitting Alexander the Great. He was in love with every button on his coat, every nail on his fingers—absolutely in love with them, and he looked it! In his behavior to me he was an absolute tyrant, spoke very little to me, and if he chanced to glance at me he gave me a firm, majestically self-confident and invariably ironical look that sometimes drove me to fury. He did his work with the air of doing me the greatest favor. Though he did scarcely anything for me, and did not, indeed, consider himself obliged to do anything, there could be no doubt that he looked upon me as the greatest fool on earth, and that the reason he did not "get rid of me" was simply that he could get wages from me every month. He consented "to do nothing" for me for seven roubles a month. Many sins should be forgiven me for what I suffered from him. My hatred reached such a point that sometimes his very walk almost threw me into convulsions. What I loathed particularly was his lisp. His tongue must have been a little too long or something of that sort, for he continually lisped, and seemed to be very proud of it, imagining that it greatly added to his dignity. He spoke in a slow, measured tone, with his hands behind his back and his eyes fixed on the ground. He maddened me particularly when he read the Psalms aloud to himself behind his partition. I waged many a battle over that reading! But he was awfully fond of reading aloud in the evenings, in a slow, even, chanting voice, as though over the dead. It is interesting that he has ended up that way. He hires himself out to read the Psalms over the dead, and at the same time he kills rats and makes shoe polish. But at that time I could not get rid of him, it was as though he were chemically combined with my existence. Besides, nothing would have induced him to consent to leave me. I could not live in a furnished room: my apartment was my privacy, my shell, my cave, in which I concealed myself from all mankind, and Apollon seemed to me, God only knows why, an integral part of that apartment, and for seven whole years I could not get rid of him.

For example, to be two or three days late with his wages was impossible. He would have made such a fuss, I would not have known where to hide my head. But I was so exasperated with everyone during that period, that I made up my mind for some reason and with some object to *punish* Apollon and not to pay him for a fortnight the wages I owed him. I had intended to do this for a long time, for the last two years, simply in order to teach him not to give himself airs with me, and to show him that if I liked I could withhold his wages. I decided to say nothing to him about it, and even to be silent purposely in order to conquer his pride and force him to be the first to speak of his wages. Then I would take the seven roubles out of a drawer, show him I have the money and have put it aside purposely, but that I don't want, I don't want, I simply don't want to pay him his wages, I don't want to just because that is *what I want*, because "I am master and it is for me to decide," because he has been disrespectful, because he is a ruffian; but if he were to ask respectfully I might be softened and give it to him, otherwise he might wait another fortnight, another three weeks, a whole month . . .

But no matter how angry I was, he always got the better of me. I could not even hold out for four days. He began as he always did begin such cases, for there had been such cases already, there had been attempts (and it may be observed I knew all this beforehand, I knew his nasty tactics by heart), to wit: he would begin by fixing upon me an exceedingly severe stare, keeping it up for several minutes at a time, particularly on meeting me or seeing me out of the house. If I held out and pretended not to notice these stares, he would, still in silence, proceed to further tortures. All at once, for no reason at all, he would softly and smoothly walk into my room when I was pacing up and down, or reading, stand at the door, one hand behind his back and one foot forward, and fix upon me a stare more than severe, utterly contemptuous. If I suddenly asked him what he wanted, he would not answer, but continue to stare at me persistently for some seconds longer, then, with a peculiar compression of his lips and a very significant air, deliberately turn round and deliberately go back to his room. Two hours later he would come out again and again present himself before me in the same way. It has happened that in my fury I did not even ask him what he wanted, but simply raised my head sharply and imperiously and began staring back at him. So we stared at one another for two minutes; at last he turned with deliberation and dignity and went back again for two hours.

If I were still not brought to reason by all this, but persisted in my revolt, he would suddenly begin sighing while he looked at me, long, deep sighs as though measuring by them the depths of my moral degradation, and, of course, it ended at last by his triumphing completely: I raged and shouted, but was still forced to do what he wanted.

This time the usual maneuvers of "severe staring" had scarcely begun when I lost my temper and flew at him in a fury. I was irritated beyond endurance even without him.

"Wait," I shouted in a frenzy, as he was slowly and silently turning with one hand behind his back, to go to his room. "Wait! Come back, come back, I tell you!" and I must have bawled so unnaturally, that he turned round and even looked at me with a certain amazement. However, he persisted in saying nothing, and that infuriated me.

"How dare you come and look at me like that without being sent for? Answer!"

After looking at me calmly for half a minute, he began turning round again.

"Wait!" I roared, running up to him. "Don't stir! There. Answer, now: what did you come in to look at?"

"If you have any order to give me at the moment, it is my duty to carry it out," he answered, after another silent pause, with a slow, measured lisp, raising his eyebrows and calmly twisting his head from one side to another, all this with exasperating composure.

"That's not it, that is not what I am asking you about, you torturer!" I shouted, shaking with anger. "I'll tell you myself, you torturer, why you came here: you see, I don't give you your wages, you are so proud you don't want to bow down and ask for it, and so you have come to punish me with your stupid stares, to torture me, and you have no sus-pic-ion, you torturer, how stupid it is—stupid, stupid, stupid, stupid!"

He would have turned round again without a word, but I seized him.

"Listen," I shouted to him. "Here's the money, do you see, here it is" (I took it out of the table drawer), "here's the whole seven roubles but you are not going to have it, you . . . are . . . not . . . going . . . to . . . have it until you come respectfully with bowed head to beg my pardon. Do you hear?"

"That cannot be," he answered, with the most unnatural self-confidence.

"It will be so," I said. "I give you my word of honor, it will be!"

"And there's nothing for me to beg your pardon for," he went on, as though he had not noticed my exclamations at all. "Why, besides, you called me a 'torturer,' for which I can summon you at the police station at any time for insulting behavior."

"Go, summon me," I roared, "go at once, this very minute,

this very second! You are a torturer all the same! A torturer! A torturer!" But he merely looked at me, then turned, and regardless of my loud calls to him, he walked to his room with an even step and without looking round.

"If it had not been for Liza nothing of this would have happened," I decided inwardly. Then, after waiting a minute, I myself went behind the screen with a dignified and solemn air, though my heart was beating slowly and violently.

"Apollon," I said quietly and emphatically, though I was breathless, "go at once without a minute's delay and fetch the police officer."

He had meanwhile settled himself at his table, put on his spectacles and taken up something to tailor. But, hearing my order, he burst into a guffaw.

"At once, go this minute! Go on, or else you can't imagine what will happen."

"You are certainly not in your right mind," he observed, without even raising his head, lisping as deliberately as ever and threading his needle. "Whoever heard of a man sending for the police against himself? And as for being frightened—you are upsetting yourself about nothing, for nothing will come of it."

"Go!" I shrieked, grabbing him by the shoulder. I felt that in another minute I would hit him.

But I did not notice that suddenly the door from the passage softly and slowly opened at that instant and a figure came in, stopped short, and began staring at us in amazement. I glanced, nearly died with shame, and rushed back to my room. There, clutching at my hair with both hands, I leaned my head against the wall and stood motionless in that position.

Two minutes later I heard Apollon's deliberate footsteps.

"There is *some woman* asking for you," he said, looking at me with peculiar severity. Then he stood aside and let in—Liza. He would not go away, but stared at us sarcastically.

"Go away, go away," I commanded in desperation. At that

moment my clock began whirring and wheezing and struck seven.

IX

And into my house come bold and free,
Its rightful mistress there to be.

From the same poetic work

I stood before her crushed, crestfallen, revoltingly embarrassed, and I believe I smiled as I did my utmost to wrap myself in the skirts of my ragged wadded robe—just exactly as I had imagined the scene not long before in a fit of depression. After standing over us for a couple of minutes Apollon went away, but that did not make me more comfortable. What made it worse was that suddenly, she, too, became embarrassed, more so, in fact, than I would have expected. At the sight of me, of course.

"Sit down," I said mechanically, moving a chair up to the table, and I sat down on the sofa. She obediently sat down at once and gazed at me open-eyed, evidently expecting something from me at once. This naïveté of expectation drove me to fury, but I restrained myself.

She ought to have tried not to notice, as though everything had been as usual, while instead she . . . and I dimly felt that I would make her pay dearly for *all this*.

"You have found me in a strange position, Liza," I began, stammering and knowing that this was the wrong way to begin.

"No, no, don't imagine anything," I cried, seeing that she had suddenly flushed. "I am not ashamed of my poverty. On the contrary, I look on my poverty with pride. I am poor but honorable. One can be poor and honorable," I muttered. "However— would you like tea?"

"No——" she was beginning.

"Wait a minute."

I leapt up and ran to Apollon. I had to get out of the room somehow.

"Apollon," I whispered in feverish haste, flinging down before him the seven roubles which had remained all the time in my clenched fist, "here are your wages. You see I give them to you; but for that you must come to my rescue: bring me tea and a dozen rusks from the restaurant. If you won't go, you'll make a man miserable! You don't know what this woman is. This is—everything! You may be imagining something, but you don't know what a woman she is!"

Apollon, who had already sat down to work and put on his spectacles again, at first glanced askance at the money without speaking or putting down his needle; then, without paying the slightest attention to me, or making any answer, he went on busying himself with his needle, which he had not yet threaded. I waited before him for several minutes with my arms crossed *à la Napoléon*. My temples were moist with sweat. I was pale, I felt it. But, thank God, he must have been moved to pity, looking at me. Having threaded his needle, he deliberately got up from his seat, deliberately moved back his chair, deliberately took off his spectacles, deliberately counted the money, and finally asking me over his shoulder: "Shall I get a whole pot?" deliberately walked out of the room. As I was going back to Liza, the thought occurred to me on the way: shouldn't I run away just as I was in my robe, no matter where, and let come what may?

I sat down again. She looked at me uneasily. For some minutes we were silent.

"I will kill him," I shouted suddenly, striking the table with my fist so that the ink spurted out of the inkstand.

"What are you saying!" she cried, starting.

"I will kill him! kill him!" I shrieked, suddenly striking the table in absolute frenzy, and at the same time fully understanding how stupid it was to be in such a frenzy.

"You don't know, Liza, what that torturer is to me. He is my torturer. He has gone now to fetch some rusks; he—"

And suddenly I burst into tears. It was an hysterical attack. How ashamed I felt in the midst of my sobs; but still I could not restrain them.

She was frightened. "What is the matter? What is wrong?" she shrieked, fussing around me.

"Water, give me water, over there!" I muttered in a faint voice, though I was inwardly conscious that I could easily have done without water and without muttering in a faint voice. But I was what is called *putting it on*, to save appearances, though the attack was a genuine one.

She gave me water, looking at me in bewilderment. At that moment Apollon brought in the tea. It suddenly seemed to me that this commonplace and prosaic tea was terribly undignified and paltry after all that had happened, and I blushed. Liza even looked at Apollon with alarm. He went out without a glance at us.

"Liza, do you despise me?" I asked, looking at her fixedly, trembling with impatience to know what she was thinking.

She was embarrassed and did not know what to answer.

"Drink your tea," I said to her angrily. I was angry with myself, but, of course, it was she who would have to pay for it. A horrible spite against her suddenly surged up in my heart; I believe I could have killed her. To revenge myself on her I swore inwardly not to say a word to her all the time. "She is the cause of it all," I thought.

Our silence lasted for five minutes. The tea stood on the table; we did not touch it. I had got to the point of purposely refraining from beginning to drink in order to embarrass her further; it was awkward for her to begin alone. Several times she glanced at me with mournful perplexity. I was obstinately silent. I was, of course, myself the chief sufferer, because I was fully conscious of the disgusting meanness of my spiteful stupidity, and yet at the same time I absolutely could not restrain myself.

"I want to—get away—from there altogether," she began, to break the silence in some way, but, poor girl, that was just what she ought not to have spoken about at such a moment, stupid enough even without that to a man so stupid as I was. My heart positively ached with pity for her tactless and unnecessary straightforwardness. But something hideous at once stifled all compassion in me: it even provoked me to greater venom. Let the whole world go to pot. Another five minutes passed.

"Perhaps I am in your way?" she began timidly, hardly audibly, and was getting up.

But as soon as I saw this first impulse of wounded dignity I positively trembled with spite, and at once burst out.

"Why did you come to me, tell me that, please?" I began, gasping for breath and regardless of all logical connection in my words. I longed to have it all out at once, at one burst: I did not even trouble how to begin.

"Why did you come? Answer, answer," I cried, hardly knowing what I was doing. "I'll tell you, my good girl, why you came. You came because I talked *fine sentiments* to you then. So now you are soft as butter and longing for fine sentiments again. So you may as well know, know that I was laughing at you then. And I am laughing at you now. Why are you shuddering? Yes, I was laughing at you! I had been insulted just before, at dinner, by the fellows who came that evening before me. I came to you, meaning to thrash one of them, an officer; but I didn't succeed. I didn't find him; I had to avenge the insult on someone to get my own back again; you turned up, I vented my spleen on you and laughed at you. I had been humiliated, so I wanted to humiliate; I had been treated like a rag, so I wanted to show my power. That's what it was, and you imagined I had come there on purpose to save you, didn't you? Did you imagine that? Did you imagine that?"

I knew that she would perhaps get muddled and not grasp all the details, but I knew, too, that she would grasp the gist of it very well. And so, indeed, she did. She turned white as a handkerchief, tried to say something, and distorted her mouth painfully but she sank on a chair as though she had been felled by an ax. And all the time afterward she listened to me with her lips parted and her eyes wide open, shuddering with awful terror. The cynicism, the cynicism of my words overwhelmed her—

"Save you!" I went on, jumping up from my chair and running up and down the room before her. "Save you from what? But perhaps I am worse than you myself. Why didn't you throw it in my teeth when I was giving you that sermon: 'But you, what did you come here for yourself? Was it to read us a sermon?' Power, power was what I wanted then, sport was what I wanted, I wanted to wring out your tears, your humiliation, your hysteria— that was what I wanted then! After all, I couldn't keep it up then, because I am a wretch, I was frightened, and, the devil knows why, gave you my address in my folly. Afterward, before I got home, I was cursing and swearing at you because of that address. I hated you already because of the lies I had told you. Because I only like to play with words, to dream in my mind, but, do you know, what I really want is that you would all go to hell, that is what I want. I want peace; yes, I'd sell the whole world for a farthing right now, so long as I was left in peace. Is the world to go to pot, or am I to go without my tea? I say let the world go to pot as long as I get my tea every time. Did you know that, or not? Well, anyway, I know that I am a blackguard, a scoundrel, an egotist, a sluggard. Here I have been shuddering for the last three days at the thought of your coming. And do you know what has worried me particularly for these three days? That I posed as such a hero to you then, and now you would see me in a wretched torn robe, a beggar, an abomination. I told you just now that I was not ashamed of my poverty; you may as well know that I am ashamed of it; I am more ashamed of it than of anything, more afraid of it than of being found out if I were a thief, because I am as vain as though I had been skinned and the very air blowing on me hurt. Surely by now even you must have realized that I will never forgive you for having found me in this wretched robe, just as I was flying at Apollon like a spiteful sheep-dog at his lackey, and the lackey was jeering at him! And I shall never forgive you for the tears I could not help shedding before you just now, like some silly woman put to shame! And for what I am confessing to you now, I shall never forgive *you,* either! Yes—you must answer for it all because you turned up like this, because I am a blackguard, because I am the nastiest, stupidest, pettiest, absurdest and most envious of all worms on earth, none of whom is a bit better than I am, but who, the devil only knows why, are never embarrassed; while I will always be insulted by every louse, that is my doom! And what is it to me that you don't understand a word of this! And what do I care, what do I care about you, and whether you go to ruin there or not? Do you understand how I will hate you now after saying this, for having been here and listening? After all, a man speaks out like this once in a lifetime and then it is in hysterics! What more do you want? Why, after all, do you still stand there in front of me? Why do you torment me? Why don't you go?"

But at this point a strange thing happened.

I was so accustomed to think and imagine everything from books, and to picture everything in the world to myself just as I had made it up in my dreams beforehand, that I could not even take in this strange circumstance all at once. What happened was this: Liza, wounded and crushed by me, understood a great deal more than I imagined. She understood from all this what a woman understands first of all, if she feels genuine love, that is, that I was myself unhappy.

The frightened and wounded expression on her face was followed first by a look of sorrowful perplexity. When I began to call myself a scoundrel and a blackguard and my tears flowed (that tirade was accompanied throughout by tears) her whole face worked convulsively. She was on the point of getting up and stopping me; when I finished; she took no notice of my shouting: "Why are you here, why don't you go away?" but realized only that it must have been very bitter to me to say all this. Besides, she was so crushed, poor girl; she considered herself infinitely beneath me; how could she feel anger or resentment? Suddenly she leapt up from her chair with an irresistible impulse and held out her hands, yearning toward me, though still timid and not daring to stir. At this point there was an upheaval in my heart too. Then she suddenly rushed to me, threw her arms round me and burst into tears. I, too, could not restrain myself, and sobbed as I never had before.

"They won't let me—I can't be—good!" I managed to say, then I went to the sofa, fell on it, face downward, and sobbed on it for a quarter of an hour in genuine hysterics. She knelt near me, put her arms round me and stayed motionless in that position.

But the trouble was that the hysterics could not go on for ever. And (after all, I am writing the loathsome truth) lying face downward on the sofa with my face thrust into my nasty leather pillow, I began by degrees to be aware of a far-away, involuntary but irresistible feeling that after all it would be awkward for me to raise my head now and look Liza straight in the face. Why was I ashamed? I don't know, but I was ashamed. In my overwrought brain the thought also occurred that our parts were after all completely reversed now, that she was now the heroine, while I was just a crushed and humiliated creature as she had been before me that night—four days before . . . And all this came into my mind during the minutes I was lying face down on the sofa!

My God! surely I was not envious of her then?

I don't know, to this day I cannot decide, and at the time, of course, I was still less able to understand what I was feeling than now. I cannot get on without domineering and tyrannizing over someone, after all, but—but, after all, there is no explaining anything by reasoning and consequently it is useless to reason.

I conquered myself, however, and raised my head—I had to do so sooner or later—and I am convinced to this day that it was just because I was ashamed to look at her that another feeling was suddenly kindled and flamed up in my heart—a feeling of mastery and possession. My eyes gleamed with passion, and I gripped her hands tightly. How I hated her and how I was drawn to her at that minute! The one feeling intensified the other. It was almost like an act of vengeance! At first there was a look of amazement, even of terror, on her face, but only for one instant. She warmly and rapturously embraced me.

X

A quarter of an hour later I was rushing up and down the room in frenzied impatience, from minute to minute I went up to the screen and peeped through the crack at Liza. She was sitting on the floor with her head leaning against the bed, and must have been crying. But she did not go away, and that irritated me. This time she understood it all. I had insulted her once and for all, but—there's no need to describe it. She realized that my outburst of passion had been simply revenge, a new humiliation for her and that to my earlier, almost generalized hatred was added now a *personal, envious* hatred—though I do not maintain positively that she understood all this distinctly; but she certainly did fully understand that I was a despicable man, and what was worse, incapable of loving her.

I know I shall be told that this is incredible; that it is incredible to be as spiteful and stupid as I was; it may be added it was strange that I would not love her, or at any rate, appreciate her love. Why is it strange? In the first place, by then I was incapable of love, for, I repeat, with me loving meant tyrannizing and showing my moral superiority. I have never in my life ever been able to imagine any other sort of love, and have nowadays come to the point of sometimes thinking that love really consists in the right—freely given by the beloved object—to be tyrannized over. Even in my underground dreams I did not imagine love in any form except as a struggle. I always began it with hatred and ended it with moral subjugation, and afterward I could never imagine what to do with the subjugated object. And what is there incredible in that, since I had so succeeded in corrupting myself morally, since I was so out of touch with "real life," that I had just thought of reproaching her and putting her to shame for having come to me to hear "fine sentiments," and I did not even guess that she had come not at all to hear fine sentiments, but to love me, because to a woman true resurrection, true salvation from any sort of ruin, and true moral regeneration is contained in love and can only show itself in that form. I no longer hated her so much, however, when I was running about the room and peeping through the crack in the screen. I was only insufferably oppressed by her being here. I wanted her to disappear. I wanted "peace," I wanted to be left alone in my underground world. "Real life" oppressed me with its novelty so much that I could hardly breathe.

But several minutes passed and she still remained without stirring, as though she were unconscious. I had the shamelessness to tap softly at the screen as though to remind her. She started, sprang up, and flew to seek her shawl, her hat, her coat, just as though she were making her escape from me. Two minutes later she came from behind the screen and looked with heavy eyes at me. I gave a spiteful grin, which was forced, however, to *keep up appearances,* and I turned away from her look.

"Good-bye," she said, going toward the door.

I ran up to her, seized her hand, opened it, thrust something in it—and closed it again. Then I turned immediately and hurriedly rushed to the other corner of the room, to avoid seeing, anyway—

I meant to lie a moment ago—to write that I did this accidentally, not knowing what I was doing, through foolishness, through losing my head. But I don't want to lie, and so I will say straight out that I opened her hand and put the money in it— from spite. It came into my head to do so while I was running up and down the room and she was sitting behind the screen. But I can say this for certain: though I did that cruel thing purposely, it was not an impulse from the heart, but came from my evil brain. This cruelty was so affected, so purposely made up, so completely a product of the brain, of *books,* that I could not even keep it up for a minute—first I rushed to the corner to avoid seeing her, and then in shame and despair rushed after Liza. I opened the door in the passage and began listening.

"Liza! Liza!" I cried on the stairs, but in a low voice, not boldly.

There was no answer, but it seemed to me I heard her footsteps, lower down on the stairs.

"Liza!" I cried, more loudly.

No answer. But at that minute I heard the stiff outer glass door open heavily with a creak and slam violently. The roar echoed up the stairs. ₊ what drives a man underground

She had gone. I went back to my room in hesitation. I felt horribly oppressed.

I stood still at the table beside the chair on which she had sat and looked aimlessly before me. A minute passed. Suddenly I started; straight before me on the table I saw—in short, I saw a crumpled blue five-rouble note, the one I had thrust into her hand a minute before. It was the same note; it could be no other, there was no other in the apartment. So she had managed to fling it from her hand on the table at the moment when I had rushed into the farther corner.

So what? I might have expected that she would do that. Might I have expected it? No, I was such an egotist, I was so lacking in respect for people in actuality, that I could not even imagine she would do so. I could not endure it. A moment later I flew like a madman to get dressed, flinging on what I could at random and ran headlong after her. She could not have got two hundred paces away when I ran out into the street.

It was a still night and the snow was coming down in masses and falling almost perpendicularly, blanketing the pavement and the empty street. There was no one in the street, no sound was to be heard. The street lamps gave a disconsolate and useless glimmer. I ran two hundred paces to the intersection and stopped short. Where had she gone? And why was I running after her?

Why? To fall down before her, to sob with remorse, to kiss her feet, to beg her forgiveness! I longed for that. My whole heart was being rent to pieces, and never, never will I recall that minute with indifference. But—what for? I thought. Would I not begin to hate her, perhaps, even tomorrow, just because I had kissed her feet today? Would I give her happiness? Had I not again recognized that day, for the hundredth time, what I was worth? Would I not torment her?

I stood in the snow, gazing into the troubled darkness and pondered this.

"And will it not be better? *Will it not be better?*" I fantasied afterward at home, stifling the living pang of my heart with fantastic dreams. "Will it not be better that she carry the outrage with her forever? Outrage—why, after all, that is purification: it is the most stinging and painful consciousness! Tomorrow I would have defiled her soul and have exhausted her heart, while now the feeling of humiliation will never die in her, and however loathsome the filth awaiting her, that outrage will elevate and purify her—by hatred—h'm!—perhaps by forgiveness also. But will all that make things easier for her, though? . . ."

And, indeed, I will at this point ask an idle question on my own account: which is better—cheap happiness or exalted sufferings? Well, which is better?

So I dreamed as I sat at home that evening, almost dead with the pain in my soul. Never yet had I endured such suffering and remorse, but could there possibly have been the faintest doubt when I ran out from my lodging that I would turn back halfway? I never met Liza again and I have heard nothing about her. I will add, too, that for a long time afterward I remained pleased with the *phrase* about the utility of outrage and hatred, in spite of the fact that I almost fell ill from misery.

Even now, many years later, I somehow remember all this as very bad. I have many bad memories now, but—hadn't I better end my "Notes" here? I believe I made a mistake in beginning to write this *story;* so it's hardly literature so much as corrective punishment. After all, to tell long stories, for example, showing how I have ruined my life by morally rotting in my corner, through lack of fitting environment, through divorce from reality, and vainglorious spite in my underground world, would certainly not be interesting; a novel needs a hero, and all the traits of an anti-hero are *expressly* gathered together here, and what matters most, it all produces an unpleasant impression, for we are all divorced from life, we are all cripples, every one of us, more or less. We are so far divorced from it that we immediately feel a sort of loathing for actual "real life," and so cannot even stand to be reminded of it. After all, we have reached the point of almost looking at actual "real life" as an effort, almost as hard work, and we are all privately agreed that it is better in books. And why do we sometimes fret, why are we perverse and ask for something else? We don't know why ourselves. It would be worse for us if our capricious requests were granted. Come, try, come give anyone of us, for instance, a little more independence, untie our hands, widen the spheres of our activity, relax the controls and we—yes, I assure you—we would immediately beg to be under control again. I know that you will very likely be angry with me for that, and will begin to shout and stamp your feet. "Speak for yourself," you will say, "and for your miseries in your underground holes, but don't dare to say 'all of us.' " Excuse me, gentlemen, after all I do not mean to justify myself with that "all of us." As for what concerns me in particular I have only, after all, in my life carried to an extreme what you have not dared to carry halfway, and what's more, you have taken your cowardice for good sense, and have found comfort in deceiving yourselves. So that perhaps, after all, there is more "life" in me than in you. Look into it more carefully! After all, we don't even know where living exists now, what it is, and what it is called! Leave us alone without books and we will be lost and in a confusion at once—we will not know what to join, what to cling to, what to love and what to hate, what to respect and what to despise. We are even oppressed by being men—men with real *individual* body and blood. We are ashamed of it, we think it a disgrace and try to contrive to be some sort of impossible generalized man. We are still-born, and for many years we have not been begotten by living fathers, and that suits us better and better. We are developing a taste for it. Soon we shall somehow contrive to be born from an idea. But enough; I don't want to write more from "underground" . . .

———————

The "notes" of this paradoxalist do not end here, however. He could not resist and continued them. But it also seems to me that we may stop here.

Dostoevsky's Russian Orthodoxy
↳ may mean he intended for the narrator to be lacking God

The Grand
Inquisitor

From: THE BROTHERS KARAMAZOV

". . . Do you know, Alyosha—don't laugh! I composed a poem about a year ago. If you can waste another ten minutes on me, I'll tell it to you."

"You wrote a poem?"

"Oh, no, I didn't write it," laughed Ivan, "and I've never written two lines of poetry in my life. But I made up this poem in prose and I remembered it. I was carried away when I made it up. You will be my first reader—that is, listener. Why should an author forego even one listener?" smiled Ivan. "Shall I tell it to you or not?"

"I am all attention," said Alyosha.

"My poem is called 'The Grand Inquisitor,' it's a ridiculous thing, but I want to tell it to you."

THE GRAND INQUISITOR

"Even this must have a preface—that is, a literary preface," laughed Ivan, "and I am a poor hand at making one. You see, my action takes place in the sixteenth century, and at that time, as you probably learnt at school, it was customary in poetry to bring heavenly powers down to earth. Not to speak of Dante, in France, law clerks as well as the monks in the monasteries used to give regular performances in which the Madonna, the saints, the angels, Christ, and God Himself were brought on the stage. In those days it was done in all simplicity. In Victor Hugo's *Notre Dame de Paris* an edifying and free spectacle was provided for the people in the Hôtel de Ville of Paris during the reign of Louis XI, to honor the birth of the dauphin. It was called *Le bon jugement de la très sainte et gracieuse Vierge Marie,* and she personally appears on the stage and pronounces her *bon jugement.* Similar plays, chiefly from the Old Testament, were occasionally performed in Moscow too, up to the times of Peter the Great. But besides plays, all sorts of legends and "verses" appeared, in which the saints and angels and all the powers of Heaven took part when required. In our monasteries the monks busied themselves in translating, copying, and even composing such poems and just think when—under the Tatars. There is, for instance, one such little poem (from the Greek, of course), 'The Wanderings of Our Lady through Hell,' with descriptions as bold as Dante's. Our Lady visits Hell, and the Archangel Michael leads her through the torments. She sees the

125

sinners and their torment. There she sees among the rest, one noteworthy set of sinners in a burning lake; some of them sink to the bottom of the lake so that they can no longer swim out, and 'those God forgets'—an expression of extraordinary depth and force. And so Our Lady, shocked and weeping, falls before the throne of God and begs for mercy for everyone in Hell—for everyone she has seen there; and indiscriminately. Her conversation with God is immensely interesting. She beseeches Him, she will not desist, and when God points to the nail-pierced hands and feet of her Son and asks, 'How can I forgive His tormentors?' she bids all the saints, all the martyrs, all the angels and archangels to fall down with her and pray for mercy on all without distinction. It ends by her winning from God a respite of suffering every year from Good Friday till Trinity day, and the sinners in Hell at once thank the Lord, crying out: 'Thou are just, O Lord, in this judgment.' Well, my little poem would have been of that kind if it had appeared then. He comes on the scene in my poem, but He says nothing; He only appears and goes on. Fifteen centuries have already passed since He promised to come in His glory, fifteen centuries since His prophet wrote, 'Behold, I come quickly.' 'Of that day and that hour knoweth no man, neither the Son, but the Father,' as He Himself predicted on earth. But humanity awaits Him with the same faith and with the same love. Oh, even with greater faith, for it is fifteen centuries since man has ceased to see signs from Heaven.

> Believe what the heart says,
> There are no pledges from the heavens.[1]

"There was nothing left but faith in what the heart says! It is true there were many miracles in those days. There were saints who performed miraculous cures; some holy people, according to their biographies, were visited by the Queen of Heaven herself.

[1] From Schiller's *Sehnsucht*.

But the devil did not slumber, and men already began to doubt the truth of these miracles. And just then there appeared in the north, in Germany, a terrible new heresy, 'A huge star like a torch' (that is, a church) 'fell on the sources of the waters and they became bitter.' These heretics blasphemously began to deny miracles. But those who remained faithful were all the more ardent in their faith. The tears of humanity rose up to Him, as before, awaiting His coming, loved Him, hoped for Him, yearned to suffer and die for Him as before. And for so many centuries mankind had prayed with faith and fervor, 'O Lord, our God, hasten Thy coming,' for so many centuries called upon Him, that in His infinite mercy He deigned to come down to His servants. He had come down, He had visited some holy men, martyrs, and hermits, even before that day, as, is written in their 'Lives.' Among us, Tyutchev, with profound faith in the truth of His words, bore witness that

> Oppressed with bearing the cross,
> The heavenly King in slave's guise,
> Wandered, blessing as he went,
> Throughout our native land.[2]

and that certainly was so, I assure you. And behold, He longed to appear for a moment to the people, to the tortured, suffering people, sunk in iniquity, but loving Him like children. My story is laid in Spain, in Seville, at the worst time of the *Inquisition, when fires were lighted every day to the glory of God,* and

> in the splendid *auto da fé*
> the wicked heretics were burnt.

Oh, of course this was not the coming in which He will appear according to His promise at the end of time in all His heavenly glory, and which will be sudden 'as lightning flashing from east

[2] From Tyutchev's *These Humble Villages.*

to west.' No, He longed to visit His children only for a moment and there where the 'heretics'' flames crackled. In His infinite mercy he came once more among men in that human shape in which He walked among men for three years fifteen centuries ago. He came down to the 'hot pavement' of the southern town in which on the day before almost a hundred heretics had, *ad majorem gloriam Dei*, been burnt by the cardinal, the Grand Inquisitor, in a magnificent *auto da fé*, in the presence of the king, the court, the knights, the cardinals, the most charming ladies of the court, and the whole population of Seville. He came softly, unobserved, and yet, strange to say, everyone recognized Him. That might be one of the best passages in the poem. I mean, why they recognized Him. The people irresistibly flock to Him, they surround Him, they form about Him, follow Him. He moves silently in their midst with a gentle smile of infinite compassion. The sun of love burns in His heart, radiance, enlightenment and power shine from His eyes, and, shed on the people, stirs their hearts with responsive love. He holds out His hands to them, blesses them, and a healing virtue comes from contact with Him, even from touching His garments. An old man in the crowd, blind from birth, cries out, 'O Lord, heal me and I shall see Thee!' and, as it were, scales fell from his eyes and the blind man sees Him. The crowd weeps and kisses the earth under His feet. Children throw flowers before Him, sing, and cry hosannah. 'It is He—it is He!' all repeat. 'It must be He, it can be no one but Him!' He stops at the steps of the Seville cathedral just as weeping mourners bring in a child's open white coffin. In it lies a girl of seven, the only daughter of a prominent citizen. The dead child lies hidden in flowers. 'He will raise your child,' the crowd shouts to the weeping mother. The priest, coming to meet the coffin, looks perplexed, and frowns, but the mother of the dead child throws herself at His feet with a wail. 'If it is You, raise my child!' she cries, holding out her hands to Him. The procession halts, the coffin is laid on the steps at His feet. He looks with compassion, and His lips once more softly pronounce, 'Maiden, arise!' and the maiden arises. The little girl sits up in the coffin and looks round, smiling with wide-open, wondering eyes; in her hands the bunch of white roses that had been laid with her in the coffin. There are cries, sobs, confusion among the people, and at that moment the cardinal himself, the Grand Inquisitor, passes by the cathedral. He is an old man, almost ninety, tall and erect, with a withered face and sunken eyes from which a light like a fiery spark gleams. Oh, he is not in his gorgeous cardinal's robes, that he flaunted before the people the day before when he was burning the enemies of the Roman Church—no, at the moment he was only wearing his old, coarse monk's cassock. At a distance behind him come his somber assistants and slaves and the 'holy guard.' He stops at the sight of the crowd and watches it from a distance. He had seen everything; he had seen them set the coffin down at His feet, seen the girl rise up. His face darkens. He knits his thick gray brows and his eyes gleam with a sinister fire. He holds out his finger and bids the guards take Him. And such is his power, so completely are the people cowed into submission and trembling obedience to him, that the crowd immediately makes way for the guards, and in the midst of the tomblike silence that has suddenly fallen they lay hands on Him and lead Him away. The crowd instantly as one man bows down to the earth before the old inquisitor. He blesses the people in silence and passes on. The guards lead their prisoner to the close, gloomy vaulted dungeon in the ancient palace of the Holy Inquisition and shut Him in it. The day passes and is followed by the dark, burning 'breathless' night of Seville. The air is 'fragrant with laurel and lemon.' In the pitch darkness the iron door of the dungeon is suddenly opened and the Grand Inquisitor himself slowly comes in with a light in his hand. He is alone; the door is closed at once behind him. He stands in the doorway and for a long time, a minute or two, gazes into His face. At last he goes up slowly, sets the light on the table and speaks.

"'Is it You? You?' but receiving no answer, he adds at once, 'Don't answer, be silent. Indeed, what can You say? I know too

well what You would say. And You have no right to add anything to what You had said of old. Why, then, have You come to
hinder us? For You have come to hinder us, and You know that.
But do You know what will happen tomorrow? I do not know
who You are and I don't care to know whether it is You or only
a semblance of Him, but tomorrow I will condemn You and
burn You at the stake as the worst of heretics. And the very people who today kissed Your feet, tomorrow at the faintest sign
from me will rush to heap up the embers of Your fire. Do You
know that? Yes, maybe You know it,' he added with earnest reflection, never for a moment taking his eyes off the Prisoner."

"I don't quite understand, Ivan. What does it mean?"
Alyosha, who had been listening in silence, said with a smile. "Is
it simply a wild fantasy, or a mistake on the part of the old
man—some impossible *quid pro quo?*"

"Take it as the last," said Ivan, laughing, "if you are so
spoiled by modern realism and can't stand anything fantastic. If
you like it to be a case of mistaken identity, let it be so. It is
true," he said, laughing, again, "the old man was ninety, and his
idea might well have made him mad. He might have been struck
by the appearance of the prisoner. It might, in fact, be simply his
ravings, the delusion of an old man of ninety, approaching
death, over-excited by the *auto da fé* of a hundred heretics the
day before. But does it matter to us after all whether it was a
mistaken identity or a wild fantasy? All that matters is that the
old man should speak out, should speak openly of what he has
thought in silence for ninety years."

"And the Prisoner too is silent? Does He look at him and not
say a word?"

"That's inevitable in any case." Ivan laughed again. "The old
man has told Him He hasn't the right to add anything to what
He has said of old. One may say it is the most fundamental fea-
ture of Roman Catholicism, in my opinion at least. 'All has been
given by You to the Pope,' they say, 'and all, therefore, is still in
the Pope's hands, and there is no need for You to come now at

all. You must not meddle, for the time at least.' That's how they speak and write, too—the Jesuits at any rate. I have read it myself in the works of their theologians. 'Have You the right to reveal to us one of the mysteries of that world from which You have come?' my old man asks Him, and answers the question for Him. 'No, You have not; that You may not add to what has been said of old, and may not take from men the freedom You exalted when You were on earth. Whatsoever You reveal anew will encroach on men's freedom of faith; for it will be manifest as a miracle, and the freedom of their faith was dearer to You than anything in those days fifteen hundred years ago. Did You not often say then, "I will make you free"? But now You have seen these "free" men,' the old man adds suddenly, with a pensive smile. 'Yes, we've paid dearly for it,' he goes on, looking sternly at Him, 'but at last we have completed that work in Your name. For fifteen centuries we have been wrestling with Your freedom, but now it is ended and over for good. Do You not believe that it's over for good? You look at me meekly and do not even deign to be angry with me. But let me tell You that now, today, people are more persuaded than ever that they are completely free, yet they have brought their freedom to us and laid it humbly at our feet. But that has been our doing. Was this what You did? Was this Your freedom?' "

"I don't understand again," Alyosha broke in. "Is he ironical, is he jesting?"

"Not at all! He claims it as a merit for himself and his like that at last they have vanquished freedom and have done so to make men happy. 'For only now' (he is speaking of the Inquisition of course) 'for the first time it has become possible to think of the happiness of men. Man was created a rebel; and how can rebels be happy? You were warned,' he says to Him. 'You had no lack of admonitions and warnings, but You did not listen to those warnings; You rejected the only way by which men might be made happy, but fortunately, when You departed, You handed the work on to us. You affirmed by Your word, You gave us the right to bind and to unbind, and now, of course, You cannot even think of taking that right away from us. Why, then, do You come to hinder us?' "

"And what's the meaning of 'no lack of admonitions and warnings'?" asked Alyosha.

"Why, that's the chief part of what the old man must say."

" 'The wise and dread spirit, the spirit of self-destruction and non-existence,' the old man goes on, 'the great spirit talked with You in the wilderness, and we are told in the books that he "tempted" You. Is that not so? And could anything truer be said than what he revealed to You in three questions and what You rejected, and what in the books is called "the temptations"? And yet if there has even been on earth a real stupendous miracle, it took place on that day, on the day of the three temptations. The statement of those three questions was itself the miracle. If it were possible to imagine simply for the sake of argument that those three questions of the dread spirit had perished utterly from the books, and that we had to restore them and to invent and formulate them anew, to restore them to the books, and to do so had gathered together all the wise men of the earth— rulers, chief priests, learned men, philosophers, poets—and had set them the task to invent, to formulate three questions, such as would not only fit the occasion, but express in three words, in a mere three human phrases, the whole future history of the world and of humanity—do You believe that all the wisdom of the earth united together could have invented anything in depth and force equal to the three questions which were actually put to You then by the wise and mighty spirit in the wilderness? From those questions alone, from the miracle of their statement, we can see that we are not dealing with the fleeting human intelligence, but with the absolute and eternal. For in those three questions the whole subsequent history of mankind is, as it were, brought together into one whole and foretold, and in them are united all the unsolved historical contradictions of human nature throughout the world. At the time it could not have been so clear since the future was unknown; but now that fifteen hundred years have passed, we see that everything in those three questions were so justly divined and foretold, and has been so truly fulfilled, that nothing can be added to them or taken from them.

" 'Judge Yourself who was right—You or he who questioned You then? Remember the first question; its meaning, in other words, was this: "You would go into the world, and are going with empty hands, with some promise of freedom which men in their simplicity and their natural unruliness cannot even understand, which they fear and dread—since nothing has ever been more insupportable for a man and a human society than freedom. Do You see these stones in this parched and barren wilderness? Turn them into bread, and mankind will run after You like a flock, grateful and obedient, though for ever trembling, lest You withdraw your hand and deny them Your bread." But You would not deprive man of freedom and rejected the offer, thinking, what is that freedom worth, if obedience is bought with bread? You replied that man lives not by bread alone. But do You know that for the sake of that earthly bread the spirit of the earth will rise up against You and fight with You and overcome You, and all will follow him, crying, "Who can compare with this beast? He has given us fire from heaven!" Do You know that centuries will pass, and humanity will proclaim through the mouth of their wisdom and science that there is no crime, and therefore no sin, there is only hunger? "Feed men, and then demand virtue from them!" That's what they'll write on the banner, which they will raise against You, and with which they will destroy Your temple. Where Your temple stood a new building will rise; the terrible tower of Babel will be built again, and though, like the one of old, it will not be finished, yet You might have prevented that new tower and have cut short the sufferings of men for a thousand years; for they will come back to us after a thousand years of agony with their tower. They will seek us again, hidden underground in the catacombs, for we shall again be persecuted and tortured. They will find us and cry to us, "Feed us, for those who have promised us fire from heaven haven't given it!" And then we shall finish building their tower, for he finishes the building who feeds them. And we alone shall feed them in Your name, and declare falsely that it is in Your name. Oh, never, never can they feed themselves without us! No science will give them bread so long as they remain free. In the end they will lay their freedom at our feet, and say to us, "Make us your slaves, but feed us." They will understand themselves, at last, that freedom and bread enough for all are inconceivable together, for they will never, never be able to share among themselves. They will be convinced, too, that they can never be free, for they are weak, sinful, worthless and rebellious. You promised them the bread of Heaven, but, I repeat again, can it compare with earthly bread in the eyes of the weak, ever sinful and ignoble race of man? And if for the sake of the bread of Heaven thousands and tens of thousands shall follow You, what is to become of the millions and tens of thousands of millions of creatures who will not have the strength to forego the earthly bread for the sake of the heavenly? Or do You care only for the tens of thousands of the great and strong dear to You while the millions, numerous as the sands of the sea, who are weak but love You, must exist only for the sake of the great and strong? No, for the weak are dear to us, too. They are sinful and rebellious, but in the end they too will become obedient. They will marvel at us and look upon us as gods, because we are ready to endure the freedom which they have found so dreadful and to rule over them—so awful will it seem to them to be free. But we will tell them that we are Your servants and rule them in Your name. We will deceive them again, for we will not let You come to us again. That deception will be our suffering, for we will be forced to lie. That is the significance of the first question in the wilderness, and that is what You rejected for the sake of the freedom which You exalted above everything. Yet that question contains the great secret of this world. Had You chosen "bread,"

You would have satisfied the universal and everlasting craving of human beings and of the individual to find someone to worship. So long as man remains free he strives for nothing so incessantly and so painfully as to find as quickly as possible someone to worship. But man seeks to worship what is established beyond dispute, so indisputably that all men would agree at once to worship it. For these pitiful creatures are concerned not only to find what one or the other can worship, but to find something that all would believe in and worship; what is essential is that all may be *together* in it. This craving for *community* of worship is the chief misery of every man individually and of all humanity from the beginning of time. For the sake of common worship they've slain each other with the sword. They have set up gods and challenged one another, "Put away your gods and come and worship ours, or we will kill you and your gods!" And so it will be to the end of the world, even when gods disappear from the earth; they will fall down before idols just the same. You knew, You could not but have known, that fundamental secret of human nature, but You rejected the one infallible banner which was offered You, to make all men bow down to You alone—the banner of earthly bread; and You rejected it for the sake of freedom and the bread of Heaven. Behold what else You did. And all again in the name of freedom! I tell you that man is tormented by no greater anxiety than to find someone to whom he can hand over quickly that gift of freedom with which the unhappy creature is born. But only he who can appease their conscience can take over their freedom. In bread there was offered to You an indisputable banner; give bread, and man will worship You, for nothing is more indisputable than bread. But if someone else gains possession of his conscience—oh! then he will cast away Your bread and follow after him who has ensnared his conscience. In that You were right. For the secret of man's being is not only to live but to have something to live for. Without a firm conception of the object of life, man would not consent to go on living, and would rather destroy himself than remain on earth, though he had bread in abundance. That is true. But what happened? Instead of taking men's freedom from them, You make it greater than ever! Did You forget that man prefers peace, and even death, to freedom of choice in the knowledge of good and evil? Nothing is more seductive for man than his freedom of conscience, but at the same time nothing is a greater torture. And yet, instead of providing a firm foundation for setting the conscience of man at rest forever, You chose all that is exceptional, vague and enigmatic; You chose what is utterly beyond the strength of men, acting as though You did not love them at all—You who came to give Your life for them! Instead of taking possession of men's freedom, You increased it, and burdened the spiritual kingdom of mankind forever with its sufferings. You wanted man's free love. You wanted him to follow You freely, enticed and captured by You. In place of the rigid ancient law, man was hereafter to decide for himself with free heart what is good and what is evil, having only Your image before him as his guide. But did You not think he would at last dispute and reject even Your image and Your truth, if he were oppressed with the fearful burden of free choice? They will cry aloud at last that the truth is not in You, for they could not have been left in greater confusion and suffering than You have caused, laying upon them so many cares and unanswerable problems.

" 'So that You Yourself laid the foundation for the destruction of Your kingdom, and no one is more to blame for it. Yet what was offered You? There are three powers, only three powers that can conquer and capture the conscience of these impotent rebels forever, for their own happiness—those forces are miracle, mystery and authority. You rejected all three and set the example for doing so. When the wise and dread spirit set You on the pinnacle of the temple and said to You, "If thou be the Son of God cast thyself down, for it is written: 'He shall give his angels charge of thee, and in *their* hands they shall bear thee up, lest at any time thou dash thy foot against a stone.' And You shall know then whether You are the Son of God and shall prove

then how great is Your faith in Your Father." But You refused
and would not cast Yourself down. Oh! of course, You did
proudly and well as a God; but men, that weak, rebellious race,
are they gods? Oh, You knew then that in taking one step, in
making one movement to cast Yourself down, You would immediately be tempting God and have lost all Your faith in Him,
and would have been dashed to pieces against that earth which
You had come to save, and the wise spirit that tempted You
would have rejoiced. But I ask again, are there many like You?
And could You really believe for one moment that men, too,
could resist such a temptation? Is the nature of men such that
they can reject miracles, and at such fearful moments of their
life, the moments of their deepest, most fearful spiritual difficulties, cling only to the free verdict of the heart? Oh, You knew
that Your deed would be recorded in books, would be handed
down to remote times and the utmost ends of the earth, and You
hoped that man, following You, would also cling to God and not
ask for a miracle. But You did not know that as soon as man rejects a miracle, he rejects God too; for man seeks not so much
God as the miraculous. And as man cannot bear to be without
the miraculous, he will create new miracles of his own for himself, and will worship deeds of sorcery and witchcraft, though he
might be a hundred times over a rebel, heretic and infidel. You
did not descend from the Cross when they shouted to You,
mocking and reviling You, "If thou be the Son of God, come
down from the cross." You did not descend, for again You
would not enslave man by a miracle, and craved faith given
freely, not based on a miracle. You craved for free love and not
the base raptures of the slave before the might that has overawed
him forever. But here too You judged men too highly, for they
are slaves, of course, though rebellious by nature. Look round
and judge; fifteen centuries have passed, look upon them. Whom
have You raised up to Yourself? I swear, man is weaker and
baser by nature than You believed him to be. Can he, can he do
what you did? By showing him so much respect, You acted as

though You had ceased to have compassion for him, because You asked too much from him—You who loved him more than Yourself! Had You respected him less, you would have asked less of him. That would have been more like love, for his burden would have been lighter. He is weak and vile. So what if he is everywhere now rebelling against our power, and proud of his rebellion? It is the pride of a child and a schoolboy. They are little children rioting and chasing away the teacher at school. But their childish delight will end; it will cost them dear. They will cast down temples and drench the earth with blood. But they will see at last, the foolish children, that, though they are rebels, they are impotent rebels, unable to keep up their own rebellion. Bathed in their foolish tears, they will recognize at last that He who created them rebels must have meant to mock at them. They will say this in despair, and their utterance will be a blasphemy which will make them more unhappy still, for man's nature cannot bear blasphemy, and in the end always avenges it on itself. And so unrest, confusion and unhappiness—that is the present lot of man after You bore so much for his freedom! Your great prophet tells us allegorically and in image that he saw all those who took part in the first resurrection and that there were of each tribe twelve thousand. But if there were so many of them, they must have been gods rather than men. They had borne Your cross, they had endured scores of years in the barren, hungry wilderness, living upon locusts and roots—and You may indeed point with pride at those children of freedom, of free love, of free and splendid sacrifice for Your name. But remember that they were only some thousands and gods at that; and what of the rest? And how are the other weak ones to blame, because they could not endure what the strong have endured? How is the weak soul to blame that it is incapable of appreciating such terrible gifts? Can You simply have come to the elect and for the elect? But if so, it is a mystery and we cannot understand it. And if it is a mystery, we too have a right to preach a mystery, and to teach them that it is not the free judgment of their hearts,

not love that matters, but a mystery which they must follow
blindly, even against their conscience. That is what we have
done. We have corrected Your work and have founded it upon
miracle, mystery and *authority*. And men rejoiced that they were
again led like a flock, and that the terrible gift that had brought
them such suffering, was, at last, lifted from their hearts. Were
we right teaching them this and acting as we did? Speak! Did we
not love mankind, so meekly acknowledging their feebleness,
lovingly lightening their burden, and even permitting their weak
nature to sin, so long as it had our sanction? Why have you
come now to hinder us? And why do You look silently and
searchingly at me with Your mild eyes? Be angry. I do not want
Your love, for I love You not. And what use is it for me to hide
anything from You? Don't I know to Whom I am speaking? All
that I can say is known to You already. I can read it in Your eyes.
And is it for me to conceal our mystery from You? Perhaps it is
Your will to hear it from my lips. Listen, then. We are not working with You, but with *him*—that is our mystery. It's long—eight
centuries—since we have been on *his* side and not on Yours. Just
eight centuries ago, we took from him what You rejected with
scorn, that last gift he offered You, showing You all the king-
doms of the earth. We took Rome and the sword of Caesar from
him and proclaimed ourselves rulers of the earth, the sole rulers,
though till now we have not been able to complete our work.
But whose fault is that? Oh, the work is only beginning, but it
has begun. It will long await completion and the earth has much
to suffer yet; but we will triumph and will be Caesars, and then
we will plan the universal happiness of man. But You might have
accepted the sword of Caesar even then. Why did you reject that
last gift? Had You accepted that third counsel of the mighty
spirit, You would have accomplished all that man seeks on
earth—that is, someone to worship, someone to keep his conscience, and some means of uniting everyone in one indisputable
general and unanimous anthill, for the craving for universal
unity is the third and last anguish of men. Mankind as a whole

has always striven to organize a universal state. There have been many great nations with great histories, but the more highly they were developed the more unhappy they were, for they felt more acutely than other people the craving for worldwide union. The great conquerors, Timours and Genghis-Khans, whirled like hurricanes over the face of the earth striving to subdue its people, and they too were but the unconscious expression of the same great human craving for universal and general unity. Had You taken the world and Caesar's purple, You would have founded the universal state and have given universal peace. For who can rule men if not he who holds their conscience and their bread in his hands? We have accepted the sword of Caesar, and in taking it, of course, have rejected You and followed *him*. Oh, centuries of the confusion of free thought, of their science and cannibalism are yet to pass, for having begun to build their tower of Babel without us, they will end with cannibalism. But just then the beast will crawl to us and lick our feet and spatter them with tears of blood from their eyes. And we shall sit upon the beast and raise the cup, and on it will be written "Mystery." But then, and only then, the reign of peace and happiness will come for men. You are proud of Your elect, but You have only the elect, while we give rest to all. And besides, how many of those elect, those mighty ones who could become the elect, finally grew tired of waiting for You and transferred and will transfer the powers of their spirit and the fire of their heart to the other camp, and end by raising their *free* banner against You? But You Yourself lifted up that banner. With us everybody will be happy and will neither rebel nor everywhere destroy each other any more as they did under Your freedom. Oh, we will persuade them that they will only become free when they renounce their freedom to us and submit to us. And will we be right or will we be lying? They will be convinced that we are right, because they will remember the horrors of slavery and confusion to which Your freedom brought them. Freedom, free thought and science, will lead them into such straits and will

bring them face to face with such marvels and insoluble mysteries, that some of them, the fierce and rebellious, will destroy
themselves, while others, rebellious but weak, will destroy one
another, and the rest, weak and unhappy, will crawl to our feet
and wail to us: "Yes, you were right, you alone possess His mystery, and we are coming back to you, save us from ourselves!"

" 'When they obtain bread from us, they will of course clearly
see that we take the bread made by their own hands from them
to distribute it to them, that there is no sort of miracle there.
They will see that we did not change the stones into bread, but
in truth they will be more thankful for taking it from our hands
than for the bread itself! For they will remember only too well
that formerly, without us, even the bread they made turned into
stones in their hands, while since they have come back to us, the
very stones have turned into bread in their hands. Only too, too
well will they value the meaning of submission henceforth! And
until men know that; they will be unhappy. Who is most to
blame for their not knowing it? Speak! Who scattered the flock
and sent it astray on unknown paths? But the flock will come
together again and will submit once more, and then it will be
once for all. Then we shall give them the quiet; humble happiness of weak creatures such as they are by nature. Oh, we shall
persuade them at last not to be proud, for You had lifted them
up and thereby taught them to be proud. We shall show them
that they are weak, that they are only pitiful children, but that
childlike happiness is the sweetest of all. They will become timid
and will look to us and huddle close to us in fear, as chicks to
the hen. They will marvel at us and will be awe-stricken before
us, and will be proud at our being so powerful and clever, that
we have been able to subdue such a turbulent flock of thousands
of millions. They will tremble more weakly before our wrath,
their minds will grow fearful, they will be quick to shed tears
like women and children, but they will be just as ready at a sign
from us to pass to laughter and rejoicing, to happy mirth and
childish song. Yes, we shall set them to work, but in their leisure

hours we shall make their life like a child's game, with children's songs, choruses and innocent dances. Oh, we shall even allow them sin, they are weak and impotent, and they will love us like children because we allow them to sin. We shall tell them that every sin will be expiated, if it is done with our permission, that we allow them to sin because we love them, and the punishment for these sins we take upon ourselves. And we shall take it upon ourselves, and they will adore us as their saviors who have taken on themselves their sins before God. And they will have no secrets from us. We shall allow or forbid them to live with their wives and mistresses, to have children or not to have them—depending upon their obedience—and they will submit to us gladly and cheerfully. The most painful secrets of their conscience; they will bring everything, everything to us, and we will have an answer for everything. And they will be glad to believe our answer, for it will save them from the great anxiety and terrible agony they now endure supplying a free, individual answer. And everyone will be happy, all the millions of creatures except the hundred thousand who rule them. For only we, we who guard the mystery, will be unhappy. There will be thousands of millions of happy babes, and a hundred thousand sufferers who have taken upon themselves the curse of the knowledge of good and evil. They will die peacefully, they will expire peacefully in Your name, and beyond the grave they will find nothing but death. But we will keep the secret, and for their happiness we will tempt them with the reward of Heaven and eternity. Though if there was anything in the other world, it certainly would not be for such as they. It is said and prophesied that You will come and conquer again. You will come accompanied by Your chosen, proud and strong, but we will say that they have only saved themselves while we have saved everyone. We are told that the harlot who sits upon the beast and holds the *mystery* in her hands will be put to shame, that the weak will rise up again and will rend her royal purple and will strip naked her "loathsome" body. But then I will stand up and point out to You the thousand millions of happy children who have known no sin. And we who have taken their sins upon us for their happiness will stand up before You and say: "Judge us if you can and dare." Know that I fear You not. Know that I too have been in the wilderness, I too have lived on roots and locusts, I too blessed the freedom with which You had blessed men, and I too was striving to stand among Your elect, among the strong and powerful, thirsting "to make up the number." But I awakened and would not serve madness. I turned back and joined the ranks of those *who have corrected* Your work. I left the proud and went back to the humble, for the happiness of the humble. What I say to You will come to pass, and our dominion will be built up. I repeat, tomorrow You will see that obedient flock who at the first sign from me will hasten to heap up the hot cinders about the pile on which I will burn You for coming to hinder us. For if anyone has ever deserved our fires, it is You. Tomorrow I will burn You. *Dixi.*' "

Ivan stopped. He was carried away as he talked and spoke with excitement; when he had finished, he suddenly smiled.

Alyosha had listened in silence; toward the end he was greatly moved and seemed several times on the point of interrupting, but restrained himself. Now his words came with a rush.

"But . . . that's absurd!" he cried, flushing. "Your poem is in praise of Jesus, not in blame of Him—as you meant it to be. And who will believe you about freedom? Is that the way to understand it? That's not the Orthodox Church's view of it. That's Rome, and not even the whole of Rome, it's false—those are the worst of the Catholics, the Inquisitors, the Jesuits! And such a fantastic creature as your Inquisitor could not exist at all. What are these sins of mankind they take on themselves? Who are these keepers of the mystery who have taken some curse upon themselves for the happiness of mankind? When have they been seen? We know the Jesuits, they are spoken ill of, but surely they are not what you describe? They are not that at all, not at all. They are simply the Romish army for the earthly sovereignty of the world in the future, with the Pontiff of Rome for Emperor, that's their ideal, but there's no sort of mystery or lofty melancholy about it. It's simple lust of power, of filthy earthly gain, of domination—something like future serfdom with them as masters—that's all they stand for. Perhaps they don't even believe in God. Your suffering Inquisitor is a mere fantasy."

"Wait, wait," laughed Ivan, "how heated you've become! A fantasy you say, all right! Of course it's a fantasy. But allow me to say: do you really think that the whole Catholic movement of the last centuries is actually nothing but the lust of power, of filthy earthly gain? Is that Father Paissy's teaching?"

"No, no, on the contrary, Father Paissy did once say something of the same sort as you—but of course it's not the same, not a bit the same," Alyosha hastily corrected himself.

"But that's a valuable piece of information, despite your 'not a bit the same.' I am expressly asking you why your Jesuits and Inquisitors have only united for vile material gain? Why can there not be a single martyr among them, tortured by great sorrow and loving humanity? You see, only suppose that just one such man was found among all those who desire nothing but filthy material gain—only a single one like my old inquisitor, who had himself eaten roots in the desert and made frenzied efforts to subdue his flesh to make himself free and perfect. But yet all his life he loved humanity, and suddenly his eyes were opened, and he saw that it is no great moral blessing to attain the perfection of the will, if at the same time one becomes convinced that millions of God's other creatures have been created as a mockery, that they will never be capable of using their freedom, that these poor rebels can never turn into giants to complete the tower, that it was not for such geese that the great idealist dreamt of His harmony. Seeing all that he turned back and joined—the clever people. Surely that could have happened?"

"Joined whom, what clever people?" cried Alyosha; almost losing his temper. "They have no cleverness like that at all, and no mysteries and secrets. Perhaps nothing but atheism, that's all their secret. Your inquisitor does not believe in God, that's his secret!"

"What if it is so! At last you have guessed it. It's perfectly true, that's really the whole secret, but isn't that suffering, at least for a man like that, who has wasted his whole life on his deeds in the desert and yet could not cure himself of love for humanity? In his old age he reached the clear conviction that nothing but the advice of the great dread spirit could build up any tolerable sort of life for the weak rebels, 'incomplete, experimental creatures created in jest.' And so, convinced of that, he sees that he must follow the council of the wise spirit, the dread spirit of death and destruction, and therefore accept lying and deception, and lead men consciously to death and destruction, and yet deceive them all the way so that they may not notice where they are being led, the poor blind creatures may at least think themselves happy on the way. And note, the deception is in the name of Him in whose ideal the old man had so fervently believed all his life long. Is that not a misfortune? And if only one such stood at the head of the whole army 'filled with the lust of power only for the sake of filthy gain'—would one such not be enough to make a tragedy? More than that, even one such standing at the head is enough to create finally the actual leading idea of the Roman Church with all its armies and Jesuits, its highest idea. I tell you frankly that I firmly believe that there has always been such a single man among those who stood at the head of the movement. Who knows, there may have been some such single men even among the Roman popes. Who knows, perhaps that accursed old man who loves mankind so obstinately in his own way is to be found even now in a whole multitude of such single old men, existing not by chance but by agreement, as a secret league formed long ago for the guarding of the mystery, to guard it from the weak and the unhappy, so as to make them happy. No doubt it is so, and indeed it must be so. I fancy that even among the masons there's something of the same mystery at bottom, and that that's why the Catholics so detest the Masons as their rivals breaking up the unity of the idea, while it is so essential that there should be one fold and one shepherd. . . . But from the way I defend my idea I might be an author impatient of your criticism. Enough of it."

"Are you perhaps a Mason yourself?" broke suddenly from Alyosha. "You don't believe in God," he added, speaking this time very sorrowfully. He fancied besides that his brother was looking at him ironically. "How does your poem end?" he asked, suddenly looking down. "Or was that the end?"

"I meant it to end like this. When the Inquisitor stopped speaking he waited some time for his prisoner to answer him. His silence weighed down upon him. He saw that the prisoner had listened intently and calmly all the time, looking gently in his face and evidently not wishing to reply. The old man longed for Him to say something, however bitter and terrible. But He suddenly approaches the old man in silence and softly kisses him on his bloodless aged lips. That was His whole answer. The old man shudders. Something trembles at the edge of his lips. He goes to the door, opens it, and says to Him: 'Go, and come no more . . . Come not at all, never, never!' And he lets him out into the 'dark squares of the town.' The prisoner leaves."

"And the old man?"

"The kiss burns in his heart, but the old man adheres to his idea."

"And you with him, you too?" cried Alyosha, mournfully. Ivan laughed.

"Why, it's all nonsense, Alyosha. It's only a senseless poem of a senseless student, who could never write two lines of verse. Why do you take it so seriously? Surely you don't suppose I am going straight off to the Jesuits to join the multitude of men who are correcting His work? Good Lord, it's no business of mine. Haven't I told you, all I want is to live on to thirty, and then— dash the cup to the ground!"

"But the little sticky leaves, and the precious tombs, and the blue sky, and the woman you love! How will you live, how will you love them?" Alyosha cried sorrowfully. "With such a hell in your heart and your head, how can you? No, that's just what you are going away for, to join them . . . if not, you will kill yourself, you can't endure it!"

"There is a strength to endure everything," Ivan said with a cold smile.

"What strength?"

"The strength of the Karamazovs—the strength of the Karamazov baseness."

"To sink into debauchery, to stifle your soul with corruption, is that it?"

"Possibly, even that . . . only perhaps till I am thirty I will escape it, and then . . ."

"How will you escape it? By what will you escape it? That's impossible with your ideas."

"In the Karamazov way, again."

" 'Everything is lawful,' you mean? Everything is lawful, is that it? Is that it?"

Ivan scowled, and all at once turned strangely pale.

"Ah, you've caught up yesterday's phrase, which so offended Miüsov—and which Dmitri pounced upon so naïvely and paraphrased!" He smiled queerly. "Yes, if you like, 'everything is lawful' since the word has been spoken. I won't deny it. And Mitya's version isn't bad, either."

Alyosha looked at him in silence.

"In leaving here, brother, I thought that in the whole world I have at least you," Ivan said suddenly, with unexpected feeling; "but now I see that there is no place for me even in your heart, my dear hermit. I won't renounce the formula, 'everything is lawful.' Will you renounce me for that, will you? Will you?"

Alyosha got up, went to him and softly kissed him on the lips.

"That's plagiarism," cried Ivan, at once passing into a sort of delight. "You stole that from my poem. Thank you though. Get up, Alyosha, it's time we were going, both of us."

They went out, but stopped when they reached the entrance of the restaurant.

"Listen, Alyosha," Ivan began in a resolute voice, "if I am really able to care for the sticky little leaves I shall only love them in remembering you. It's enough for me that you are somewhere here, and I won't lose my desire for life yet. Is that enough for you? Take it as a declaration of love if you like. And now you go to the right and I to the left. And it's enough, do you hear, enough. I mean, even if I don't go away tomorrow (I think I certainly will go) and we meet again, don't say another word on these subjects. I beg that of you in particular. And about Dmitri too, I ask you specially never to speak to me about that again," he added, with sudden irritation; "it's all exhausted, it has all been said over and over again, hasn't it? And I'll make you one promise in return for it. When, at thirty, I want to 'dash the cup to the ground,' wherever I may be I'll come to have one more talk with you even though it were from America, you may be sure of that. I'll come on purpose. It will be very interesting to have a look at you, to see what you'll be by that time. It's rather a solemn promise, you see. And we really may be parting for seven years or ten. Come, go now to your Pater Seraphicus, he is dying. If he dies without you, you will be angry with me for having kept you. Good-bye, kiss me once more; that's right, now go."

APPENDIX

The appendix presents material relevant to *Notes from Underground,* much of it hitherto unavailable in English. As indicated in the introduction, the *Notes* are in part a direct reply to Chernyshevsky's novel *What Is to Be Done?* From that novel I have given here a discussion of man's rational actions and calculations; the Eulogy of Marya Alexeevna, in which the theories of environment and advantage are stated fully, if ironically; a passage directly refuted by the episode on the Nevsky with the officer; and two of Vera Pavlovna's dreams: the first, that deals with liberating man's spirit from underground, or more specifically, from cellars (the image recurs in the novel), and the fourth, Vera's utopian dream of man's perfectibility, the immediate predecessor for the notion of the "crystal palace." The last has been given fully, even though only the last part is clearly pertinent to the *Notes,* as it is a vital and frequently anthologized passage in Russia. In its own way it is an interesting and revealing addition to the tradition of utopian literature.

The passages from Dostoevsky's correspondence and *Winter Notes* deal with the composition and elaboration of the *Notes.* Two satires arising out of *Notes from Underground* end the volume. The first, "The Swallows," attributed to Shchedrin, attacks the ostensible fatuity and confused ideas of Dostoevsky and his collaborators. The *Notes* themselves are parodied in the Fourth Swallow's speech near the end of the playlet.

Dostoevsky's vigorous rejoinder, "Mr. Shchedrin, or, Schism among the Nihilists," took advantage of a temporary rift in the radical camp to repay Shchedrin and his collaborators in kind. After parodying the radicals' aesthetic and political ideas, Dostoevsky uses some of the ideas expressed in the *Notes* in new and effective forms to expose the bankruptcy of the radicals' positions.

R. E. M.

Excerpts from *What Is to Be Done?*

by

N. G. CHERNYSHEVSKY

PART II, CHAPTER 8

A Hamletic Trial

. . . There were two windows in Vera's room. A writing table stood between the windows. At one window, at the end of the table, Vera sat and knitted a woolen muffler for her father, diligently fulfilling Marya Alexeevna's orders. At the other window, at the other end of the table, sat Lopukhov. He leaned one elbow on the table, and held a cigar in that hand, while the other hand was placed in his pocket. The distance between them was two yards, if not more. Vera primarily looked at her knitting, Lopukhov primarily looked at his cigar. A reassuring disposition. Marya Alexeevna heard the following:

"Must one look at life that way?" Marya Alexeevna started to hear at this point.

"Yes, Vera Pavlovna, one must."

"Then what cold, practical people say, that only calculated advantage rules man is true?"

"It is. What are called higher feelings, ideal strivings, all that is completely insignificant in ordinary life in comparison to each person's striving for his own benefit, and fundamentally life is itself composed of that same striving for benefit."

"And you, for example, are you like that?"

"What else, Vera Pavlovna? I will tell you what the real mainspring of my whole life is. Up to now the essence of my life has consisted in the fact that I have studied, that I have prepared myself to be a doctor. Fine. Why did my father send me to school? He repeated over and over again to me: 'Study, Mitya. After you have finished your studies you will become a functionary, you'll support your mother and me, and you yourself will be well off.'

That is why I studied. Without that calculation my father would not have let me study. After all, the family needed a worker. Why, even I, though I liked learning, would I have spent time on it if I had not thought that the time spent would be rewarded with interest? I was finishing my secondary school. I convinced my father to let me attend medical school instead of becoming a government functionary. How did that come about? My father and I both saw that doctors live much better than civil servants and department chiefs, and that was the limit of my expectations. There you have the reason why I came to be in the Academy and stayed there—a good piece of bread. Without that calculation I would not have entered the Academy and I would not have stayed there."

"But after all you liked to study in secondary school, and after all you later liked your medical studies?"

"Yes. That is the frosting. And it is useful to make the thing a success. But the thing ordinarily occurs without the frosting, while it does not take place without that calculation. Love for science was only a product stemming from study, not the reason for study. The reason was only one—advantage."

"Let us assume that you are right, yes, you are right. Every deed that I perform can be explained by advantage. But that is a cold theory."

"A theory must in itself be cold. The mind has to judge things coldly."

"But it is merciless."

"To fantasies, which are empty and harmful."

"But it is prosaic."

"Poetic forms do not suit science."

"Then that theory, which I cannot fail to admit, dooms people to a cold, merciless, prosaic life?"

"No, Vera Pavlovna, the theory is cold, but it teaches man to attain warmth. A match is cold; the match-box against which it is struck is cold; wood is cold; but we get from them fire, which makes warm food for man and provides him with heat. The theory is merciless, but according to it, people will not be pitiful subjects of idle compassion. A lancet must not bend, otherwise one would have to pity the patient, who would be none the better for our pity. That theory is prosaic, but it discloses the real motives of life, while poetry lies in the truth of life. Why is Shakespeare the greatest poet? Because there is more of life's truth in him than in other poets, less deception than in other poets."

"Then I will be merciless as well, Dmitri Sergeevich," said Vera with a smile. "Don't deceive yourself by the idea that you have a stubborn opponent to your theory of calculated advantage, and that you have gained a new adherent to it. For a long time I had myself thought along the same lines that I read in your book and heard from you. But I thought that these were my private thoughts, that intelligent and learned people thought differently, and that a conflict would arise therefrom. It would happen, sometimes, that everything one read was written from an opposing point of view, full of reproaches and sarcasm against what you note in yourself and in others. Nature, life, reason lead in one direction, books draw one in another and say that is bad, low. Do you know, in part, the objections I made to you seem funny even to myself!"

"Yes, they are funny, Vera Pavlovna."

"Only we are paying each other marvelous compliments," she said, laughing. "I tell you 'Don't be too haughty, Dmitri Sergeevich.' You tell me 'You are ridiculous with your doubts, Vera Pavlovna!' "

"So what?" he said, also smiling, "there is no reason for us to pay compliments, because we are not paying compliments."

"Very well, Dmitri Sergeevich. People are egoists, isn't that right? You have just spoken about yourself, I too want to speak about myself."

"That is logical. Each person thinks about himself most of all."

"Very well. Let us see if I don't catch you in questions about myself."

"Let us see."

"I am engaged to a rich man. I don't like him. Should I accept his proposal?"

"Calculate what is most useful for you."

"What is most useful for me! You know that I am quite poor. On one hand, a dislike for a person; on the other, domination over him, an enviable position in society, money, a host of admirers."

"Weigh everything. Choose whatever is most useful for you."

"And if I choose a husband's wealth and a host of admirers?"

"I would say that you chose whatever seemed to you to conform most to your interests."

"And what would one have to say about me?"

"If you proceeded coolly, after thinking it over intelligently, then one would have to say that you acted deliberately, and that you will probably not regret it."

"But will my choice deserve censure?"

"The sort of people who say all sorts of nonsense may talk about it as they like. People who view life correctly will say that you acted as you should have. If you did things that way, it means that your personality was such that you could not have acted otherwise under the circumstances. They will say that you acted as necessity dictated, that really you could not have made a different choice."

"And my action will not be censured at all?"

"Who has the right to censure conclusions drawn from a fact, if the fact exists? Your personality under the circumstances is a fact. Your actions are necessary conclusions from that fact, performed by the nature of things. You are not responsible for them and to censure them is stupid."

"You won't abandon your theory. Then I won't deserve your censure if I accept my fiancé's proposal?"

"I would be foolish if I were to censure you."

"Therefore, that means permission, perhaps even approval, perhaps even the outright advice to do as I have said."

"There is only one advice: to calculate what is useful to you. Approval comes as soon as you act upon that advice."

"Thank you. Now my personal affairs have been decided. Let us return to the first question, the general one. We started with the view that man acts according to necessity, that his actions are determined by the forces under which they occur. Stronger forces prevail over others. That is where we left the proposition that when an action is a matter of life and death, those motives are called advantageous, their struggle inside man is called the consideration of advantage, that man will therefore always act according to calculated advantage. Am I expressing your chain of thought correctly?"

"Yes."

"You see what a good pupil I am. Now that special question about actions that are a matter of life and death is settled. But difficulties remain about the general question. Your book says that man acts according to necessity. But there are cases, after all, when it seems that I decide arbitrarily whether I will act one way or another. For example, I am playing the piano and turning pages. Sometimes I turn them with my left hand, sometimes with my right. Let us suppose that now I turned them with my right hand. Couldn't I have turned them with the left? Does not that depend on my arbitrary will?"

"No, Vera Pavlovna. If you turn pages without thinking which hand you use, you will turn with whatever hand does so more conveniently. There is nothing arbitrary about it. If you think 'I'll turn it with my right hand,' you turn the page under the influence of that idea. But that idea did not occur arbitrarily in you either. It was the necessary outcome of other ideas. . . "

PART II, CHAPTER 12

Vera's First Dream

And Vera dreams.

She dreams that she was locked up in a damp, dark cellar. And suddenly the door opens and she finds herself in a field. She runs, she gambols and thinks: "How come I did not die in the cellar? That is because I had not seen the field. If I had seen it, I would have died in the cellar." And again she runs and gambols. She dreams that she is paralyzed, and she thinks: "How come I am paralyzed? Old men and women are paralyzed, but not young women." "They are, they are," someone's unknown voice says to her—"but now you will be cured, as soon as I touch your hand—you see, you are cured. Arise, then." Who is that speaking? And how light she feels! The whole illness has passed, and Vera gets up, walks, runs, and is again in the field, and again gambols, and again thinks: "How could I endure paralysis? That is because I was born with paralysis, I did not know how people walk and run. And if I had known, I could not have endured it," and she runs and gambols. And there a young woman is walking in the field. How strange! Her face and her walk, everything is changing in her, everything is constantly changing. Now she is an Englishwoman, a Frenchwoman, now she has become a German, a Pole. Now she has become a Russian, too, then again an Englishwoman, again a German, again a Russian. How come she constantly has the same face? After all, an Englishwoman does not resemble a Frenchwoman, a German a Russian, while her face constantly changes and yet remains the same. How strange she is! How gentle! How wrathful! Now sad, now gay— constantly changing. Yet always good. How come she is still good even when she is angry? But what a beauty she is! No matter how her face changes, with every change she becomes more and more beautiful. She comes up to Vera. "Who are you?" "Formerly he called me Vera Pavlovna, but now he calls me 'my dear.' " "Ah, then you are that Vera Pavlovna who fell in love with me?" "Yes, I love you very much. But who are you?" "I am your fiancé's bride." "What fiancé?" "I do not know. I do not know my fiancés. They know me, but I cannot know them: I have many of them. Choose one of them as a fiancé for yourself, only choose from among them, from among my fiancés." "I choose . . ." "I do not need the name, I do not know their names. But do you choose only from among them, only from among my fiancés. I want my sisters and my fiancés to choose only each other. Were you locked up in the cellar? Were you paralyzed?" "Yes, I was." "Now you have gotten rid of it?" "Yes, I have." "It was I who released you, who cured you. Remember then, that there are many who have not been released, who have not been cured. Release them, cure them. Will you?" "I shall. Only tell me, what are you called? I do so want to know." "I have many names. I have various names. Whatever name one needs to call me, that is the name I give him. You may call me 'love for people.' And that is really my true name. Not many call me that, but you may call me so." And Vera walks through the town. There is a cellar, in the cellar young women are locked up. Vera touches the lock—it falls down. "Come!" They come out. There is a room, in the room lie young women, paralyzed. "Arise!" They arise, walk and they are all again in the field, running, gamboling—ah, how gay! Together with them it is much gayer than just being alone! Ah, how gay!

PART II, CHAPTER 24

Eulogy of Marya Alexeevna

You are about to stop being an important character in Vera's life, Marya Alexeevna, and in parting from you the author of this tale begs you not to complain that you are leaving the stage after a denouement somewhat disadvantageous to you. Do not think that you will thereby lose respect. You have been duped, Marya Alexeevna, but that in no way affects the opinion we have of your intelligence. Your mistake does not testify against you. You met people unlike those you used to come in contact with, and you cannot be blamed for being deceived in them, if you judged by your previous experience. Your entire life previously led you to the conclusion that people can be divided into two classes, into fools and rogues. "Anyone who is not a fool is a rogue, unquestionably a rogue, you thought. And only a fool can fail to be a swindler." That view was very true, Marya Alexeevna, until recently it was completely true, Marya Alexeevna. You met people, Marya Alexeevna, who spoke very well and you saw that all these people, without exception, were either sly, taking people in with fine-sounding words, or grown-up stupid children who do not understand life and do not know how to go about anything. Therefore you did not believe fine words, Marya Alexeevna, thought them stupid or a deception, and you were right, Marya Alexeevna. Your view of people had already been completely formed when you came across the first woman who was neither stupid nor a rogue. It was forgivable for you to be confused, to stop in hesitation, not to know what to think of her, how to deal with her. Your view of people had already been completely formed when you came across the first noble man who was not simple-minded, a pitiful child, who understood life as well as you did, who judged it as truly as you, who was capable of doing something just as thoroughly as you. It was forgivable for you to make a mistake and take him for an old fox like yourself. These mistakes, Marya Alexeevna, do not diminish my respect for you as an intelligent and sensible woman. You drew your husband out of poverty, made your old age secure, these are good things, and they were difficult things for you. Your means were bad, but your environment did not give you other means. Your means belong to your environment, not to you personally, their dishonor does not fall upon you, but you gain honor for your intelligence and strength of character.

Are you satisfied, Marya Alexeevna, with the acknowledgment of these virtues of yours? Of course you would have been satisfied even with this, because you would never have thought of claiming that you were kind or good. In a moment of involuntary candor you admitted yourself that you were a spiteful and dishonorable person, and you did not consider your spitefulness and dishonor dishonorable to yourself, for you proved that you could not be otherwise considering the circumstances of your life. Therefore you would probably not be very interested that praise for your virtues was not added to the praise of your intelligence and strength of character. You do not even consider yourself as possessing them, and do not consider it a merit, but rather an attribute of stupidity to have them. Therefore you would probably not start to demand other praise in addition to the former one. But I can say one more thing in your honor. Of all the people I do not like and with whom I would not want to have to deal, I would just the same rather deal with you than with others. Of course, you are merciless where that is necessary for your own advantage. But if it is not to your advantage to harm someone, you would not do so out of trivial emotions. You do not consider it worth wasting time, work and money without utility. Of course you would be glad to roast your daughter and her husband on a spit, but you would restrain your vengeful inclinations in order to judge the affair coldly, and you would understand that you would not succeed in harming them. And after all, that is a great merit, Marya Alexeevna, to be able to understand what is impossible to do. Once you have understood it, you would not start a trial that would not ruin the people who irritate you. You would calculate that those minor irritations caused them by troubling about the trial, would subject you to much greater troubles and loss, and therefore you would not start the trial. If you cannot defeat an enemy, if the insignificant loss you impose on him causes you much greater loss, it is not worthwhile to start the battle. Once you understand that, you have the good sense and courage to submit to necessity without harming yourself and others in vain, and that, too, is a great merit, Marya Alexeevna. Yes, Marya Alexeevna, one can still deal with you, because you do not believe in evil for evil at a loss to yourself—that is a very rare, very great merit, Marya Alexeevna! Millions of people, Marya Alexeevna, are more harmful than you to themselves and others, though they do not look as terrible as you. Among those who are not good, you are better than others because you are not reckless and obtuse. I would be glad to wipe you off the face of the earth, but I respect you. You do not spoil anything. Now you are occupied with evil things because your environment demands it, but if you had a different environment, you too would gladly become harmless, even useful, because you do not want to do evil without financial gain, and if it were advantageous, you could do what you liked, perhaps, therefore, even act honorably and nobly if it were necessary. You are capable of it, Marya Alexeevna, it is not your fault that that quality is inactive in you, that other, opposite qualities are active in place of it. But you have it, and one cannot say that about everyone. Worthless people are incapable of things. You are only a bad person, not a worthless person. You are also higher than others on a moral scale.

"Are you satisfied, Marya Alexeevna?"

"What should I be satisfied with, my dear fellow? Am I badly off?"

"That's fine, Marya Alexeevna."

PART III, CHAPTER 8

. . . What kind of man was Lopukhov? This is the kind of man he was. He was walking along the Kamennoostrov Avenue in a ragged uniform (on the way back from a lesson for a pittance, two miles away from the school). Toward him comes a dignitary, taking a constitutional, and as a dignitary he comes straight toward him, without moving aside. At that time Lopukhov practiced the following rule: "Except in the case of women, I will not move aside first for anyone." They banged into each other's shoulder. The individual, making a half turn, said, "What a pig you are, you beast," and was ready to continue the edifying discourse, but Lopukhov turned fully toward the individual, picked the individual up bodily and deposited him, very carefully, in the gutter. He stood over him and said, "If you make a move, I'll push you in farther, where the mud is deeper." Two peasants passed by, looked, and praised him. A functionary passed by, looked, did not praise, but smiled broadly. Carriages passed but no one looked out of them. One could not see him lying in the gutter. Lopukhov stood for a while, again picked up the individual, not bodily, but by the hand, raised him, drew him up to the sidewalk, and said: "Alas, dear sir, what have you done? I hope you did not hurt yourself? Will you permit me to wipe you off?" A peasant passed and helped to wipe him off, two townspeople passed and helped to wipe him off, they all wiped the individual and went away.

PART IV, CHAPTER 16

Vera Pavlovna's Fourth Dream

Vera Pavlovna dreams that from the distance a familiar voice—
oh, how familiar now!—reaches her ears, coming ever nearer:

> Wie herrlich leuchtet
> Mir die Natur!
> Wie glänzt die Sonne!
> Wie lacht die Flut![1]

And Vera sees that it is so, it is all like that: a field glimmers
with a golden tint. The field is covered with flowers, hundreds,
thousands of flowers display themselves on bushes that surround the field, a flourishing forest that rises behind the bushes
rustles, and it too displays variegated flowers. A scent carries
from the field, from the meadow, the bushes, from the flowers
that fill the forest. Birds flutter among the branches and thousands of voices are wafted from the branches together with the
scent. And beyond the field, beyond the meadow, bushes and
forest, one again sees similar fields, glimmering with gold,
meadows covered with flowers, and bushes in flower as far as
the distant mountains covered with forests and illuminated by
the sun. Above their peaks, here and there radiant, silver,
golden, purple, transparent clouds lightly tint the clear azure
along the horizon. The sun rises, nature rejoices and is glad-
dened, showers light and warmth, scent and song, love and
bliss into the heart, from the heart pours a song of joy and
bliss, love and goodness—"Oh earth! Oh bliss! Oh love! Oh

[1] Goethe's *Das Mailied.*

love, golden, splendid as the morning clouds above those mountain tops!

> O Erd! O Sonne!
> O glück! O Lust!
> O Lieb, O Liebe,
> So goldenschön,
> Wie Morgenwolken
> Auf jenen Höh'n!

"Now do you know me? Do you know that I am beautiful? But you do not know, none of you knows me in all my beauty. Look, what was, what is, what shall be. Listen, and look:

> Wohl perlet im Glase der purpurne Wein,
> Wohl glänzen due Augen der Gäste.[2]

At the foothills, on the edge of the forest, among the flowering bushes of the tall, thick alleys, a palace arises.

"Let us go there."

They go, they fly there. A sumptuous feast. Wine sparkles in the glasses. It is noisy, and beneath the noise, there are whispers, laughter and hands pressed in secret, and at times a stealthy, silent kiss. "A song, a song! Without a song the joy is incomplete!" A poet rises. His brow and his thought are illuminated by inspiration, Nature tells her secrets to him, she discloses her idea of history. Thousands of years of life sweep into his song in a series of tableaux.

I

The poet's words ring out, and a tableau arises.

Nomads' tents. Sheep, horses and camels graze around the

---

[2] Schiller's *Die Vier Weltalter.*

tents. A forest of olives and figs lies in the distance. Much, much farther, at the edge of the horizon to the northwest, a double chain of high mountains. The mountain tops are covered with snow, the slopes are covered with cedars. But these shepherds are shapelier than cedars, their wives shapelier than palms. Their life of indolent bliss is without care. They have but one object—love. All their days one after the other pass in caresses and love-songs.

"No," says the radiant beauty. "That was not sung of me. I did not exist then. That woman was a slave. I cannot be found where equality does not exist. They called the queen Astarte. There she is."

A sumptuous woman. Heavy golden bracelets hang on her arms and legs. A heavy necklace of pearls and coral mounted in gold is worn around her neck. Her hair is anointed with myrrh. Her face expresses sensuality and servility, her eyes, sensuality and vacuity.

"Obey your master. Sweeten his leisure during the pause between campaigns. You must love him because he has bought you and if you will not love him, he will kill you," she says to the woman who lies before her in the dust.

"You see, it is not I," says the beauty.

II

Again the inspired words of the poet sound. A new tableau appears:

A city. Far to the north and east are mountains; far to the east and south, near on the west, a sea. A marvellous town. The houses in it are not large, and from the outside not elegant. But how many marvellous temples in it! Particularly on the hill at the top of stairs that issue from gates of remarkable size and beauty. The whole hill is covered with temples and public buildings, each one of which would suffice today to magnify the beauty and fame of the most magnificent capital. Thousands of statues stand in the temples and throughout the city, any one of which would suffice to make the museum that possessed it the foremost museum in the world. And how splendid the people who crowd the squares and streets are: each of those youths, each of those girls and young women could serve as models for the statues. An active, lively, gay people, a people whose whole life is bright and elegant. Those houses that do not appear elegant from the outside—what a store of elegance and great capacity for enjoyment they display inside! One could admire each article of furniture, each dish. And all those people, so fine, so able to understand beauty, live for love, live to serve beauty. Now an exile returns to the city that had overthrown his power. He returns to take power—everyone knows it. Why is not a single hand raised against him? In the carriage, a woman of loveliness remarkable even among these beauties rides with him and exhibits him to the people, begging the people to accept him, telling them that she is his patroness. And bowing to her beauty, the people confer upon her lover, Pisistratus, power over them. Now there is a trial. The judges are grim old men. The people may be carried away, but not they. The Areopagus is famous for its merciless strictness, its inexorable impartiality. Gods and goddesses have granted it jurisdiction over their affairs. And now a woman whom all consider guilty of fearful crimes is to appear before it, a woman who must die, the destroyer of Athens. Each judge has already condemned her in his heart. The accused Aspasia appears before them, and they all fall to the ground before her saying "You cannot be condemned, you are too beautiful." Is not that the kingdom of beauty? Is not that the kingdom of love?

"No," says the radiant beauty, "I did not exist then. They worshiped woman, but did not recognize her as their equal. They worshiped her, but only as a source of pleasure. They did not yet recognize her human dignity. I do not exist where there is no respect for woman as a human being. They called that queen Aphrodite. There she is."

There are no adornments on that queen. She is so beautiful, her worshipers did not want her to be clothed, did not want her marvellous contours to be hidden from their enraptured eyes.

What does she say to the woman, almost as beautiful as herself, who throws incense upon her altar?

"Be a source of pleasure to man. He is your master. You live for him, not for yourself."

And her eyes express only the bliss of physical pleasure. Her bearing is proud, and pride shines in her face, but only pride in her physical beauty. And to what sort of a life was woman consigned during her reign? Man shut her up in a harem so that no one but he, her master, could revel in the beauty that belonged to him. She lacked freedom. They had other women, who called themselves free, for they sold their beauty for pleasure, they sold their freedom. No, they did not have freedom. That queen was a half a slave. "Where there is no freedom, happiness does not exist, I do not exist."

III

Again the poet's words sound. A new tableau appears:

An arena before a castle. Around it an amphitheatre with a brilliant crowd of spectators. Knights are in the arena. Above it, on the balcony of the castle, sits a young lady. She holds a scarf in her hand. The winner will receive the scarf and permission to kiss her hand. The knights fight to the death. Torrenburg wins. "Knight, I love you as a sister would. Demand no other love. My heart does not throb at your approach, it does not throb when you recede." "My fate is settled," he says, and journeys to Palestine. The fame of his deeds spreads throughout the Christian world. But he cannot live without seeing the queen of his heart. He returns, he has not found forgetfulness in battle. "Do not knock, knight. She is in a nunnery." He builds himself a hut, from whose windows, unseen by her, he can see her when she opens the window of her cell in the morning. And his whole life consists in waiting, until, beautiful as the sun, she appears at the window. He has no other life than to see the queen of his heart, and he had no other life, until life ran out in him. And when his life dimmed, he sat by the window of his hut and thought only of one thing: Shall I see her again?

"That was not sung of me at all, not at all," says the radiant beauty. "He loved her so long as he did not touch her. When she became his wife, she became his subject. She had to tremble before him. He locked her up, he ceased to love her. He hunted, he left for war, he caroused with his companions, he violated his vassals while his wife was discarded, locked up, despised. At that time man ceased to love a woman he had touched. No, I did not exist then. They called that queen 'Chastity.' There she is."

A modest, gentle, delicate, beautiful woman, more beautiful than Astarte, more beautiful than Aphrodite herself, but pensive, sad, sorrowful. Before her, knees are bent, garlands of white roses are brought her. She speaks: "My soul is sad unto deadly sorrow. A sword has pierced my heart. Do you sorrow as well. You are unhappy. The earth is a vale of tears."

"No, no, I did not exist then," says the radiant beauty.

IV

"No, those queens did not resemble me. They all still continue to rule, though their reign is declining. The birth of each begins the decline of the previous one's reign. And I was only born when the reign of the last of them began to decline. And since my birth their reign has started to decline quite quickly and will cease completely. Among them the successor could never replace her predecessor and so the latter stayed with her. I shall replace them all, they will disappear, and I shall remain alone to rule over the whole world. But they had to rule before me. My reign could not begin without theirs.

"People used to be like animals. They stopped being animals when man started to prize beauty in woman. But woman is weaker than man, and man was coarse. At that time everything was decided by force. A man would master the woman whose beauty he came to prize. She became his possession, his thing. That was Astarte's reign.

"As he developed man started to prize her beauty more than hitherto, began to admire her. But her consciousness had not yet developed. He only prized beauty in her. She could then only think what he told her to. He said that only he was a human being. She was not a human being, she still saw in herself only a pretty treasure that belonged to him. She did not consider herself a human being. That was Aphrodite's reign.

"But now the consciousness that she too was a human being began to awake in her. What sorrow must have gripped her at the manifestation of the slightest thought of her human dignity. After all, she was not yet recognized as a human being. Man still did not want her as a companion in any other form than that of a slave. And she said 'I do not want to be your companion!' Then his passion for her made him beg and submit, and he forgot that he did not consider her a human being, and he loved her, the unattainable, inviolable, chaste maiden. But as soon as she acceded to his supplications, as soon as he touched her—woe to her! She was in his hands, and these hands were stronger than hers. He was coarse and he turned her into his slave and despised her. Woe to her! That was the maiden's sorrowful reign.

"But centuries passed. My sister—do you know her?—she who started to appear to you before I did, she did her work. She had always existed, she existed before everyone, she already existed when people were created, and she always worked indefatigably. Her work was hard, success slow, but she worked and worked, and success grew. Man became more intelligent, woman more and more firmly recognized herself as a human being equal to him. And then came the time when I was born.

"That was recently, oh, that was very recently. Do you know who first felt that I had been born and said it to others?

Rousseau said it in his *La Nouvelle Héloïse*. In it, through it, people heard about me for the first time.

"And from that time my reign spreads. As yet I still rule over a small number. But it spreads quickly, and you can already fore-see the time when I shall rule over the whole world. Only then will people feel completely how beautiful I am. Now those who admit my power cannot yet obey all my will. They are sur-rounded by a crowd hostile to my force. The masses would tor-ment them, would poison their lives, if they had known and fulfilled my will completely. I need happiness, I don't want any kind of suffering, and I tell them: 'Do nothing that will make them torment you. Know my will now only to the extent that you can know it without harm to yourselves.' "

"But can I know all of you?"

"Yes, you can. Your situation is very happy. You have nothing to fear. You can do anything you like. And if you know my will completely, my will desires nothing that will harm you. You do not have to desire, you will desire nothing for which those who do not know me might torment you. You are even now satisfied with what you have. You do not think, nor will you think of any-thing or anyone else. I can disclose myself to you completely."

"Tell me your name yourself, you told me the names of the preceding queens, but you have not yet once named yourself."

"You want me to tell you my name? Look at me, listen to me."

V

"Look at me, listen to me. Do you recognize my voice? Do you recognize my face? Have you seen my face?"

No, she had not yet seen her face, had not seen it at all. Why did it seem to her that she saw it? She has talked with her for a year, has kissed her, has seen her so frequently, that radiant beauty, the beauty does not hide for her, she does not hide from it, but rather continually appears before her.

"No, I have not seen you, I have not seen your face. You appeared before me, I saw you, but you were surrounded by a radiance. I could not see you, I could only see that you were the most beautiful of all. I hear your voice, but I only hear that it is the most beautiful voice of all."

"Look. For you, for this minute, I shall dim the radiance of my aureole and my voice will sound to you for this minute without the fascination I always give it. For a minute I shall stop being a queen for you. Did you see, did you hear? Did you recognize me? Enough, I am again a queen, and henceforth shall always remain a queen."

She is again surrounded with all the glitter of her radiance, and again her voice is inexpressibly ravishing. But in that minute, when she ceased being a queen in order to let herself be recognized, was it really so? Did Vera Pavlovna really see that face, really hear that voice?

"Yes," says the queen. "You wanted to know who I was and you found out. You wanted to know my name. I have no name apart from her in whose guise I appear. My name is her name. You have seen who I was. There is nothing higher than man, there is nothing higher than woman. I am she in whose guise I appear, who loves, who is loved."

Yes, Vera Pavlovna saw. It was she herself, it was she herself, but a goddess. The goddess's face was her own face, was her real face, whose features are so far from perfection. Every day she sees many faces more beautiful than hers. It was her face illuminated by the radiance of love, more beautiful than any ideal bequeathed to us by the sculptors of antiquity and the great painters of painting's great era, yes, she herself, but illuminated by the radiance of love. In Petersburg, where there is so little beauty, there are hundreds of faces more beautiful than hers. But she, she is more beautiful than the Venus de Milo, more beautiful than all the beauties known hitherto.

"In a mirror you see yourself such as you are by yourself without me. In me you see yourself as you are seen by one who loves you. For him I merge into you. For him there is nothing more beautiful than you. For him all ideals dim before you. Is it not so?"

It is so, oh, it is so!

VI

"Now you know who I am. Learn, too, what I am.

"In me is the sensuous delight that was in Astarte. She is the ancestress of all us other queens that replaced her. In me is the rapture in the contemplation of beauty that was in Aphrodite. In me is the reverence before purity that was in 'Chastity.'

"But in me all that is not as it was in them but fuller, higher, more forceful. What 'Chastity' possessed is united in me with that possessed by Astarte and that possessed by Aphrodite. And uniting in me with other forces, each of these forces becomes more powerful and better through this union. But more, much more power and splendor are given to each of these forces in me by that new element which is in me, which did not exist in a single one of the preceding queens. That new element in me, by which I am distinguished from them, is the equality of rights in lovers, and equal relationship between them as people, and from this single new element everything in me is much, oh much more beautiful, than it was in them.

"When man recognizes woman's equality of rights, he renounces the view of her as his property. Then she loves him, as he loves her, only because she wants to love, and if she does not want to, he has no rights over her or she over him. Hence Freedom exists in me.

"From equality of rights and freedom, even those elements in me that existed in the preceding queens acquire a new meaning, a greater splendor, a splendor unknown before me, and one that makes everything that existed before me seem insignificant.

"Before me sensual delight was not fully known, because without the free inclination of both lovers, neither of them experiences radiant rapture. Before me complete rapture in the

contemplation of beauty was unknown, because radiant rapture
in its contemplation cannot exist, unless beauty discloses itself
willingly. Without free inclination, both enjoyment and admiration pale in comparison with their existence in me.

"My chastity is purer than the 'Chastity' that is considered
only physical purity. I am pure in heart. I am free, for I lack de-
ceit and pretense. I do not say what I do not feel, I do not kiss
without sympathetic feeling.

"But that new element in me, which gives a greater splendor
to that which existed in the preceding queens, it alone creates a
splendor in me that is higher than everything. A master feels constrained in the presence of a servant, a servant is constrained before his master. Man is completely free only with his equal. With
a lower being, one is bored. Full gaiety can only exist when one
is with an equal. For this reason even man did not know the full
joy of love before me. What he felt before me was not worth
calling joy. It was but a momentary intoxication. And woman,
how pitiful she was before me! She was then a dependent, slav-
ish creature, she lived in fear, before me she knew too little the
meaning of love. Where there is fear, love does not exist.

"Therefore, if you wish to express what I am in one word,
that word is equality. Without it physical delights, ecstasy in
beauty are dull, gloomy, foul. Without it there is no purity of
heart, there is only the deception of physical purity. From it,
from equality, also stems freedom in me, without which I cannot
exist.

"I have told you everything that you may tell others, everything that I am now. But at present my kingdom is as yet small,
I must still protect mine from the calumnies of those who do not
know me, I may still not divulge my complete will to everyone.
I shall tell it to everyone when my kingdom will extend over all
men, when everyone will be beautiful in body and pure in heart,
then will I disclose all my beauty to them. But you, your fate is
particularly auspicious. I will not trouble you, I will not harm
you by telling you what I shall be when everyone will be worthy

to acknowledge me their queen, not merely a few, as now. To you alone I shall divulge the secrets of my future. Swear that you will say nothing, and listen."

VII

■ ■ ■ ■ ■ ■ ■ ■ ■ ■ ■ ■ ■ ■ ■ ■ ■ ■

                                                                    1

■ ■ ■ ■ ■ ■ ■ ■ ■ ■ ■ ■ ■ ■ ■ ■ ■ ■

VIII

"Oh, my love, now I know your entire will. I know what it will be. But how will it be? How will people live then?"

"I cannot tell you that alone. For that I need my older sister's aid, she, who appeared to you long ago. She is my sovereign and my servant. I can only be what she makes of me, but she works for me. Sister, come to my aid."

The sister of her sisters, the bride of her bridegrooms appears.

"Greetings, sister," she says to the queen. "Are you here too?" she says to Vera Pavlovna. "You wish to see how people will live when my pupil, the queen, will reign over everyone? Look."

A building, an enormous, enormous building, such as are now in but a few capitals, and those the very largest—or no, there is not a single one like that now! It stands in the midst of fields and meadows, gardens and woods. The fields grow our grains, only not as they were with us, but very thick, very abundant. Is that really wheat? Who has ever seen such ears of wheat? Who has ever seen such grains? Only in a hothouse would it be possible to grow such ears with such grain now. The fields are our fields. But such flowers now exist only in flower gardens. Gardens, lemons and oranges, peaches and apricots—

---

[1] Clearly an ineffable vision! (R. E. M.)

how can they grow in the fresh air? Oh, but those are columns around them, they are open for the summer. Yes, that is a hothouse open for the summer. The groves are our groves, oak and linden, maple and elm. Yes, the groves are the same as our present ones. They are very carefully maintained, there is not a single diseased tree among them. The groves are the same, but only they have remained as they are now. And that building, what kind of architecture is that? We have none like that now. Yes, it is already hinted at in the palace that stands on Saidenham Hill. Glass and steel, steel and glass, and that is all. No, that is not all, that is only the shell of the building, that is its exterior walls. But there, inside, there is a real house, an enormous house. It is covered by this crystal and steel building as by a sheath. It is surrounded by broad galleries on every floor. What graceful architecture in that inner house, what small pillars between windows. And the windows are huge, tall, the whole height of the wall! Its stone walls look like a row of pilasters making a frame for the windows that look out upon the balconies. But what kind of floors and ceilings are these? What are these doors and window frames made of? What is that? Silver? Platinum? And even the furniture is constructed almost entirely of that same material. Wooden furniture is merely a whim here, it is here only for variety. But what is the rest of the furniture made of, and the floors and ceilings? "Try to move this armchair," says the older queen. That metallic furniture is lighter than our walnut furniture. But what kind of metal is that? Ah, now I remember, Sasha showed me a plank of it. It was as light as glass, and earrings and brooches made from it already exist. Yes, Sasha said that sooner or later aluminum would replace wood, and perhaps even stone. But how rich all this is! Aluminum everywhere, and all the spaces between windows are hung with mirrors. And what rugs on the floor! There in that hall half the floor is uncovered; one can see it is made of aluminum. "You see, there it has a dull finish, so that it won't be too slippery. Children play there, and grown-ups also. In that hall the floor is also uncovered, for dancing." And there are tropical trees and flowers everywhere. The whole house is a huge winter garden.

But who lives in this house that is more splendid than a palace? "Many people live there, very many. Come, we will take a look at them." They go out on the balcony that leads off the gallery on the top floor. How could Vera Pavlovna have failed to notice before? "Groups of people are scattered throughout those fields. Everywhere there are men and women, old people, young people and children, all together. But mostly young people; there are few old men, even fewer old women, there are more children than old people, but nonetheless not very many. More than half the children stayed home to occupy themselves with the housework. They do almost all the housework. They like very much to do it. A few old women are with them. There are so few old men and women because they become old very late here. Life is healthy and quiet here. It preserves freshness." Almost all the groups working in the fields are singing. But what kind of work are they doing? Ah, they are gathering the wheat. How quickly their work goes! And why should it not go quickly, why should they not sing? Machines do almost everything for them, they reap, and bind sheaves, and carry them away. Almost all that people have to do is walk, or ride, and drive the machines. And how comfortable they have made themselves. The day is very hot, but to them, of course, it does not matter. A large canopy is spread over that part of the field where they are working. As the work moves on, so does it—how cool they have made themselves! Why shouldn't they work quickly and joyfully, why shouldn't they sing? I too would start reaping under those conditions! And songs, one song after another, unknown songs, new ones. Now they have remembered one of ours, too. I know the song:

> You and I will live in riches,
> These people are our friends,

Whatever your heart may desire,
With them I can all acquire.[1]

But now the work is finished. They are all going to the building.
"Let us go into the hall again to see how they dine," says the
older sister. They go into the largest of the huge halls. It is half-
filled with tables, and the tables are already set. "How many of
them there are! How many diners will there be?" "A thousand
or more. Not everyone is here. Whoever likes may dine privately,
in his quarters." Those old women and men, those children who
did not go into the fields prepared all that. "To prepare food, do
the housework, clean up the rooms—that work is too easy for
other hands," says the older sister. "It is only for those who cannot yet do, or can no longer do any other work." What splendid
tableware—all aluminum and crystal. Flowers are set in the center of the broad tables, the food is already on the table, the
workers enter and everybody sits down at table, both the workers and those who prepared dinner. "But who will serve the
food?" "When, during the meal? Why? After all, there are only
five or six courses. Those that have to be served hot are put in
places where they will not cool off. Do you see, in the hollow
places—those are steam trays," says the older sister. "You live
well, you like to eat well. Do you frequently dine that well?" "A
few times a year." "That is their regular fare. Whoever likes,
may have better food, whatever he wants. But then there is an
additional charge. But whoever is satisfied with the common
fare need not pay at all. And everything is done that way. Whatever everyone can afford is gotten free. For every special thing or
whim, there is a charge."

"Is that really us? Is that really our country? I heard a song
of ours, they speak Russian." "Yes, you see that river nearby?
That is the Oka. Those people are we. After all, we are both
Russians!" "And you accomplished all that?" "That was all

[1] Kol'tsov's *Flight*.

done for me, but I inspired it, I inspired its completion, but it is she, my older sister who does it, she is the workman, and I only enjoy it." "And will everyone live that way?" "Everyone, says the older sister, for everyone there will be eternal spring and summer, eternal happiness. But we have only shown you the end of my part of the day, of worktime, and the beginning of hers. We shall look at them again on an evening two months hence."

IX

The flowers have started to fade. The leaves are beginning to fall off the trees. The scene is becoming cheerless. "You see, it would be boring to look at this, it would be boring to live here," says the younger sister. "I don't like to live that way." "The halls are empty, there is no one in the fields or gardens either," says the older sister. "I have arranged all that according to the will of my sister, the queen." "Is the palace then really empty?" "Yes, after all, it is cold and damp here, why should people remain. Out of two thousand people only ten or twenty eccentrics have remained here now, to whom it seemed a pleasant change to stay here for once, in a remote corner, in isolation, to look at a northern autumn. In a short time, when winter comes, there will constantly be new people here. Little groups of people who like winter excursions will arrive to pass several days of winter here."

"But where are they now?" "Oh, everywhere that it is warm and pleasant," says the older sister. "When it is pleasant here and there is a great deal of work, a multitude of guests of all sorts comes here for the summer from the south. We were in a house populated entirely by a group from your country. But there are many buildings built for guests, and in still others, guests from foreign lands and their hosts live together. Everyone may choose whatever group he wishes. But you who in the summer receive many guests, helpers in your work, you yourself leave for the south during the six or seven bad months of the year. But there is a special region in the south of your land where the greater part of your people go. And that part is called 'The New Russia.' " "Is that where Odessa and Kherson are?" "That was in your time, but now, look, that is where New Russia is."

Mountains, covered with gardens. Narrow valleys and broad precipices lie between the mountains. "Those mountains were formerly bare cliffs," says the older sister. "Now they are covered with a thick layer of earth, and forests of the tallest trees grow on them among gardens. At their bottom, in the damp hollows, there are coffee plantations. Somewhat higher there are dates, palms and figs. Vineyards are interspersed among sugar cane plantations. There is some wheat in the fields but mostly rice." "What country is that?" "Let us rise up higher for a minute. You will see its borders." In the distant northeast there are two rivers, which flow together due east from Vera Pavlovna's observation point. Farther to the south, still in the same southeastern direction, there is a long and broad bay. The land extends far to the south, continually broadening to the south between that bay and the long, thin bay that forms its eastern border. There is a thin isthmus between the thin eastern bay and the sea that lies far to the northeast. "But we are in the center of the desert," says the astounded Vera Pavlovna. "Yes, in the center of the former desert. But now, as you can see, that whole expanse from the north, from that large river to the northeast, has already been turned into a fertile land, into such a land as that strip along the sea to the north of it once used to be and has now become again, the strip that was called of old 'the land of milk and honey.' As you see we are not very far from the southern border of that cultivated expanse. The mountainous part of the peninsula still remains a sandy, barren steppe, such as the whole peninsula was in your time. With each passing year, people, you Russians, push the edge of the desert farther and farther to the south. Other people work in other countries. Everyone has ample room and ample work, both space and abundance. Yes, from the big river in the northeast up to the middle of the peninsula, the whole expanse is covered with vegetation and flowers. Throughout the whole region, as in the north, huge buildings stand two or three miles from each other, as though they were numerous huge chessmen on a gigantic chessboard." "Let us go down to one of them," says the older sister.

It is the same sort of huge, crystal house, but its columns are white. "They are made of aluminum," says the older sister, "because after all it is very warm here. White heats up less in the sun. It is somewhat more expensive than iron, but more comfortable for local conditions." But they have thought of something else as well. For a considerable distance around the crystal palace there are rows of thin, extremely high columns, and on top of them, high above the palace, covering the whole palace and for a half mile around it, stretches a white canopy. "It is constantly sprinkled with water," says the older sister. "Look, from each column a little fountain rises above the canopy and sprays water upon it. As a result it is cool there. You see, they change the temperature as they like." "But what if someone likes the heat and the bright sun that shines here?" "Do you see, in the distance there are pavilions and tents. Everyone may live as he likes. I am striving toward that goal, I work only to attain that." "Then there must be cities left for those who want to live in cities?" "There are not very many people like that. There are fewer cities left than there were before and then almost only to serve as centers of communication and the exchange of goods, near the best harbors, in other centers of communication, but these cities are larger and more splendid than the earlier ones. Everyone goes there for a few days, for variety. A large part of their population constantly changes. People go there for work, for a short time." "But what if someone wants to live there constantly?" "They can live there, as you live in your St. Petersburgs, Londons, Parises—what business is it of anyone? Who would stop them? Let everyone live as he likes. Only the overwhelming majority, ninety-nine out of a hundred, live in the manner shown to you by my sister and me, because that is more pleasant and advantageous for them. But enter the palace, the evening is already quite far gone, it is time to look at them."

"No, I want to know how all this was done, first." "What?" "The turning of that barren desert into an abundant land where almost all of us spend two-thirds of the year." "How was it done? What was so hard about it? After all, it was not done in one year or in ten years. I made the work progress gradually. From the northeast, from the banks of the great river, from the northwest, from the coast of the large sea—they have so many powerful machines—they brought loam, it bound the sand, they dug canals, irrigation trenches, greenery started to appear and with it more moisture in the air. They advanced step by step, several miles, sometimes only a mile a year, just as now they keep going farther south. What is so special about it? It is just that they have become intelligent, started to turn to their own use the enormous quantity of means and force that they wasted previously, or used to their own detriment. After all, I do not work and teach in vain. It was only difficult for people to understand what was useful. In your time they were still such savages, so coarse, cruel, imprudent. But I kept teaching them. And when they started to understand, fulfilling the work was no longer difficult. You know that I never demand anything difficult. You do something in my way, for me is that so bad?" "No." "Of course not. Just remember your own workshop. Did you have extensive means, more than others had?" "No, what kind of means did we have?" "Nevertheless your sewing women have ten times more comfort, enjoy life twenty times as much, experience unpleasantness a hundred times less than others who have the same means you had. You yourself proved that even in your time people could live quite untrammelled. One only had to be intelligent, to know how to settle oneself, to find out how to use one's means most effectively." "Yes, yes. I know that." "Go see for a little while longer how people live some time after they started to understand what you have already understood."

X

They enter the house. Another such enormous, splendid hall. The evening is in full swing and merriment. Three hours have already elapsed since sunset. The very height of merriment. How brightly the hall is lit, though by what means? Neither candelabra nor chandeliers are visible anywhere. Ah, that's where! In the cupola of the hall there is a large square of dull glass, and the light pours through it. Of course, that is how it should be. Just like the sun—white, clear, soft—well, yes, that is electric light. In the hall there is a crowd of about a thousand, but a crowd three times as large could easily be accommodated there. "And sometimes, when guests visit," says the radiant beauty, "there are even more." "Then what is that? Isn't that a ball? Is that really an ordinary workday evening?" "Of course." "But according to today's standards, that would be a royal ball, so luxuriously are the women dressed. Yes, the times have changed, that is even apparent by the style of the clothes. There are also some ladies in clothes like ours, but it is clear that they dressed that way for variety, for a joke. Yes, they are joking, jesting at their own costumes. The others are wearing other costumes, of the most various kinds, various eastern and southern styles. They are all more graceful than our style. But a costume similar to that worn by Greek ladies during Athens' most elegant era predominates— very light and loose, and the men also wear a long garment without a waist, something like a mantle or toga. It is clear that that is their habitual domestic attire, how modest and beautiful that garment is! How softly and elegantly it outlines their bodies, how it enhances their graceful movements! And what an orchestra—more than a hundred musicians and especially, what a choir!" "Yes, in all of Europe you did not have ten voices comparable to those hundreds that are just in this hall, and in every other hall there are as many more. The way of life is not the same, it is very healthy and at the same time very elegant and therefore both chests and voices are better," says the radiant beauty. But the people in the orchestra and chorus constantly change. Some leave, others come to take their place. Some go to dance, others leave the dance to play.

Their evening is an ordinary, workday evening. They enjoy themselves and dance like that every evening. But when did I ever see such energetic merrymaking? But why should their merriment not have an energy unknown to us? They have worked a great deal in the morning. Whoever has not worked enough, did not prepare the nerve that would let him experience the merriment fully. And now the merriment of simple people, when they have occasion to enjoy themselves, is more joyous, lively and fresh than ours. But our simple people have meager means for merriment and here means are more ample than ours. And our simple people's merriment is troubled by the memory of inconvenience and privation, of poverty and suffering, is troubled by a foreboding of the same thing in the future, it is a passing hour in which need and grief are forgotten, though can need and grief really be forgotten completely? Will the desert sand not be dissipated? Will not the marsh's miasma contaminate even the small strip of good earth and good air that lies between the desert and the marsh? While here neither the memory nor the danger of need or grief exists. Here only the memory of free and willing work, of satisfaction, good and enjoyment exist, here only the expectation of the same things in the future exists. What a comparison! And moreover, our workers' nerves are only strong because they are capable of enduring much merriment, but they are coarse, unreceptive. While here nerves are as strong as our workers' nerves, and as developed, as impressionable as ours. A readiness for merriment, a healthy, strong desire for it, such as we do not possess, such as is vouchsafed only to powerful health and physical labor, is united in these people with all the delicacy of feeling we possess. They have our whole moral development together with our strong workers' physical development. Obviously their merriment, their enjoyment, their passion are more lively and stronger, broader and sweeter than ours. Lucky people!

No, real happiness is not yet known, because the kind of life necessary for that does not yet exist, nor do such people. Only such people can enjoy themselves fully and to the full delight of enjoyment. How they bloom with health and power, how shapely and graceful they are, how energetic and expressive their features are! They are all happy, handsome men and women, leading a free life of work and enjoyment, oh, the lucky ones, the fortunate ones!

Half of them noisily enjoy themselves in the huge hall, but where is the other half? "Where are the others?" she asks the radiant beauty. "They are everywhere. Many are in the theatre, some as actors, others as musicians, still others as spectators, each as he likes. Some have scattered to the auditoriums, the museums, or are sitting in the library; some in the garden alleys, others in their rooms, either to rest alone, or with their children. But the greatest number, the greatest—that is my secret. You saw in the hall how their cheeks burnt, how their eyes shone. You saw that they left and that they returned. It was I who drew them away, here is a room for each and all—my shelter. In it my mysteries are inviolable, the doors are curtained, luxurious carpets deaden the sound, there there is quiet, there there is mystery. They returned—it was I who brought them back from the realm of my mysteries to light merriment. I reign here.

"I reign here. Here everything is done for me! Work is the preparation of fresh feelings and forces for me, merriment is a preparation for me, a rest after me. Here I am the goal of life, here I am all life."

XI

"In my sister, the queen, lies life's greatest joy, says the older sister, but you see, here there is every kind of joy, whatever anyone desires. Here everyone lives as he likes best, here each and everyone has complete will, free will.

"What we have shown you will not soon exist in its full development as you saw it now. Many generations will pass before that which you previewed here will be fully accomplished. No, not many generations. My work is progressing quickly now, more quickly each year, but nevertheless you will not enter into my sister's completed realm. At least you have seen it, you know the future. It is radiant, it is beautiful. Tell it to all: that is what lies in the future, the future is radiant and beautiful. Love it, strive toward it, work for it, bring it closer, transfer into the present as much of it as you can. Your life will be radiant and good, rich in happiness and enjoyment, to the extent that you have been able to incorporate the future in it. Strive for it, work for it, bring it closer, transfer into the present from it everything that you can."

Excerpts from

Winter Notes on Summer Impressions

by

FYODOR DOSTOEVSKY

CHAPTER 5

Baal

. . . I spent only eight days in London, and, at least on the surface, what broad spectacles, what clear yet individual settings, that do not only conform to a fixed plan, impressed themselves in my mind. Everything is so huge and sharp in its individuality. One could even be deceived in this individuality. Each sharply differentiated thing, each contradiction, exists side by side with its antithesis and stubbornly goes hand in hand with it, contradicting each other and, apparently, in no way excluding each other. Everything here, apparently, stubbornly insists upon its own way and exists in its own fashion and, apparently, does not harm anything else. Yet at the same time, here too the same stubborn, obscure and by now chronic struggle, the struggle unto death between the whole Western world's individualistic bent and the necessity to live together at least in some form, to create at least some communal form, and to set up house in a single anthill: at least one can turn to the anthill, only in order to live there without eating each other up—without that we would turn to cannibalism. In this respect we find, on the other hand, the same thing that exists in Paris as well: the same desperate striving to remain *in status quo* out of desperation, to rip out of oneself by the roots all hopes and desires, to curse one's future, in which perhaps the foremost leaders of progress have insufficient faith, and to bow down to Baal. Please do not be carried away by the fancy oratory, however. All this is consciously recognized only in the minds of the most advanced consciously thinking people, while they are unconsciously, instinctively recognized in people's life functions. But the Parisian bourgeois, for example, is almost consciously quite satisfied, and is convinced that all is as it should be, and would even beat you if you question the fact that all is as it should be, he would beat you because until now he is still somewhat afraid, despite all his self-assuredness. While the same may be true in London, yet what broad, overwhelming spectacles! Even on the surface, what a difference from Paris. That city, as unfathomable as the ocean, bustling day and night; the shrieking and howling of machines, those iron machines passing above the houses (and soon to pass under them as well); that boldness of enterprise, that apparent disorder which in actuality is the highest degree of bourgeois order; that polluted Thames, that air saturated with coal dust; those splendid squares and parks; those fearful sections of the city like Whitechapel, with its half-naked, savage and hungry population. The city with its millions and its worldwide trade, the Crystal Palace, the International Exposition. Yes, the exposition is striking. You feel the terrible force that united here all these innumerable people drawn from all corners of the globe, into one fold. You recognize a gigantic idea. You feel that something is almost achieved here already, that this represents a victory, a triumph. You almost seem to begin to fear something. No matter how independent you may be you begin to be terrified for some reason. "Isn't this really the ideal that has already been attained?" you think. "Isn't this the goal? Isn't that really the 'one fold'?" Must one not really accept this as the ultimate truth and to become silent forever? This is all so triumphant, majestic and proud, that it takes your breath away. You look at these hundreds of thousands, these millions of people, who stream here humbly from corners of the globe, people who come with a single thought, who quietly and persistently mill around that colossal palace, and you feel that something final has taken place here, something has taken place and ended. That is some sort of biblical spectacle, something like Babylon, some prophecy out of the Apocalypse coming to pass before your very eyes. You feel that a great amount of eternal spiritual fortitude and denial would be necessary in order not to submit, not to capitulate to the impression, not bow down to the fact and not worship Baal, that is, not to accept the existing as your ideal.

"But that is nonsense," you will say, "a sick man's ravings, nerves, exaggeration. No one would stop at that, and no one would take it for his ideal. Moreover, hunger and slavery are not easy to bear, and they prompt negation and breed skepticism better than anything else. Well-fed dilettantes, taking a walk for their own pleasure, of course, can create spectacles out of the Apocalypse and thereby soothe their nerves, exaggerating and distorting every phenomenon in order to arouse strong feelings in themselves."

"All right," I answer. "Let us suppose that I was carried away by the setting, I will agree to that. But if you had seen how proud the powerful spirit that created that colossal setting was, and how proudly that spirit was convinced of his victory and triumph, then you would have trembled for his pride, persistence and blindness, you would have trembled for that over which this spirit hovers and rules. In the presence of such colossal things, in the presence of such gigantic pride in the ruling spirit, even a hungry soul frequently is benumbed, makes peace, submits, seeks salvation in gin and vice and begins to believe that everything should be so for everyone. The fact overwhelms, the mass becomes ossified and grabs at any escape, and even if skepticism were to rise, it would gloomily and with a curse seek salvation in something like Mormonism . . ."

CHAPTER 6

An Essay on the Bourgeois

. . . Western man talks about brotherhood *[fraternité]* as the great moving force of civilization, but he does not realize that there is no place to obtain brotherhood if it does not exist in reality. What can be done? One has to create brotherhood at all cost. But it seems that one cannot create brotherhood, because it creates itself, comes of itself, is found in nature. But in French nature, in Western nature generally, it does not readily appear. Instead you find there a principle of individuality, a principle of isolation, intense self-preservation, of personal gain, self-definition in terms of one's own *I*, in placing this *I* in opposition to all nature and all other people, as an autonomous, independent principle completely equal and equally valuable to everything that exists outside it. Well, such a position cannot bring brotherhood about. Why? Because in brotherhood, in real brotherhood, individual personality, the *I*, cannot trouble about its equality of value and importance to *everything else*, and rather that *everything else*, must come *of itself* to that personality that demands equal rights, to that individual *I* and by itself, without his requests, would have to recognize him as equal in value and importance to itself, that is, to everything else that exists in the world. Moreover, that rebellious and demanding personality would have to sacrifice all of its *I* to society first of all, and not demand its rights but rather resign them all to society with no strings attached. But Western personality is not used to such procedure. It fights for what it demands, it demands rights, it wants to *separate itself*—well, brotherhood does not emerge out of such conditions. Of course, there could be a regeneration. But such regeneration would be accomplished after thousands of years, since ideas like those must first be incarnated in flesh and blood to become reality. Tell me, does one really have to be without individuality to be happy? Does redemption lie in impersonality? On the contrary, on the contrary, say I, not only must one not be without individuality, but that is just what one has to become, an individual, even more and to a higher degree than it is known in the West today. Understand me: voluntary, completely conscious and totally unconstrained self-sacrifice for the benefit of all, is, in my opinion, a token of the greatest achievement of individuality, of its greatest power, its greatest self-control, the greatest freedom of its own will. To sacrifice one's life willingly for others, to be crucified, burned at the stake for others willingly, can only be done at the highest point of the attainment of individuality. A highly developed individuality, completely convinced of its right to be individual, no longer fearing anything for itself, cannot possibly do anything else with its individuality, that is, can find no greater use for itself than to give itself up entirely for others, so that others too may become equally autonomous and happy individualities. That is nature's law. Normal man aspires to it. But there is a tiny hitch here, the tiniest little hitch, which, however, will destroy and ruin the whole thing if it occurs. It consists in the presence of even the smallest calculation for the benefit of one's own advantage. For example, I sacrifice myself completely for others. Well, that is what is required, that I sacrifice myself completely, entirely, without any thought of advantage, without in the slightest thinking that here now I am sacrificing myself entirely for society, and that therefore society will in turn give itself entirely to me. One has to sacrifice oneself precisely in such a way as to give up everything and even wish that nothing will be given to you for it in turn, that as a consequence no one will be put to any loss through your action. But how can that be done? After all, it is just like trying not to think of a polar bear. Try setting yourself the task of not thinking of a polar bear and you will see that the cursed animal keeps coming to mind every minute. What can be done? There is absolutely nothing to be done, it *has to do it by itself, to be in one's nature,* to be contained unconsciously in the nature of the whole race. In short, in order for a brotherly, loving principle to exist, one has to love. One must be drawn instinctively to brotherhood, community, harmony, and one must be drawn, without paying attention to the age-old sufferings of the nations, without paying attention to the savage crudeness and ignorance deeply rooted in the nation, without paying attention to age-old slavery, to foreign invasions, in short, the need for brotherly communality exists in man's nature, that he is born with it or that he had assimilated it from time immemorial. Of what would this brotherhood consist, if we were to explain it in rational, conscious language? In this, that each separate individual would of himself, without any coercion, without any advantage to himself would say to society, "We are only strong when united, take me completely if you need me, do not consider me when making your laws, do not trouble yourself about me in any way, I cede all my rights to you, and, if you please, dispose of me. That would be my greatest joy, to sacrifice myself completely and that you would suffer no harm from it. I will annihilate myself, melt into the general mass, so long as your brotherhood remains and flourishes." And brotherhood, on the other hand, would have to say, "You give us too much. We have no right to take what you offer us, as you yourself said that your whole joy consists in that. But what can be done if our heart constantly aches for your happiness as well? Take everything from us. We will strive every minute, with all our power, to assure you as much personal freedom, as much opportunity to reveal yourself, as possible. Have no fear of any enemies now, neither people nor nature. We all support you, we all guarantee your security, we work for you indefatigably, because we are brothers, we are all your brothers, and we are many and strong. You can be completely tranquil and bold, fear nothing and depend upon us."

After that, of course, there is no longer any reason for wanting to separate oneself; everything would now be shared of itself. Love one another, and all this shall be given unto you.

Now there, after all, is a real utopia for you, gentlemen! Everything is founded on feeling, on nature, not on intellect. After all, that almost seems to slight reason. What do you think? Is it a utopia or not?

But just the same, what is a socialist to do, if Western man does not possess that brotherly principle, but, on the contrary, possesses a principle of singleness, of individuality, constantly standing apart, demanding its rights sword in hand? The socialist, seeing that there is no brotherhood, begins to exhort brotherhood. Because brotherhood does not exist, he wants to create, to make brotherhood. In order to make rabbit stew, you have to have a rabbit first. But there is no rabbit, that is, there is no nature capable of brotherhood, no nature believing in brotherhood, which of itself strains toward brotherhood. In despair the socialist starts to make, to define the brotherhood of the future, to calculate its size and shape, tempts one with its advantages, talks, teaches, explains how much advantage would accrue to each from this brotherhood, how much each will gain. He will define what each individual would look like, what his tasks would be and will determine in advance the list of the earth's blessings, to what extent each individual will merit them, and how much each must willingly bring to the community, at the expense of his own individuality. But what kind of brotherhood is that, when what everyone must do and what he will merit is divided and defined in advance? However, the formula "One for all and all for one" has already been proclaimed. And, of course, one could not even conceive of anything better than that, the more so as that formula is bodily taken from a little book known to everyone. But now they have started to apply that formula to reality, and after six months the brothers dragged their founder Cabet to court. It is said that the Fourierists have taken the last 900,000 francs of their capital, and are apparently trying to found a brotherhood. They are not successful. Of course, there is a great attraction to live if not in brotherly fashion, at least simply on some rational basis, that is to live well, with everything guaranteed to you and only work and acquiescence demanded in turn from you. But there is another joker here. It seems that man is guaranteed everything, is promised food, drink, work, and in turn only the smallest iota of his personal freedom is asked for the general good, the smallest, smallest iota. No, man does not want to live according to those calculations, he will not surrender the single iota. It seems to him, in his stupidity, that it is a prison, and that he would be better off by himself, because he would be completely free that way. And after all, though he is beaten when he is free, though he has no work, though he dies of hunger and has no freedom at all, the queer fellow still prefers his freedom. Of course, all the socialist can do is throw up his hands and tell him that he is a fool, immature, a child, that he does not understand his own advantage. That an ant, some mute, insignificant ant is more intelligent than he, because life in the anthill is good, everything is well ordered, everyone is well fed, happy, each knows what his task is. In short: man is still a long way from the anthill!

Excerpts from Dostoevsky's *Letters*

To his brother Michael, November 19, 1863

. . . Various troubles literally do not leave me a moment to write. I have already had two attacks [of epilepsy] and one of them, the last, was very bad. The new name for the journal, *Truth,* will have no bearing on *the leading article.* An analysis of Chernyshevsky's novel and of Pisemsky's would create a big stir, and most important of all, would be appropriate for the journal. Two contradictory ideas, and both in vogue. Therefore, it will be true. I think that I will write all three articles. (If only I could work in peace for as little as two weeks) . . .

To I. S. Turgenev, 23 December, 1863

Dear and respected Ivan Sergeevich:

P. V. Annenkov told my brother that you did not want to publish "Phantoms" because there is too much of the fantastic in the story. That disturbs us terribly. First of all, I will say frankly that we, that is, my brother and I, are counting on your story. It will help us greatly in the first issue of our journal, which has been *started anew,* and consequently has to make a name for itself. I am forewarning you of that purposely, so that you will not suspect that the reasons I give in the rest of the letter stem only from motives of personal advantage. I will add still another circumstance and assure you of its veracity on my word of honor. We need your story much more than the attraction of your name on the cover.

Now I will tell you a couple of things about your story, based on my impressions of it. Why do you think, Ivan Sergeevich (if you really do think that), that your "Phantoms" are untimely now and will not be understood? On the contrary, mediocrity, after imitating the masters for six years, has brought the positivists to such vulgarity that they would welcome a purely poetical work (a very poetical one). Many will greet it with a certain bewilderment, but a pleasant bewilderment. That is what would happen with everyone who understands anything at all, both in the old and new generation. As for those who understand nothing, do we really have to consider them? You would not believe how they approach literature. Limited utilitarianism—that is all they demand. Write them the most poetic work, they will put it aside for one that describes someone's being whipped. *Poetic truth* is considered rubbish. All one need do is copy facts from reality. Our prose is a terrible lot of Quakerism. After that, there is no point in considering them. The healthy portion of society which is awakening is eager for a bold sally from art. And your "Phantoms" is very bold and it will serve as an example (for all of us) if you are the first to dare present such a sally. The form of "Phantoms" will puzzle people. But their real aspect will provide a solution to all the puzzles (except the puzzlement of fools and those who *do not want* to understand anything except their Quakerism). Incidentally, I know one representative of pure utilitarianism (nihilism) who, though dissatisfied with your novel [*Fathers and Sons*], said she could not put it down, that it made a deep impression. After all, we have a lot of nihilists out of affectation. But the most important thing here is to understand that realistic side. I think that too much is realistic in "Phantoms." That reality is the *sorrow of a cultivated and conscious being living in our day,* a sorrow that you have captured. All of "Phantoms" is permeated by that sorrow. That "sound rings in the mist" and it does well to ring. "Phantoms" is similar to music. And incidentally, how do you look upon music? As enjoyment or as a positive necessity? I think that it is the same language, but capable of expressing what consciousness has *not yet mastered* (not just intelligence, but all of consciousness), and therefore it has a *positive* use. Our utilitarians won't understand that. But those among them who like music have not *given it up* but engage themselves in it as previously.

The form of your "Phantoms" is excellent. After all, if there is anything to be questioned here, then, of course, it is a question of form. And therefore the whole question will be "does fantasy have a right to exist in art?" Well, who can answer such questions! If anything in "Phantoms" can be criticized, it is that it *is not completely* fantastic. It should be even more so. Then it would be more *daring*. A creature who is called a vampire appears in your story. I think that she should not be called that. Annenkov did not agree with me, and presented the argument that there are allusions here to loss of blood, that is, to real forces, and so on. I do not agree with him, either. I am content to have understood—even too tangibly—the sorrow and wonderful shape into which it has been molded, that is, wandering throughout reality *without any relief*. And the *mood* is good, a mood of some kind of tender sorrow, without special force. And the pictures, as the rock, and others, hint at an elemental, still unresolved idea in Nature (the idea that exists throughout Nature), which may someday solve man's questions, but which now only induces sorrow and frightens one still more, though one does not want to tear oneself away from her. No, such an idea is timely now, and such fantastic things are *completely positive*.

To his brother Michael, February 9, 1864

My dear friend, Misha:

I delayed answering you because I really thought I would go to Petersburg at any moment. However, I have been sick for the last two weeks, and lately worse and worse. I had two attacks, although that would not have been too bad, but the worst of it is that I have gotten hemorrhoids in the bladder [sic] and it is very unpleasant. I am afraid I will really get ill. If I do, *then*, of course, I would have to be treated soon. In that case I would leave for Petersburg immediately. I won't risk it now, first, because I am improving a little and second, because I would have to sit in a train for twenty hours, and I cannot sit down at all.

Incidentally, I do not lie down either, but sort of half sit, half stand. . . .

To his brother Michael, February 29, 1864

. . . I have thought up another excellent article on theorizing and the fanaticism of theorizing (of the *Contemporary*). It will not be untimely, especially if they keep harping on us. It will not be a polemical article, but a real work. . . .

To his brother Michael, March 20, 1864

. . . I have started to work on the story. I am trying to get it off my hands as soon as I can, but at the same time I want to make sure that it turns out as good as possible. It is much harder to write it than I had thought. And yet, it is absolutely necessary that it turn out well. It is necessary for *myself*. The story's tone is too strange, it is a sharp and wild tone. Perhaps people will dislike it. Therefore, "poetry" must soften it and carry all before it.

As a result of all this, my work has come to a complete stop. You can imagine the torments I have undergone because of the idea that the first issue will have nothing of mine in it. But it cannot be helped. I finally have to admit it. Until today I tormented myself with the idea that perhaps I would finish in time. There will not be enough with just Turgenev's story. Find anything you can, my dear, and do not spare material. I will have something toward March. I will not hide from you that what I wrote turned out to be bad. I suddenly started to dislike the story. And I have become negligent there myself. I do not know how it will all end. . . .

I will never forgive myself for not finishing it earlier. The whole story is trash, and even at that it was not ready in time. It shows that I have written myself out. And it did not come out right. I have become terribly anxious. . . .

To his brother Michael, March 26, 1864

. . . Some of the articles [in the first two issues] are quite good: "Phantoms" (I think there is a lot of trash in it: something nasty, diseased, senile, *disbelieving* out of weakness, in short, all of Turgenev and his convictions. But the poetry redeems a great deal. I reread it) . . . I am also bewailing [the first part of my *Notes*]. Terrible misprints, and it would have been better not to print the penultimate chapter at all (that chapter where the very idea is stated), than to print it in that form, that is, with sentences left out and contradicting itself. But what is to be done? Those swinish censors left in the passages where I railed at everything and *pretended* to blaspheme; but they deleted the passages where I deduced from all this the *necessity of faith and Christ*. What are they doing, those censors? Are they in league against the government, or something? . . .

To his brother Michael, April 2, 1864

. . . I *probably* will not finish the article this month, and not only that article, but I will not publish anything this month in the critical section . . . I am writing the story now, but it is going badly. My friend, I was ill the greater part of the month, then I got better, but up till now I have not recovered completely. My nerves are ragged and I have not regained my strength yet. My torments *of every kind* are so oppressive that I do not even want to mention them. My wife is dying, *literally*. Every day a moment arrives when we expect her to die. Her sufferings are terrible and tell on me as well because—after all, writing is not mechanical work and I write and write just the same, in the mornings, but it is just beginning. The story is stretching out. Sometimes it seems to me that it will be trash, but still I write with enthusiasm. I do not know how it will turn out. But the thing is, it requires a lot of time. Even if I finish half, I will send it to be set up in type, but I want it all published together—*sine qua non.* In general, there is little time for writing, though it would seem that all my time is my own. But this is not a productive period for me, and sometimes I have other things in mind. And moreover I am afraid that my wife will die soon, and then I will have to interrupt my work. Without that interruption, I think I would be able to finish it. . . .

To his brother Michael, April 5, 1864

. . . If only I have the strength and leisure, and *no interruptions,* my story could be finished this month, but not during the first half. . . . Will I be able to finish the story this month? Judging by all signs—no. And the worst thing is there may be an interruption that does not depend upon me and for whose consequences I cannot answer. Therefore, my dear, I ask you to write to me as soon as possible the *very latest* date by which you must have my story. I will be able to judge from your reply whether or not I can finish. . . .

To his brother Michael, April 9, 1864

. . . I wrote to you that I probably would not finish the story in time. I repeat, Misha: I am so exhausted, so oppressed by circumstances, that I cannot even answer for my physical circumstances at work. . . . The story is growing in scope. It may run to 150 pages, I do not know, and therefore even with the greatest exertion of effort, it can simply not be finished *physically.* What shall we do? Publish it unfinished? Impossible. It cannot be divided. And then I do not know how it will come out, it may be trash, but personally I place great hope in it. It will be a powerful and frank work. It will be the truth. Even if it is bad, it will create a stir. I know it. And it may turn out to be very good. . . . If possible, spare me from the March issue, be good to me. To make up for it, for April you will have both my story of considerable length and a critical article. I swear it *by my head* if only I do not die. Let me finish my story and then you will see what activity I am capable of.

To his brother Michael, April 13, 1864

. . . The story keeps growing in scope. It will probably be effective. I am working as hard as I can, but I move ahead slowly because my time is occupied by other things. The story is divided into three chapters, of which each will be at least 50 pages. The second chapter is in chaos, the third is not yet begun, the first is being revised. The first chapter is 50 pages long and can be revised in about five days. Should we really publish it separately? It will be laughed at, the more so as it loses all its impact without the other two chapters. You know what a musical *transition* is. The same thing occurs here. The first chapter is apparently empty chatter. But suddenly that chatter resolves itself into an unexpected catastrophe in the last two chapters. If you tell me to send only the first chapter, I will. I can still sacrifice such trifles and will send the chapter. . . .

To his brother Michael, April 15, 1864

. . . This morning [my wife] died. . . . I cannot send the story (even the beginning) now in any case. What is to be done? . . .

THE SWALLOWS

by

M. E. Saltykov-Shchedrin

THE SWALLOWS

(A DRAMATIC FABLE)

Cast of Characters

FIRST SWALLOW, an editor of a journal [Michael M. Dostoevsky] [1]

SECOND SWALLOW, a philosopher [N. N. Strakhov]

THIRD SWALLOW, an aesthetician [A. A. Grigor'ev]

FOURTH SWALLOW, a despondent novelist [Fyodor M. Dostoevsky]

FIFTH SWALLOW, a gay novelist (currently absent) [G. P. Danilevsky]

SIXTH SWALLOW, } poets { [N. Gerbel']
SEVENTH SWALLOW } { [F. Berg]

FIRST BAT, clerk in the editorial office

SECOND BAT, watchman

SEVERAL RATS

The set shows an empty, damp cellar; the doors flaunt a sign "Saturn Revived: Chief Editorial Office"; *shelves along the walls; on one of them are several empty tubs, upon which perch swallows; lean, hungry rats run about the floor.*

FIRST SWALLOW. First of all, gentlemen, we must examine our past. Why have they insulted us?

ALL THE SWALLOWS *(together)*. Why have they insulted us?

FIRST SWALLOW. For eight solid months I have not stopped thinking of the question "Why have they insulted us?" for a moment. For more than two years they accused us of being swallows! We met, talked, passed the time, caught flies—

[1] The satire is directed at the Dostoevsky brothers' journal, *The Epoch* (and its predecessor, *Time*). The contributors' names are here indicated in brackets.

what other guarantees could they need? And then, one terrible moment, Second Swallow had the unfortunate idea to fly to some ill-starred region.

ALL THE SWALLOWS *(together, without Second Swallow).* "Suddenly, one of them desired to travel, to fly . . ."

FIRST SWALLOW. At that time a certain Peterson,[2] who had plenty of spare time—but why did they insult us?

SECOND SWALLOW *(justifying himself).* I am the only swallow among countless other swallows who has taken up philosophy. And therefore, as a pupil and follower of Hegel, I supposed . . .

VOICE FROM ABOVE. In the future don't suppose. *(The swallows are terrified.)*

SECOND SWALLOW *(unheedingly continuing his speech).* I supposed . . .

FIRST SWALLOW. Enough. *(Bitterly)* Evidently they do not even let you justify yourself *(Voice from Above:* "And what did you think?") so let us forget the past *(Aside:* "Why did they insult us?"), and occupy ourselves exclusively with the future. First of all, I suppose, we have to agree about our program.

SEVENTH SWALLOW. As you are moulting at the moment, pluck out a quill and give it to First Bat. And so, gentlemen, what shall we say in our policy editorial? Frankly, I would like to leave that to the typesetters' will! *(The swallows emit a weak chirp.)* Are you surprised by that? But I remember very well that in the year *Notes from the Fatherland* was founded, a certain Andrew the Wise said to me: My friend! Though you are but a swallow, when you publish your own journal remember . . .

Soft music is heard. The voice of Mr. Albertini carries in from the street, singing to the tune of "Jadis regna en Normandie":

---

[2] A contributor to the *Moscow News* whose attacks on *Time* brought about the government's suppression of that periodical. The refrain "Why have they insulted us?" is connected with this fact.

In a certain widespread land
Once lived Andrew the Wise;
Not raised as a gentleman, above his station,
He asked for several roubles
Directly, without intermediaries.

The voice dies in the distance. The swallows faint. The first to come to himself is the Second Swallow. He looks around timidly to see if Peterson is not visible anywhere.

SECOND SWALLOW. Despite the remarkable resemblance of that song to the words of my respected friend and fellow swallow (I am not pointing to the inner meaning of both, but rather to the fact that in both the famous name of Andrew the Wise is mentioned), I consider that in this instance, one ought not, just the same, to depend completely on the typesetters' perspicacity. In the first place, the typesetters, in order to cut their work short, might allow themselves to pick letters in stacks rather than in order. In the second place they may, in order to spite us, print in the policy editorial that our journal is published for "light reading" and who could answer for the consequences of such an act!

THIRD SWALLOW. Yes, then a new influence may again pass here.

SECOND SWALLOW. And we can avoid all that the more successfully as we have a living example before us in the journal *The Epoch*, published since the beginning of this year, 1864. In a manner similar to it, we can simply say that the journal's views are dearly enough indicated by the fact that swallows publish it . . .

FOURTH SWALLOW. And that the time is not far off when it will be enough to say the word "swallow" and everyone will understand that it means precisely swallows, and not eagles!

FIRST SWALLOW. Excellent. I have always maintained myself that we are swallows and nothing else. *(Aside)* Why did they insult us? *(Aloud)* And if Peterson knew . . .

VOICE FROM ABOVE. He knows! *(The swallows are terrified.)*

FIRST SWALLOW. Done, the policy editorial is finished. Now the important thing we have to discuss is the articles. Seventh Swallow! Do you have greetings to the public ready?

SEVENTH SWALLOW *(modestly)*. I call my greeting "Hail Anew." This song is supposed to describe the joy of a young swallow on the occasion of the return, at springtime, to their old nests. *(Declaims.)*

> In the dark day!
> In the bright night!
> Gathered the swallows!
> Gathered the brave lads!
> Look at the swallows, sitting-standing!
> Look at the brave lads silent-talking!
> Chirp-cheep-a-ling!
> Chirp-cheep-a-ling!
> Gay-gloomy swallowing![3]

FIRST SWALLOW. Enough. I consider, gentlemen, that this poem will make our journal's intentions even clearer. For, what is it we want to say in reality, I ask you?

ALL *(answer in a chorus)*.

> Chirp-cheep-a-ling!
> Chirp-cheep-a-ling!

FIRST SWALLOW. Precisely. Consequently, all I can say to our young poet and fellow swallow is that he needlessly ends each of his lines with an exclamation point!

THIRD SWALLOW *(turning to the Seventh Swallow)*. With all due fairness to your "chirp-cheep-a-ling!" as a critic of ornitho-

---

[3] Though this poem is nothing but an ill-disguised imitation of Mr. F. Berg, it is quite satisfactory for a swallow. *(Author's note.)*

logical arts I cannot fail to note that I much prefer your romance that starts with the lines

> Flying, recently. Over the Fontanka?
> I languish. I long to assuage . . .

It is true that the exclamation points are completely inappropriate here, but that poem, if it is permissible to express oneself that way, reeks of Vsevolod Krestovsky's "Sandpipers," while your "Chirp-cheep-a-ling" reeks of yourself.

FIRST SWALLOW. In general, Seventh Swallow, we will place upon you the duty to write poems without exclamation points in the future. The proofreader will place them there for you. And so, one poem is ready *(Seventh Swallow, delighted, cleans his tail feathers with his beak.)* And now, sir, you, Mr. Sixth Swallow!

SIXTH SWALLOW *(smoothly).* The poem I shall now read is meant to describe the sorrow of a middle-aged swallow at the sight of life's agitations. *(Reads.)*

> Long have I not rowed along the Moika—[4]
>   I was afraid—but suddenly I wished to!
> I softly dozed in that rowboat, as in a hammock,
>   I lay peacefully on its bottom!
> Getting a splinter in my paws, I dreamt I was fighting,
>   That a hundred oceans roared under me!
> That even in a rowboat, I was ready
>   To battle oppressive fate!
> But, alas! a clumsy bark laden with manure
>   Grazed my poor skiff!
> I almost perished! Like an innocent flower
>   By the cold frozen stiff!

---

[4] The Moika and Fontanka are rivers traversing St. Petersburg, used for local transportation.

Gathering the fragments, I repaired my boat,
    I stopped up, I caulked as best I could!
And directed my course toward central Meshchansky:
    There, a certain fabulous castle
At Bank bridge shines all in flames . . .[5]

FIRST SWALLOW. Enough, thank you. *(Aside)* Why did they insult us? *(Aloud)* One thing troubles me, however: "Gathering the fragments"—What fragments? Why fragments? What did Sixth Swallow have in mind when he expressed himself that way?

SIXTH SWALLOW *(faltering)*. I—I had in mind—I simply thought—

FIRST SWALLOW. Perhaps you had in mind some organic fragments?[6]

THIRD SWALLOW. Perhaps you had in mind the fragments of our former intentions? *(Aside)* Why did they insult us?

FIRST SWALLOW. That is just what I fear most of all. I admit that I even question whether one can publish such a poem under current circumstances, a poem that can give rise to various interpretations . . . Of course, if Peterson were to assure me that it is permissible . . .

VOICE FROM ABOVE. It is permissible! *(General joy.)*

FIRST SWALLOW. Excellent. Consequently we can reprint Maykov's poem from *The Epoch* after this, and then we will be completely secure. I propose, gentlemen, that we reprint I. S. Turgenev's new work from that same issue of *The Epoch*.

THIRD SWALLOW. I even think that it would not be a bad thing to reprint it in each issue of our new journal.

FIRST SWALLOW. Quite so, that will make us secure. Then I pro-

---

[5] This poem too is an obvious imitation of Mr. Gerbel's *Long Have I Not Seen the Azure Skies*, published in No. 1–2 of *The Epoch* of this year, 1864. *(Author's note.)*

[6] In addition to the interpretation provided by the poem, there is a hint here at Grigor'ev's (Third Swallow's) "Organic Criticism."

pose to publish an article entitled "The Accidental Killing of a Certain Swallow During the Battle of Solferino," and a very interesting story entitled "Old and New Swallows" sent to me from the provinces. Then, I must admit with sorrow, that while our friend Fifth Swallow sent us ten whole novels, they turned out to be soaked. First Bat! Read us our Russian Cooper's letter!

FIRST BAT (reads). "I was in Poltava, and flew all over it. I wrote a novel and flew to Kharkov; in Kharkov Kulish gave a ball in my honor; there were little ladies . . . Just now I thought, what a pity that I did not manage to visit Poltava . . ."

FIRST SWALLOW (aside). Well, why, why did they insult us?

SECOND SWALLOW. But excuse me—after all, just two lines before that he wrote that he had flown all over Poltava, and now he regrets that he did not manage to visit it?

FIRST SWALLOW. Oh, Second Swallow! Don't you know that he has a habit of doing that?

THIRD SWALLOW. I even consider that there is nothing reprehensible in that habit, for art cannot exist without some deviltry.

FIRST SWALLOW. In any case, our situation is very unpleasant, because only the following could be clearly made out in all those ten novels: "On a high cliff, washed by the turbulent waters of the placid Devoury, proudly rises a huge white castle, surrounded on all sides by a moat. In that castle the old Marquis de Chassé-Croisé lives, with his daughter, the beautiful Oxana" . . . then, with the greatest of difficulties the following could be made out as well: "Ro-ro-ro—traveller in boots—once Gerbel', Grigorovich, Fyodor Berg and I dined with Turgenev"—and that is all!

THIRD SWALLOW. Too bad; but Fourth Swallow, whose works are eagerly read not only by swallows, but by the whole feathered race, will save us!

FOURTH SWALLOW. The new work I have finished is entitled *Notes on the Immortality of the Soul*. This is a question of the gravest importance for swallows, and as we must first and foremost show that our journal is an organ of swallows that is published by swallows and for swallows, it is completely natural that I took that into account in my choice of subject as well. The *Notes* are written by a sick and spiteful swallow. At first he talks about all sorts of nonsense: that he is sick and spiteful, that everything in the world is topsy-turvy, that his guts hurt, that no one can predict whether there will be plenty of mushrooms next summer, and finally that everyone is trash, and will not become good until he becomes convinced that he is trash, and in conclusion, of course shifts to the real subject of his meditations. He draws most of his proofs from Thomas Aquinas, but as he does not mention the fact, the reader thinks that the ideas belong to the narrator himself. Then there is the setting of the story. There is neither dark nor light, but some sort of gray in the story; no human voices are heard, only hissing; no human figures are seen, but it is as though bats were flitting about in the dusk. It is not a fantastic world, nor yet a real one, but, as it were, a Cockaigne. Everybody cries, not about anything; but simply because their guts hurt *(sneezes from emotion and falls silent)*.

FIRST SWALLOW. What do you say to that, Third Swallow?

THIRD SWALLOW. I don't quite understand—that is, I do understand and yet at the same time am somehow afraid to understand! It is—it is, so to speak, albinism of thought—there is something senile—yes! On the one hand, a stirring *furioso*, on the other, a delightful *cantabile!* On the one hand, demons draw Don Juan into hell, on the other, a ballad is heard behind the stage—it is terrifying! Terrifying!

For some time the swallows are silent and cannot come to themselves.

FIRST SWALLOW *(to Third Swallow)*. Please express everything you have just said about Fourth Swallow's new work in the form of a letter to me and get it ready for the second issue of the journal. That will be our critical section. Then, gentlemen, so far as the current sections of the journal are concerned, I hope that we will be guided in this case by the examples of former years. You will write letters to me, and I will remain silent. Then you will write letters to each other, and that way the year will pass before you know it! You have, of course, already prepared something of that sort, have you not, gentlemen?

SECOND SWALLOW. I have prepared a letter, in which I ask you to explain to me what I am talking about . . .

FIRST SWALLOW. Excellent I think that in view of current circumstances, we need above all articles in which the ventriloquial element, so to speak, predominates. *(catching himself suddenly)* But excuse me—have you been purified?

SECOND SWALLOW. I offered repentance and received absolution.

FIRST SWALLOW. That is the way. It indicates you understand that if a man commits an indiscretion he must without fail seek absolution. And you, Third Swallow?

THIRD SWALLOW. I have written an article on the effect of upset stomachs on the state of dramatic art in Petersburg.

FIRST SWALLOW. Splendid. And so, gentlemen, we are set, and I hope that henceforth no one will ever insult us. *(Aside)* And why did they insult us? *(Aloud)* On the one hand, we will completely convince the public that we are swallows, on the other . . .

A crash is heard. M. N. Katkov, lit by a tallow candle end, comes down into the cellar. The rats die. The swallows cry "Excuse us!" and fall into the tub. Odor.

(Curtain)

MR. SHCHEDRIN, or,
SCHISM AMONG THE NIHILISTS

by

FYODOR DOSTOEVSKY

AN EXCERPT FROM THE NOVEL
<u>MUNIFICENT</u>

I

MUNIFICENT JOINS THE STAFF
OF THE "OPPORTUNIST" AS CO-EDITOR[1]

And so they went and made Munificent a co-editor of the *Opportunist*. That occurred about a year and a half ago. Munificent still went about freely and enjoyed life without a care, but the *Opportunist* was thrown into disorder. The former regular contributors disappeared: Pravdolyubov died, the others were not physically present. The editors and closest contributors met immediately in order to consult. They may even have sat in a circle at the time, but in order to avoid personal comments we will dispense with such trifles.

"We are in a bad way," began one of the editors. "You know, gentlemen, that Pravdolyubov has died, that others—"

"And how we know!" they answered in a chorus.

"Let's get down to business! We alone are left. That's not all. Few of us are literary men. At the first opportunity, of course, we will mouth commonplaces—"

"Mouth commonplaces, mouth commonplaces," a chorus again sounded.

"—but commonplaces will not last for long. Life marches on. New problems rise, new facts. We, too, will have to deal with them. And without our former main contributors we can make a blunder. What is to be done?"

---

[1]Shchedrodarov (Munificent) is the satirist Shchedrin (Liberal) who will also figure under Shchedrin's alias "Young Pen." The periodical the *Contemporary* becomes the *Opportunist* in Russian by a minor transposition. The defunct contributor is Dobrolyubov, and the absent one Chernyshevsky, the author of *What Is to Be Done?* and of the aesthetic theories given later.

"First of all, to print the novel *What Is to Be Done?*" the staff answered.

"That goes without saying. But then what?"

"Then, I have thought up a very good thing," one of the company decided. "When somebody drives us against the wall and in general in all those cases where a definite and positive opinion is necessary, we will immediately announce that this will all be explained when 'new economic relations are established'; follow that by a dash and we're all set. That will do for a year and a half, even two."

"Hm! A lovely idea, the more so as it can be used in absolutely any situation. I ask you, what does not depend upon economic relations? That way, even the most common idea will seem to assume the stature of real thought. And the more we use it, even, the more sense it will assume in the eyes of the ignoramuses, and thereby will spare us from the responsibility of really doing something. But I think that even that is not enough—"

"Not enough, not enough!"

"You see, gentlemen, in our journalistic work, if somebody sits silently, if he does not snap at and attack everything, he always seems to the majority of subscribers to be neither powerful nor smart, though he may have considered the business very conscientiously and understood it better than anyone. Whoever attacks first, barks and bites, and brazenly and impudently refuses to answer the most specific inquiries, doesn't give a hang about them, whistles, caricatures and rushes to abuse everyone indiscriminately, will seem powerful and cunning to the common man and the majority. That is the way we too will act, particularly because we have acted that way frequently in the past. That is why we need a mutt now, a barking and biting mutt. I hope you understand, gentlemen, that I am using the term 'mutt' in its most noble, in its highest literary sense. And in what way is a mutt inferior to any other kind of animal or bird? What is important here, strictly speaking, is not the mutt, but its muttish characteristics. As soon as we say 'sick 'em,' the mutt we have chosen should jump up from its place, fly, sink its teeth into whoever we show it, and harass it until we yell *ici!* to it. Of course, the fewer ideas the mutt has, the better. On the other hand it must be sportive, wield a pen, be spiteful, have unparalleled vanity and—and—speaking in literary style—be innocent, so that it would guess nothing. I think that if our famous humorist and satirist Mr. Munificent were invited to join the staff, he could successfully serve us along those lines as a permanent contributor."

"Yes, yes!" everyone shouted, but an objection was raised.

"I agree," the objector said, "that Munificent has no ideas of his own, and that this is a considerable advantage. I also agree that he is vain. But what does he have in addition to these advantages? After all, he only has his 'Trumpoulos and Spuds.' That's all he lives on!"

"You're right," they answered him, "but he is sportive, agile, he has sallies, boundless and groundless spite, spite for spite's sake, something like art for art's sake. A spite of which even he understands nothing. And that is the most valuable thing of all. All one has to do is direct that spite and he will bite everything you show him because that is all he has to do. Read Mr. Skribov's article about him, Mr. Objector, which will appear in a year and a half in the journal *The Foreign Word*. There they quite successfully evaluate him as a humorist and point to his 'Trumpoulos and Spuds.'[2] But we will use these shortcomings to our own

---

[2] Evidently our young author has Mr. Pisarev's article in the *Russian Word* in mind. Here is an excerpt from that article:

Mr. Shchedrin, without noticing it himself, has superbly characterized the typical traits of his own special humor, in one scene of his Numbskulls. The Numbskulls are playing cards:

"The Greek Trumpoulos!" he (the infantry commander) exclaims, playing trump. We all laugh, though that Trumpoulos regularly appears on the scene every time we sit down to play cards, which happens almost every evening.

"Spuds!" the commander continues, playing spades.

"Oh, do stop it, you joker!" says General Darling, dying of laughter. "After all, I am spoiling the whole hand through your joking."

advantage. Trumpoulos is vulgar, we know, but then it is within everybody's range. It is ordinary, but an ordinary success, though it may be short-lived, though it may pass quickly, nevertheless spreads quickly and we only need Munificent for two, or perhaps three, years. Finally, if Munificent were more intelligent, what would we do with him? He would start to argue and would not listen. And most important, and the final argument is, that so far as I can judge from his works, he has not an iota of civic feeling. Nothing matters to him but himself, and therefore as soon as you flatter his vanity, he will agree to anything."

"Flatter, but not very much," a voice was heard. "Severity does no harm."

"Oh, of course, severity and even the strictest severity. But he will be enticed simply by the prospect of becoming a staff member. Are we agreed, then?"

"Excuse me, an unforeseen circumstance. What if he finally begins to understand, and a feeling of literary merit rises in him?"

"Hm. Well, we'll consider that later."

"And finally, how will you say to him 'You're a mutt, therefore bark!' That does not even seem to me to be literary."

"Oh, that's nonsense. There is an appropriate phrase for everything. For example, one does not have to say 'bark!'—one could say 'emit sounds!' or something on that order. Don't worry, he will understand, all the more because that is just what he himself needs. Well, is it settled or not?"

Does it not seem to you, dear reader, after reading the above, that Mr. Shchedrin says "Trumpoulos" and "Spuds" to you and you, like General Darling, wave your arms and, dying of laughter, weakly cry "Oh, do stop it, you joker, I am spoiling the whole hand." But the implacable wit will not stop and, you really spoil the hand, that is, are led astray and take the numbskullish jester for the Russian satirist. Of course, "secret little suckling pig amours," "a new stopgap for an old chasm" and particularly "son of a bitch of an ace" are not up to "the Greek Trumpoulos," Mr. Shchedrin's witticisms are more daring, unexpected, and complicated than the infantry commander's jokes, but then many numbskullish General Darlings laugh at his witticisms, as does our whole reading public, including our intelligent, fresh, and active youth. (Fyodor Dostoevsky)

"It is settled, it is settled!"

And that is how Munificent came to join the staff of the *Opportunist*.

II

TERMS

Munificent was hired under very harsh terms. But as he was terribly glad to join, he did not even notice them, the poor thing! He hardly even heard them, and probably did not understand them. He appeared at the editorial offices all spruced up, and all these points were proposed to him immediately, at a general meeting. Here are some of them:

First Point. "Young Pen! Learn that you have come here—to emit sounds. Forget 'Umbilicus City' now. All those Trumpouloses are nonsense. You may, of course, fill our literary columns with them even now, but nevertheless you must strive for something else, for a higher ideal, namely: to popularize natural science, presenting it under the guise of stories and tales. That is every writer's and poet's highest goal. But that is still in the future. In the meantime just emit sounds. Note that I do not tell you 'to bark,' because that is not a literary expression, but I tell you to emit sounds. I hope you understand what that means?"

"And how, sir!" answered Munificent, and assumed greater dignity. The editor cast a glance over the whole meeting as though to say "He says, after all, that he understands!"

Second Point. "Young Pen! Henceforth you must adopt our tactics and follow them unconditionally. You must respect, screen and protect all those who declare themselves to be progressives. Even if they are not worth it, even if they are high-school juniors, even if they are obviously behaving improperly. But if they have published even four progressive lines, or if they have contrived in two years some little couplet, say even one like

Bek and Bek and Lev Kambek,
Lev Kambek and Bek and Bek,

this then, learn that we consider him sacred. But even if they
have been behaving far out of line and babbling away, then you
must just the same simply keep silent about them, and under no
circumstances emit even a single sound, that is, if you cannot
praise them. If anyone writes in verse or prose about a 'Civic
Tear' and publishes it, that person at the very least must become
inviolable for you. And even if such a one appeared before
you—"

"In a drunken state," Munificent interrupted humorously,
expecting everyone to die with laughter immediately, as from his
"spuds," and to praise him for his gaiety. But he had not reck-
oned with his superiors. They were a gloomy bunch, not sus-
ceptible to humor. The interrupted orator frowned and
distinctly, emphatically, and sternly pronounced:

"E-ven in a drun-ken state, sir!"

Munificent lost courage.

Third Point. "Young Pen! You will participate in the critical
section. Therefore instill in yourself the principle that a real
apple is better than a painted apple, the more so as one can eat
a real apple, but one cannot eat a painted apple. Consequently
art is nonsense and a luxury and can only serve to amuse children. That 'new idea,' so grand in its simplicity, must henceforth
replace all courses in aesthetics for you and will immediately
give you the necessary point of view for analyzing all so-called
'works of art.' Do you understand?" But Munificent grew so
courageous with joy, while on the other hand he started to lose
his courage, that he did not dare to say anything even against
that. That, in the first place, a real apple and a painted apple are
two entirely different subjects and cannot in any way be compared; that, in the second place, let us grant that a real apple can
be eaten, but a painted apple is painted specially to be *looked at,*
not to be eaten; that, after all, not everything in the world can

be eaten, and that one cannot limit the utility of all things and works to their edibility. But Munificent kept quiet for the reasons given above."

Fourth Point. "Young Pen! Henceforth you must instill in yourself the principle that shoes are in any case better than Pushkin, because you can walk around without Pushkin very well, but it is impossible to walk around without shoes, and consequently Pushkin is nonsense and a luxury. Do you understand?"

But Munificent again kept quiet. He did not even bring himself to ask how, for example, those people who already had shoes should look at Pushkin.

"Homer and Alexandre Dumas and all the others are equally nonsense, because in Homer there is a world of prejudices and spirits, he believes in miracles and in the gods, and consequently he can infect our youth with those prejudices. Thus the enlightened Karochkin, who destroys prejudices, in any case stands incomparably higher than the unenlightened Homer. Ostrovsky can only be printed because he revealed the flaws of Moscow merchants; there is not the slightest value in him beyond that. Only perhaps also that he is a *name,* and for the same reason one can even print 'Minin,' but only in subscription months.

"Even Shakespeare himself is nonsense and a luxury, because he even has witches appearing, and witches are the very lowest order of reaction and are particularly harmful to Russian youth, which, even without Shakespeare, is already beset with witches by their nurses. But note, Young Pen, that one can still have patience with Shakespeare, and consequently refrain from emitting sounds, only because (and the Devil only knows why!) it occurred to Büchner to praise him in *Stoff und Kraft,* and as one must stand behind every progressive, and the more so behind Büchner, then one can spare Shakespeare, until the right time comes, of course.

"But all that is so insignificant," the orator added, "that I will not make a special point of it, but simply add it to the fourth, that is, the point about shoes and Pushkin."

Fifth Point. "Young Pen! You will be shown five 'rational books,' which you must read without fail, in order to resemble us. In six months you will have to pass an examination about your reading, in the presence of all members of the editorial staff and the most important contributors."

Sixth Point. "Young Pen! You must become convinced of the most important concept of our policy, namely, that for the happiness of all mankind, and equally for the happiness of each separate individual, first and most important of all, is the belly, or in other words, the stomach. Why are you laughing, my dear sir?" Munificent started to wag and claimed that he had not laughed at all.

"I just remembered the 'bellybutton of the world' that the people believe is so senselessly infected by pernicious prejudices, sir," he mumbled in the hope of amusing them and thereby turning anger into favor. But again he was not successful.

" 'Bellybutton of the world!' My dear sir!" The orator raised his voice. "You dare place your senseless 'bellybutton of the world' next to the greatest economic idea of our age, together with the last word of real and social sciences? Learn, that the belly is everything, and everything else, almost without exception, is a luxury and even a useless luxury! What is the good of politics, what is the good of nationalism, what is the good of senseless 'native soil,' what is the good of art, what, even, is the good of science, if the belly is not full? Fill the belly and everything else will take care of itself, and if it does not, then it still does not matter because all the rest is a luxury and useless. Ants, insignificant ants, uniting for self-preservation, that is, for the belly, to our shame be it said, were able to invent the anthill, that is, the highest ideal of social organization one can imagine. And what on the other hand did people do? Nine out of ten people throughout the world constantly go hungry! Why is that? Because people are stupid, because they cannot figure out where their real advantage lies, because they rush after some childish toy, after some sort of art, after the useless, because they are steeped in prejudice, live separately and haphazardly, according to their will, rather than according to the rational books, and therefore they are poor, wasted away, unable to undertake anything. But as soon as you attain a state where everyone has enough to eat, that is, as soon as you have taken the first step, then humanity will grab the moon by its horns if that were necessary. Do you understand?"

Munificent wanted to answer that, of course, it would be very useful to satisfy one's belly first and then proceed to everything else. But that one could also remain at the point of desires and anger for a thousand years with such an idea without attaining the slightest practical result, and that on the contrary, one would have overlooked all of life and spoiled it. He also wanted to add that it is perhaps not at all so easy as it seems, and that perhaps it would be much easier to grab the moon by its horns than to attain satisfied bellies everywhere by the preliminary and intentional paralyzing of all man's other capacities. But Munificent was already so exhausted and frightened, and, moreover, he was so little constructed for making similar objections, that he meekly kept silent, in the hope that the other would soon finish.

"And therefore," the orator continued, "if, on occasion, you have to write, let us say a political article, let us suppose on the Pan-Slavic Question, then you write straight off that *The Day* babbles nonsense. That the Slavs' groans and their desires to free themselves from the Austrians and Turks are also nonsense. That such desires are a luxury, and even an unpermissible one. That it should not matter to them at all whether they are independent or under the Austrians or Turks, precisely because their first duty is to think about the belly, and then perhaps they can drive the Turks away as well, but only as a luxury. Do you understand?

"Similarly, if someone should say to you 'I want to think, I am tormented by the eternal unresolved questions, I want to love, I agonize over questions of faith, I search for a moral ideal, I love art,' or anything along those lines, answer him immediately, decisively, and bravely, that that is all nonsense, metaphysics, that all that is a luxury, childish dreams, unnecessary things. That first of all comes the belly. And finally, if that man has such an overwhelming itch, advise him to take a pair of scissors and cut out the itching place. If he wants to dance, cut off his legs; if he wants to draw, cut off his hands; if he agonizes, wants to dream, off with his head. The belly, the belly, and only the belly—that, my dear sir, is a profound conviction! Do you understand, Young Pen?"

Young Pen wanted to observe that if everything else were cut off, then, after all, the sole remaining belly too would be dead. But he did not observe it because he could not observe it, and he could not because his head was not at all constructed for thinking that way. Therefore he only blinked his eyes and was terribly weary.

"I see by your face that you did not understand me at all. You are still impulsive. Read the five rational books, take the examination, and then we will see."

"I do not have my own thoughts as yet," timidly affirmed Munificent.

"We know. But you have a sportive mind, you have a pen. And if the five rational books are useful to you, then you will emit good sounds. We have hopes for you. But you must drop the 'town of Umbilicus' without fail. 'Trumpoulos and Spuds' are nonsense."

Munificent was jarred. After all, he, too, was proud.

"I have other things than 'Trumpoulos and Spuds,' " he said with modest discretion. "In one place I wrote that 'the lawyer bit the mayor on the belly.' "

"What? Really? Where is that place?" asked the orator, pleasantly surprised.

"In such-and-such a story," answered Munificent, becoming more gay and as pleased as a child.

"Well—that, of course, is something. But after all, that is still far from being everything."

"Really, sir? And here I thought that that was everything," Munificent answered sincerely, the praise having immediately and terribly emboldened him.

"That is precisely it, young man," the orator admonished him impressively. "Go, take with you the rational books given to you, and good luck, emit sounds. So the lawyer bit the mayor—how did you put it? on the belly?"

"On the belly, sir."

"I particularly like the fact that it was the belly. It reminds one of our theory, but with this difference, that we want to fill the belly, rather than bite it. Of course, you, too, introduce a new idea there, but that is still far from being everything. And so, good luck! I see that you are tired. Go and emit sounds."

III

MUNIFICENT'S REVOLT

Munificent emitted sounds for a little more than a year. And at whom he emitted sounds! In his innocent zeal he reached the point of attacking people without any reason, for no cause, but simply to fulfill his duties as humorist. Sometimes he was praised and patted on the head. It was felt in the *Opportunist* that his work could in its own way be fruitful. Ordinary readers, who were even prepared to laugh at "spuds" repeated a hundred times in a row (and there was an enormous number of those), were satisfied. What more was necessary? Moreover, in addition to really talented things, Munificent could sometimes write page after page of humor, in which neither the editors, nor the readers, nor he himself could understand a single line, but in which there seemed to be a hint of something so secret, so intelligent and cunning, in short, so much in the style of the journal, that the simple-minded reader was enchanted and said to himself

"There you have something!" It is true that he did not have the slightest trace of civic feelings, and that therefore he shamelessly barked, scoffed at and disgraced the most honorable and sensible people side by side with the most odious ones, so long as it was humor. He was really a follower of art for art's sake, humor for humor's sake. So long as it was "Trumpoulos" it did not matter to whom it was applied.

But time passed, he read, and involuntarily ideas started coming into his head, previously untroubled by any questions. As he was obliged to read the matter he was instructed to make fun of, he involuntarily became enlightened, and involuntarily a new light started to shine upon him. True, not for long. But little by little something akin to consciousness started to stir in him. I will not say that signs of civic feelings appeared in him. His giddiness and constantly wounded vanity created the situation that on the very next day, he obligatorily "emitted sounds" against the very things he had mentally agreed with the day before. In general, he started to be troubled. He wanted to say, to express something. What and where did he not rush to! The most diverse, the most contradictory opinions and even theories came from his pen, and if the public had not simply taken all of this as "humor," it would sometimes have been very amazed. So far as the editors were concerned, they had confidence in him and did not very much interfere with his emitting sounds. They heard the "sounds" and were satisfied. When Munificent got so confused that he lost his head, he appeared before the public and played a trick on it. The public laughed, that flattered him, having an artistic temperament, he immediately calmed down. But happiness is not eternal. It was not so much the new ideas that wandered into his mind in snatches, as his envy of *The Foreign Word*'s feuilletonist Krolichkov that aroused his vanity. It was then he brandished in the *Opportunist* his famous articles on children and on stale new ideas, which clearly violated the second point of the terms by which he had been hired by the *Opportunist*.

Skribov and Krolichkov rose in fury and triumphantly ac-

cused the *Opportunist* of being reactionary. Cowardice and up-
roar started among the *Opportunist's* editors. They hurriedly
gathered and looked as though the house were on fire. They immediately called Munificent before them. But he had already
prepared himself. He walked in independently. Emancipation
shone on his brow. He stood at the door, leaning on the door-
post with his hand, gazing at the window, as though the matter
did not concern him in the least, and that he would not look at
it. The editors looked at each other in horror.

IV

STORM IN A TEACUP

"What have you done? What have you done, you wretch?" The
editors and staff fell on him in a chorus.
"What have I done? I have done nothing," answered Munificent, as though to say "You will not scare me now."

"What do you mean, nothing! We did not check up on you
lately and look at the trash you've come up with!"

"There is nothing trashy about it. It simply means that I now
have my own ideas and that is all."

"But, you wretch, you have no ideas, you never had your
own ideas. We hired you with the understanding that you would
have no thoughts of your own, that you would only emit
sounds, and you—"

"And now I have ideas of my own, too. *Que diantre! The
Day* has its ideas, even *The Voice* claims it has ideas of its own,
why can I not have my own ideas?"

"But, you wretch, that is a completely different question, why
you cannot have them. But where, where could you have gotten
your ideas? You took them from *Time!* Look, look, read: here is
The Foreign Word. They have published a tirade against brats
from an 1862 issue of *Time*. Listen:

'But we hate the shallow, brainless brawlers that drag

everything they touch through the mire, that soil every pure, honorable idea simply by participating in it, whistlers whistling for bread and solely in order to whistle, riding somebody else's stolen phrase as though it were a hobbyhorse, and whipping themselves with a toy whip of common liberalism.'

"Did you hear? Learn, you wretch, that *The Foreign Word* says outright that you took that out of *Time*, that there is a striking resemblance to it in your article in everything, even in expression. Listen! here is your humorous article on that score:

'But without a doubt no one contributes so much to the public's misconception as certain flap-eared cracked characters who with audacious ease attach themselves to the work done by the young generation. By their mere presence they render anything in which they participate unrecognizable, just as in the summer, flies in a second taint any object at all, even the most valuable. There is no idea our flap-ears would not defame, no deed they would not taint.'

"What do you mean not out of *Time*? Even the expressions are similar!"

"Well, so what if it is out of *Time*?" answered Munificent, piqued in turn. "I admit, certainly, that I adapted it from *Time*, as many others do, too, because it is a good journal, and it is useless for you to make me emit sounds against it. But I did not steal it from *Time*, my thoughts simply agreed with theirs. So what? My thoughts, too, can agree with theirs. My expressions are different. I write 'taint a deed like flies.' That is a splendid phrase, and it is too bad you don't appreciate it!"

"But, you wretch! it might be good, after all, if you used it for us, but after all, you are using it against us. Against us! Do you hear?"

"But, after all, I wrote about brats, not about you."

"About brats! But after all that is just like raising a hand against yourself! What did we teach you when we let you join the staff? He doesn't understand! Doesn't understand? And, moreover, *Time* has many subscribers, and he supports it!"

"But why are you attacking me, really?" Munificent shouted, losing his temper completely. "And why do you keep harping on *Time* all the time? I repeat, it is a good journal and I have taken a lot out of it! You made me laugh at it, stick my tongue out at it! Through your kindness, for example, I laughed at *The Day*, too. There are serious-minded people at *The Day*, there is science there, successive and honorable analyses of many years' standing. They want the useful. No one can accuse them of anything uncivic. Their idea is gaining greater and greater popularity. It is recognized even by their longtime and declared foes. One can fail to agree with it, but one cannot deal with *The Day* disrespectfully. Though through your kindness I made faces and stuck my tongue out at them, almost compared them to Askochensky. That is what emitting leads to!"

"But who ordered you to act so zealously? It means you were amusing yourself."

"And why do you fall on me like that about the brats? For goodness' sakes! They taint and spoil everything. *Time* only talked about rascals then, and with reason. After all, they used whatever they liked with us lately, liberalism, progressivism, or anything at all. I mentioned the flap-ears. Though there may be some honorable ones among them, yet they spoiled everything. We could have had positive results. Where are they? We missed everything with your system and your flap-ears! And what is the meaning of a 'civic tear'? After all, all they do is write that they shed them, but show me a real one. And even if it were real, they would taint that one, they would contrive to stain it. After all, that way one can finally debase and taint everything to such an extent that it will disgust a new man.[8] After all, we are repelling our very own from us.

---

[8] It seems to us that the young novelist who offered *Munificent* to us does not know how to describe characters. The Munificent of Chapter I cannot speak as he speaks here, and that is no longer artistic. However, this is a satiristic, a caricature novel, and *in its own way* this is all true. (Fyodor Dostoevsky)

"Civic tear! But, after all, that is only a phrase, a trite phrase! I respect a person who really sheds it, but I will not start to respect the fashion of civic tears simply because the word 'civic' is written there. For, after all, this may be followed by civil tears, private tears, commissariat tears, tears of the society for the preparation of dry goods—is all that also to be respected? *Morgen früh, je t'antipathe!—*"

"What a tone! Listen to his tone! My God, what is he saying?" the staff shouted in horror.

"Why tone? There is no tone here at all. Recently you published the following in the *Opportunist,*

> A flowerless field
> Lies behind past days.
> *In it sleep* requited
> A citizen's tears.

Surely that is written as a joke? How can tears sleep in a field? And you worship it!"

But here the member of the editorial board also flew into a rage.

"What, my dear sir! You laugh! But, after all, those are a citizen's tears! And what business is it of yours if they sleep in a field? Let them sleep, let them do what they like, for they are not common tears but a citizen's. Look, see: 'A citizen's' is written. Our convictions—"

"I no longer believe in your convictions."

"Our convictions are the belly, my dear sir! Our convictions about the belly! The belly, the belly—do you hear?"

"I don't give a hang about your belly, I have heard enough about it. I no longer believe in your belly! To fill the belly at the cost of preliminary paralyzing of all the organism's parts and capacities is absurd. But you, on the contrary, have gone so far in your fanaticism for the belly as to consider in turn all the organism's other organs and capacities except the belly as absurdities. That is what you did with art, with moral ideals, with the historical march of events, with all life. Where is your practical sense? You are going against life. We are not supposed to prescribe laws for life but to study life and extract laws from life itself for ourselves. You are theoreticians!"

"But that is word for word out of *Time*. He has learned it by heart!"

"So what? I really have learned many places out of *Time* by heart. Even though I emit sounds against *Time*, I am obliged to *Time* for a great deal. I do not understand how one can stand on air, without feeling the soil under one. An Englishman, German, or Frenchman, each is particularly strong because each stands on his own soil, and because he is first of all an Englishman, German, or Frenchman, and not an abstract general man. Before you can do anything you have to make yourselves into something, to assume your own shape, to become yourselves. Then and only then will you be able to have your say, to present your own form of a world-view. But you are abstractions, you are shadows, you are nothing. And nothing can come from nothing. You are foreign ideas. You are a mirage. You do not stand on soil but on air. The light shines right under you—"

"How itchy he is! How itchy he is!"

"Well, yes, I am itchy! I myself have written a dozen times 'when new economic relations will begin.' But what sense is there in that? It even began to seem funny to me. Why will they begin, how will they begin? Will they fall down from the sky? That is an empty phrase! You can sit and wait with such a phrase for a thousand years, and absolutely nothing will come of it."

"He is a freethinker!" all those around Munificent shouted. "How dare you!"

"No, I am only an overbaked nihilist, and I really wanted to be useful. I wanted to have my own thoughts and you did not even notice my efforts. I purposely went away to the country last February for my ideas (read my clever February feuilleton in the

Opportunist). I saw peasants there and I was very surprised that they were poor. I had seen peasants before, but I had never thought about them. Of course, it is not the readers' fault that I saw it for the first time. But I was so surprised that I took it for a 'new idea.' Even more, I created 'a new economic relation'—"

"You, *you* created 'a new economic relation'?" all shouted in amazement.

"Yes, I, I myself, *moi-même!* Because I too can have my ideas. I concluded that if you hired a coachman in Moscow, you would not bargain with a peasant because he is poor, and would not give him fifteen cents if he asks for twenty. Give him a quarter instead, if he asks for twenty cents, and that would create a new economic relation and that, of course, would be worth more than all your ideas."

But at this point such an Homeric was heard that Munificent was completely bewildered. Even without that he had been agitated by the whole scene. For some time he looked at the laughing staff with amazement. But then he suddenly covered his face with his hands and started to sob like a little baby—

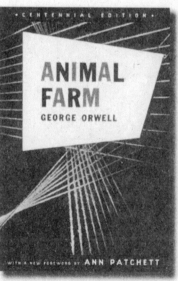